The Pre-nup Problem

Ophelia Gold

Contents

Prologue

God I'm so stressed out. Well, being the best in the business can do that to you, I'm always getting new clients. Just today I've had three new clients all coming to me for the same reason. Wanting to know what a prenup is. All three of them were women, panicked women at that. You see, I see the nasty side of love and marriage all the time. I'm more shall we say ... realistic? Being a divorce attorney I get to see the wrong side of love daily. Yeah sure it starts off nice ...dating, kissing, restaurants, romance, and promises of eternal love. That however changes the moment they hear those three dreaded words... the prenuptial agreement.

Chapter One

The Prenup Problem

"**J**ill, have you managed to sign the prenup yet? My attorney is waiting to process the documents" says Bill with a little annoyance in his voice.

OWH GOD I COMPLETELY FORGOT!

"Honey I've been busy, trust me I'll get round to it soon" I practically sing back in response. Well it's better than telling him I forgot, it should buy me some time. Anyway, I love the fact that I'm finally engaged and planning my wedding, nothing could bother me now.

"Well you'd better hurry up; anyone would think you don't want to get married the way you're stalling."

"Don't be silly honey you know I can't wait to marry you. That's why I've had no time to look through the prenup. I'm too busy trying to make plans for the wedding" I try and reassure him.

"Plans can wait Jill! Just sign the damn thing soon will you, or there will be no wedding to plan." Bill has such a stressful job so I'm used to his serious mood swings by now.

"Ok Bill, I hear you loud and clear" I say cheerily, trying to hide my horror. Oh god I wish he wouldn't joke about there being no wedding, I'm too excited about it. Right all I have to do is sign the damn thing then he will get off my back.

"Good, right I'm off to work now, see you tonight" he kisses me on the forehead as usual, part of our morning routine.

The minute Bill leaves for work I run to the door and wave to him whilst he waits for the elevator to come up. Bill waves back almost on autopilot neither of us really thinking of our actions because everything between us runs like clockwork. When I finally see him get in I close the door behind me. When he leaves for work, I can let go and return to my normal self. Thank god he's gone. SHIT SHIT SHIT! I keep putting that damn prenup off. I've been too busy to think about it, right today I'm going to sign it.

But I'm not just going to scribble my signature on a legal document before I've had chance to read through it, after all I am my father's daughter. He taught me to never sign anything until I know the document backwards and have seen the small print. My father's a lawyer, a great lawyer at that. That's how I came to be with Bill. My father introduced us; he said that Bill was a massively intelligent man and that he would one day soon be making a lot of money (obviously father only wants the best for his daughter) He was right; Bill went to Harvard law and graduated top of his class now he's a partner in one of the biggest law firms in New York City': Richman&co. I don't know exactly how much money Bill makes, he won't tell me. But all I know is it's enough to provide him with a Lamborghini, this penthouse suite on Lexington Avenue, fine wine, designer clothes and the rest. Now I'm going to be Mrs. Swanson! Part owner to this life and all it's luxuries. He proposed with a 10ct canary diamond. It's just the most gorgeous thing ever. It was so romantic and unexpected.

Well kind of unexpected, I suppose I have hinted at marriage once or twice or...... anyway the time has come. I'm 36 years old and I already have my man, my canary diamond, now all I need to do is plan the most amazing wedding anyone has ever seen. I want to be the envy of every woman because I've now got it all. If life was a race I WOULD BE WINNING!

So my father has promised me that the budget for the wedding is going to be huge. He said he will spare no expense (naturally) because he knows how much this means to me, I'm high maintenance and I don't mind admitting it. I want the best of the best and I only intend on doing this once. So I need to get to work, I need to call and make an appointment to get my measurements took, pick fabric for my dress, choose centre pieces, find the perfect venue.....oh god I'm hopeless, he said no prenup no wedding. I keep forgetting, right that's it I'm not doing another thing until I have signed this god forsaken pre-nuptial agreement.

—⁓⦵⦵⦵⦵⦵⦵⁓—

Three hours later and I have read and re read the document over and over at least fifty times. I don't believe it, I don't really understand it. It looks like......but that can't be right!? No way am I signing this. I need help, I need a professional... a second opinion, confirmation... This can't be happening. I won't let this happen! That's it I'm calling my father and getting the number of the best divorce attorney money can buy.

Chapter Two

Divorce Attorney Extraordinaire

Exactly forty- five minutes later I arrived at Jack Hornski's office. This is the man that knows everything there is to know about prenup's. (My father called him for me and booked an emergency appointment, I think he could hear how stressed out I was) As I run into the building clutching the papers to my chest, I skid down the hall frantic to find Mr. Hornski's office. Within seconds of my arrival a voice follows my direction.

"Please sign in and take a seat in the waiting area" come's the voice of an arrogant, beautiful twenty-five year old model playing the role of the receptionist.

"I'm here to see Mr. Hornski It's an emergency appointment, my father paid good money to get me in so quickly." I pant from my sudden sprint down the hall.

"Not that quickly." she smiles smugly and points towards the waiting area where another two people are waiting

"You will have to wait your turn, Mr. Hornski has other clients to see before you"

I immediately hate this woman! Her name tag reads "Felicity" but she's definitely trying to be Marilyn Monroe, with the short blonde curls, false lashes, low slow seductive voice all tied up into a busty long legged package. She doesn't intimidate me, I'm taller and slimmer. I know exactly how she got this job and qualifications had nothing to do with it. Fine if she wants to play this game I'll play along.

I sign in and try to sit patiently in the waiting area. I can't stop my feet from marching to their own beat. I can tell I'm bothering people because the two in front of me keep staring and look rather agitated but I don't care, adrenaline has crept in and is here to stay. I'm constantly fiddling with my canary diamond I can't wait much longer. God this is gonna be some wait - I'm third in the queue! In an attempt to distract myself I try to read a law leaflet, but it's boring as hell. My constant clock watching seems to slow time to a glacial drip. With every agonizingly slow second that drags by my panic, eagerness and fear are slowly turning into a knot in my stomach. I feel sick then angry then upset. God NO, I have the sudden urge to cry. Not now Jill, not here I'm sure this is just a misunderstanding, I'll have all this straightened out before long.

Staring in a daydream I realize I have been listening to my own problems, hearing only my own thoughts, I haven't been taking in my surroundings. I suddenly become fully in the present and find my eyes resting on the door I will be walking through shortly. There's a large onyx plaque nailed to the mahogany door, and in bold gold is the name "J.Hornski". Beyond the door I can hear mumbling. He's clearly with a client; my interest peeks when I begin to hear sobs. It sounds like a woman. My heart is breaking for her. She's probably going through a divorce, after all why else would women come here? WAIT! Are those people looking at me like that? Is that why the receptionist was looking down her nose at me? No way is this happening, I'm cleaning this up right now. I'm going to stage a call to Bill and let them all know I'm not divorced, in fact I'm happy and in love and I am currently making plans for my overpriced wedding.

Pretending to dial I place the phone to my ear and act as though Bill has just answered.

"Hey honey I miss you, I was just thinking about you. *Pause.* Awgh I love you too! *Pause.* I know honey I can't wait to plan our wedding either (so loud am I, my voice is returning to me off the walls) fake laugh. *Pause.* Baby I'm so lucky to have you; you know everyone has been complimenting my canary diamond today. (Fake Marilyn Monroe spins her head so fast I think she may have fractured her neck. That got her attention.) Ok babe, well have a fab day at the office, I'll see you tonight. *Pause.* Love you. *Pause.* Bye"

Ha nailed it.

I pretend to hang up the phone and place it back into my new Chanel purse. The room suddenly feels eerily quiet now I've stopped shouting. All of two seconds go by when I hear the "clack clack clack" of cheap imitation Manolo Blahniks on polished marble. It's fake Marilyn, galloping toward me. I feel like telling her to slow down and sign in first but the pleasure of knowing my stage call had, had its intentional effect has overrode my sarcastic tongue. (For now)

Fake Marilyn approaches wanting to inspect my ring. She seems suddenly very interested in me and wants to know when and where I'm getting married, what's my fiancé like, how long have we been together, where did he buy my ring, what's the budget for the wedding, and the questions just keep coming. Of course I'm completely blasé about the whole thing I'm not about to open up and tell my personal plans to my new found enemy. Bless fake Marilyn (think I'll start referring to her as Farilyn) she's very obviously dying to be my new best friend, knowing now that I'm not a sad lonely woman here to get a divorce. In fact I know with utter certainty that I lead a far more glamorous life than she could even dream of.

I very elegantly flash my diamond ring in her direction once more, long enough for her to be completely mesmerised and jealous, then I pull back and blank her giving her the cold shoulder. (That's it now Farilyn I just wanted to make you mad jealous, I'm done now, go and pretend to work like you were doing)

Now feeling completely satisfied I start to relax I'm no longer impatient about going in, actually I'm quite enjoying the silent attention around me. The two men in the queue are looking at me with interest and Farilyn just can't get enough, I keep catching her sneakily peaking in my direction no doubt in hope to admire and lust after my ring once more (seriously I'm telling you I even saw her lick her lips, my ring is literally making her drool. Man I'm enjoying this.)

Just as I'm starting to enjoy myself the door finally opens and a sobbing woman emerges holding a snotty looking rag in one hand and holding a box of Kleenex in the other, she's in bits I wonder what's happened. The distraught woman shakes the man's hand whilst still holding onto her snot rag (I'm assuming the man is Mr. Jack Hornski himself) her eyes are red, puffy and streaked with tears. I don't usually feel sorry for people in fact I've always felt showing any signs of weakness makes people look pathetic. I could never cry in public I would die of shame I'd never be able to look anyone in the eye again. But I don't feel that way for this woman for whatever reason, there seems to be something vulnerable about her an almost childlike quality about her. Just her outfit tells me she's not overly fond of fashion or in fact takes any pride in her appearance at all. She looks about my age, mid 30's a natural looking blonde, cut into a dishevelled looking bob, unless she's so upset she's been pulling her hair out by the roots. Yes that explains it a little, but the rest of her has no explanation.

She has three quarter length sweat pants on with a tiny print of hello kitty on the bottom, a lime green spaghetti strap top on that seems to enhance her little bump of a stomach (she's definitely not pregnant just chubby, trust me I've got an eye for these things) and if she came to the office with make-up on there are no apart signs of it now, unless she's cried it all off which I doubt because there's no mascara smudge in sight and I'm sorry but no one can cry that hard.

Trust me I know, one day I ordered a package and when they rang the bell I rushed to the door and tripped over the bear skin rug and fell. I hit the side of our glass coffee table, which of course didn't smash but it hurt like hell. I dislocated my shoulder and fractured my ankle from the fall. Naturally I had to go to the hospital; I've never been in so much pain in my life. I cried openly on my own but immediately stopped the moment the paramedics arrived (that's what I mean even when my bones are on the point of breaking I will not cry in front of anyone, well maybe my father but that's to be expected I am after all daddy's girl) it was embarrassing enough lying in that hospital bed with doctors and nurses staring at me whilst mascara and eyeliner where spread all over my face I must have looked like Pennywise the clown.

So yes I would definitely have noticed it, had this woman cared for beauty products. But I suppose in her own way she's almost sweet looking, not attractive or glamorous just sweet, vulnerable and simple. (SIMPLE! yes that word sums this woman up to perfection)

She finally let's go of Mr. Hornski's hand and I watch him whip out a handkerchief to wipe his hand the minute she turns her back to him.

"Take care Sally; I'm sure everything will be fine." Jack Hornski says in a very low gruff voice, it's quite a sexy voice actually.

Sally that's the simple woman's name (mmm simple Sally it's got a ring to it) she replies to Mr Hornski half-heartedly with just a whimper and a nose blow and a weak "yes......errmm...ok... thanks...I... think" Sally stutters between emptying her nose for the tenth time on that revolting rag, holding a box of Kleenex as she makes her way to the seat next to mine.

One down two more to go before it's my turn; I'm going to be here all day I won't have any time to make any plans for the wedding by the time I get out of here.

My attention wanders back to Sally, *simple Sally. Simple sweet Sally...* well if I'm forced to stay here I suppose there's no harm talking to someone, I'm bored and she looks lonely, and it's not like I'm ever going to see her again. One final look at the clock tells me I've been here for nearly one hour, god that's dragged, right that's it I've got to find another way to pass the time but how do I start the conversation ......*erm hey why are you crying?* No to direct......*ergh hey how are you?* No that's a daft question she's obviously upset. Oh for god's sake she's blowing her nose so loudly straight into my ear, it's deafening. Ok she's clearly crying out for attention (literally) I know what I'll do I'll get her some water (I think I could do with some also)

I head over to the water cooler, relieved to stretch my legs after an hour on that uncomfortable chair. My next move is to hand the water to her and let her do the talking because I'm out of ideas at this point.

After I pour two cups of cold water I reluctantly go back to my seat and cautiously hand Sally hers. "Oh…thanks…thankyou… god I'm such a mess."

"That's ok I bet you're not the first woman to have broken down in here before" I try to justify her behaviour even though I personally disagree with it, but really I'm just looking for gossip.

Simple Sally chugs the whole cup load down in one fell swoop. Damn, apparently crying can make you seriously thirsty, no wonder as she's drained herself of all liquid, through her tears. Think she needs a refill. I gesture if she would like me to get her another drink and she nods emphatically with her head bowed down to her knees, clearly she isn't in the mood for talking just yet. I pass Sally her second cup of water and again in one shot, gulps the entire contents down as though it was made of something stronger.

"God I could really do with a cocktail right about now" Sally wines (I knew she was thinking about alcohol)

"Really is it that bad?"

"Worse! I was so happy this morning, now look at me!"

"Well what happened?" This is like pulling teeth.

"Why can't people just get married and live happily ever after like they do in the movies? You never read a romance novel filled with love and happiness and marriage, but then the story suddenly turns ugly with lawyers and legal documents to fill out. All this prenuptial agreement drama is giving me a headache."

Prenuptial agreement!? That's what I'm here for, she's not getting divorced after all, her tears are over the prenup. Please God don't let me come out of Mr. Hornski's office looking like Sally I couldn't bare it. No I know what I'll do, I'll ask Sally to fill me in on some of the details before I go into my appointment. That way I'll have a heads up, I won't have the element of surprise like she did, this way it will soften the blow.

"So Sally......erm...what's so terrible about your prenup...exactly?" (Ok calm down Jill it won't be half as bad as what your expecting, will it?) I sit back slowly trying to control my nerves about what may come out of Sally's mouth, I anxiously wait for her response with a bated breath.

"Basically if we ever get divorced I'll get nothing. I'll be out on the street, HOMELESS! I can't believe it, I mean I just can't believe it I have been with Allan for over ten years, planning our wedding should be the happiest time of my life I didn't think we would ever get married but now here we are, so why do we have to discuss such an awful topic. I mean what happened to the vow: till death do us part? What's the point in even saying those words if we don't mean them? I know I'll mean them from the bottom of my heart I don't want anyone else and I never have, so why does he insist on me signing a prenup unless he intends on divorcing me one day?"

WOW

Well I wasn't expecting that. My god its worse than I expected. Sally has more than opened up to me now; she is like a huge exposed wound filled with hurt, fear and pain. Wracked in sobs she tries to pull another Kleenex out of the box and finds it empty. In a fit of rage she flings the empty box half way down the hall only to get Farilyn's evil glare.

"Pick that up right now or I'm calling security!" (Jeez, talk about drunk with power)

Sally immediately jumps to attention and races for the empty Kleenex box and throws it in the trash followed along by a million apologies. Farilyn apparently enjoys when people do exactly what she says, exactly when she says it. Looking smug she returns to her computer in a vain attempt of looking superior only she can't fool me, I can see that she is bidding on a black neck scarf on eBay. God what I'd give to get this woman fired.

Before I can get to intently engrossed in my idea to sabotage Farilyn's little life, Sally slumps back in her chair with all the weight of the world on her ... hips.

"I'm so sorry to have dumped all this on you; it's not your problem just mine. Listen to me going on and on; this is probably nothing to what you're going through. Are you here to get a divorce? I'm so sorry for you it must be so hard. Do you want me to run to the store and get you some tissues, I'm all out and I think I need a few more myself."

Sally starts rubbing my leg in such a sympathetic way, I cringe.

"I am absolutely not getting a divorce! I just came for the same reason you did. To get some clarity on the prenup, that's all so please remove your hand at once."

Sally rips her hand away with a start. She looks really shocked and frightened but I don't care. Oh god everyone's staring at me. I didn't want anyone to know my business; great Farilyn's head has started to rise up to the height of a swan. For god's sake why did Sally have to ruin everything for me? Farilyn was totalling jealous of me a minute ago!

"You're here about a prenup? You're going through the same thing as me. It's so awful isn't it" Sally starts whimpering again only this time I could hit her.

"Yes I am, but could you please keep your voice down everyone is staring." I hiss through gritted teeth.

"Owh gosh I'm so sorry, didn't you want anyone to know? I suppose that makes sense because after all it is rather embarrassing, maybe I shouldn't tell anyone else either"

This snivelling little weasel has just ruined my reputation round here. I'll be damned if I ever come back here again.

"Yes I suggest you keep everything to yourself from now on. Now if you don't mind I'd rather just sit in silence now, I'm beginning to get a headache"

"Yeah......sure...I understand...but can I just ask you one more thing?"

I'm going to beat this woman over the head very soon I can feel it, I'm so angry right now and embarrassed, I can barely hide it.

"Only if you whisper for god's sake what is it?"

"Well I was just wondering what your prenup says, is it as bad mine?"

"My prenup has got to be a mistake, there's no way my prenup is the same as yours! I need mine looking over by a professional"

"I see, so in you prenuptial agreement has he stated he will leave you the house or some money or something if you two ever get a divorce?"

(No of course he bloody hasn't that's why I'm here, you evil nosey woman. Would I be this panicked over this if he had?)

"Obviously...yes, yes he's leaving me everything that's why I'm here, I'm just shocked that's all I just need it confirmed" I smile back bewildered by my own lie, I even dramatically flip my hair and adjust my blouse for emphasis on how our two circumstances couldn't be more different.

"Wow, god I'm so jealous, he must love you a lot"

Stupid, simple, Sally has said far too much for my liking. She's right; if he did love me why leave me nothing? Why ask me to sign it? Why even mention a divorce? I thought marriage was for life. Sally's staring back at me in awe, but I can barely keep my poker face up for much longer, my smile is slipping and it just plain hurts to look this naïve creature in the eye.

I'm no longer confident that this is all a big mistake, in fact I think I believed it the minute I read it, perhaps that's what's frightened me all along. I'm even more disturbed and worried now, but I still want to go through with my appointment I haven't waited all this time to go back now. I try and keep my mind of Sally's words and focus on the floor. I no longer care to discuss this with her I just want to leave already and never return to this sad place where dreams are crushed, ever again.

Picking up on my silent treatment Sally's attention goes to her handbag in search of candy. I notice this because she tries to hand one to me, but I would never eat candy anytime any place, especially out of a stranger's handbag. As I decline the offer, a nerdy looking woman joins the queue to see Jack Hornski. This Jack Hornski man is obviously very popular. He's an acquaintance of my father although I've never met him before.

As Sally sucks the life out of a butterscotch candy the new woman is hovering around the chairs, hesitating whether to sit down or not. She's sticking out like a saw thumb just standing there, everyone's looking at her who knows maybe she has a phobia of chairs? Or maybe the sight of Sally's red blotchy tear smeared face has given her second thoughts on staying.

As everyone is gawking at her she turns a certain shade of crimson, deeper than her hair colour. (She's a red head from a bottle, it screams artificial) Looking nervous she starts rummaging around in her bag to avoid our gazes.

After what feels like too long, she pulls a packet of hand wipes out of her bag and starts cleaning a chair. I don't mean just the handles on the chair I'm talking the legs, the seat and all the steel too. My god what a freak! This woman is brave I wouldn't dare embarrass myself like that. Even Sally has stopped sucking to watch this woman quite contently going about cleaning her chair like it's the most natural thing in the world. Everyone is momentarily transfixed to be a witness to this.

She's got Farilyn's attention too.

"Excuse me what do you think you're doing? There's no need to clean it I assure you we have a cleaner here morning, noon and night nothing is ever dirty at Hornski and co." (Ha, what a joke Farilyn! You're a dirty thing at Hornski and co.)

"Sorry I hate sitting on public seats, unless I've personally cleaned it" The red head replies.

She looks like a nerdy school teacher type but with burgundy shoulder length hair. She has glasses on and a blouse that's buttoned up to her neck, she's also wearing the ugliest pencil skirt I have ever seen. Pencil skirts are meant to flaunt your figure not drown it. She's slim and trim so god knows why she's trying to hide it; she should probably swap clothes with Sally, I think even they would look better on her than this circus tent.

Farilyn doesn't really know how to respond to this new found information and just nods for the woman to carry on. Pleased with this the woman carries on cleaning at full speed to prevent the agony of being gawked at any longer. Finally the red head takes to her thrown with a look of relief and everyone immediately loses interest. (Great now what do I have to look at; at least she was providing me with a little entertainment)

"I'm the same you know, I love a clean home" Sally decides to chirp in, directing it at the red head

The red heads baffled by Sally's directness, I can tell she's not really a people person. I feel like laughing because Sally is no longer pestering me to talk, she's found a new woman to pry information from. Things seem to be looking up.

"Yeah, well I'm a bit more anal about cleaning than your average person" the red head quips back obviously uncomfortable about discussing it.

"Well that's good, you can never be too clean can you" how does Sally not pick up on people's body language? This woman clearly doesn't want to talk.

The red heads had enough of her now I can tell. She just nods in response to her last comment but Sally's like a dog with a bone.

"Are you here about a prenup too?"

(Are you kidding, How rude you can't just come out with that. Doesn't she have any boundaries?)

"Ergh...ergh... well...I...erm" red head is all flustered, no wonder I thought I was direct before I bumped into Sally.

"Don't be frightened to tell me, that's what I'm here for and this lady too. Sorry I didn't ask you what your name is I'm Sally by the way" she directs it at me and the red head. Extending her hand out as if to be formal, but there's nothing formal or normal about this woman. Why won't she just disappear? Telling everyone my personal business, I could slap her.

Well she's not getting my name she can think again. I'm totally blanking her now, like a defiant child I take one look at her extended hand and look away.

Seeing that she isn't getting any joy out of me she continues on to the red head.

"Hi I'm Sally, Sally willow and you are?"

"I'm Anne Beckety"

Finally Sally shakes Anne's gloved hand, and Sally continues to pull out the reason why she's here.

"So are you here for a divorce?"

16

"God no, no, I....erm...yes I suppose I am here about a pre-nuptial agreement as well. Not to draw one up or anything just ....you know, just to find out the finer details on mine" I feel for this Anne beckety, forced to talk about her problems with Sally. It would never have happened if we were all getting seen to a little quicker.

Help us anyone, we are trapped in her with Miss Sally Willows the nosiest woman alive!

"Yes I understand, me and her are here for the same thing to. My fiancé is leaving me nothing if we get divorced and her fiancé is leaving her everything! What about you? Are you un-lucky like me?" That's it I can't take any more of this.

"Look here Miss Willow; I don't appreciate you talking about me to anyone, especially as I'm sat right next to you. Leave this woman alone, mind your own business and shut up!" God that felt good.

I didn't mean to come across that mad, now everyone's looking at me again even Farilyn. This is the day from hell. Sally is staring at me and even Anne looks a little frightened from my burst of rage, I hate making a scene, can't anyone see what she's doing to me. Christ is that water coming into Sally's eyes now? I can't handle this.

A few minutes go by in eerie silence, I try wishing the time away and it almost works as one man left Jack Hornski's office and another entered. Meaning I'm next in line and I can't wait to get out of here.

As Anne stares into oblivion and Sally's head is bowed in shame, I hear snivels. Please not again.

"I'm sorry" come's a tiny high pitched voice.

"What was that?" I couldn't stop myself it was like a reflex.

"I said I'm sorry, I totally forgot you didn't want anyone knowing about the prenup, god I'm so forgetful really I didn't mean it. But when you think about it isn't it nice knowing you're not the only one?"

"I suppose, but don't do it again" I snap at her.

"I won't, I won't promise"

I feel exhausted like handling a child; she's uncontrollable and totally dependent on people liking her. I can tell she thinks she's back in my good books and I try to soften up a bit but I'm still not in the mood for talking.

"It is actually quite nice knowing I'm not the only one going through this. I guess all this legal stuff drives everyone mad. I mean we're not really told about this stuff as kids. We all just dream about the wedding not the paper work with it" this is the first time Anne has willingly spoken up on her own, without the persuasion of Sally or Farilyn.

"That's so weird I just said that, like we only ever really think about the happily ever after, but talking about possible divorce and prenup's and all this kind of stuff just puts a big dark cloud over everything"

"That's exactly how I feel." Anne nods back.

Anne and Sally seem to be getting on well enough now that they're bonding over their mutual problems. I mean their right, that's how I feel too. I don't really have anyone in my life to open up to about this stuff accept my father and he's a man so I guess I can't talk to him about everything like sex and stuff, some things are just meant to be girl talk. I don't know why I don't have any female friends I've always assumed it's because they envy me and I probably remind them of everything they don't have. That's what my father says too and I believe him.

"Do you feel that way too miss…" Sally stares at me expectantly; I guess I could always give girl talk a try. What have I got to lose accept my dignity and she's already taken that.

"Yeah I guess I do. I don't really see the need in a prenup

if you're going to be together forever like me and Bill are, but I suppose not all marriages last so this is really just to cover their backs in case, and I'm Miss green, Jill Green soon to be Mrs. Swanson"

Sally looks at me with admiration, as though I'm right in what I'm saying, and Bill and I will stand the test of time. They both look jealous of me, well that's better than before.

"Jill that's a nice name" Sally smiles up at me, (I guess she's on ass kissing mode for pissing me off before)

"Yeah I guess that makes sense, still doesn't make it any less worrying for us though does it?" Anne stares me out, as though she senses my secret lie about being left everything in the prenup. Sally looks from Anne to me as though we are discussing something she missed.

"Yes I guess we all have reason's to be worried"

Anne nods knowingly at me. Yeah she knows I was lying to Sally earlier. She's far smarter than Sally I can immediately tell, she looks the respectful type I don't think I need to worry in her knowing. In fact I bet she's in the same boat as Sally and I.

"So Anne have you got as much reason to worry as us?" this is my way of talking to her in code without fully revealing anything to Sally, even though a person with half a brain would know what me and Anne are getting at.

"I absolutely do, it's not nice is it. I don't really have anyone to confide in this sort of stuff to, so I've had to come here for clarity"

I understand that alright translated it means, I have no friends, I'm scared to death that my fiancé will divorce me and leave me with nothing but a broken heart. This woman's good, Anne knows instinctively we are all in the same boat; she's looking at me as if to say "we're all in this together stop pretending to be better than us, its ok to be scared"

Fantastic, now I have a brainless blunt butterscotch sucker, now a nerdy know it all nut.

"I can relate to that Anne, I don't really have friends either. I kind of keep myself, to myself if you know what I mean" this coming from sally?

Anne and I keep eye contact with a small grin forming on our faces, god we're like Sally's mothers that find her an irritating handful but she still has the ability to be amusing and not even know it. Weird that she picked up on Anne's subtle choice of words, maybe Sally's not brain dead after all.

Sally pops another candy and gets comfortable like this is her prenup support group and we are now fully in session.

"What about you Jill, do you have friends you can confide this sort of stuff to? Weird that none of us have decided to talk this over with our partners isn't it? Maybe it's just a girl talk thing, do you think?"

Will she ever stop talking? I can see Sally's new statement has got Anne thinking but I won't let myself go there. Sally's weird one minute she's like a child you can't control from making a fool out of herself, and then the next minute she will say something so earth shatteringly true it forces you to really examine your life and I don't like either.

"Well" Sally keeps pushing, I look to Anne for support but she's looking at me almost as intently as Sally. Oh great I guess she wants an answer too?

"Yes… Alright…yes I don't really have anyone but my father. He's a lawyer, a great lawyer and he recommended I come here to have the best of the best thoroughly look through my prenup" I relent, not feeling as though I've lost, I feel kind of liberated to have someone to listen to me. My father does but I don't want to bother him about every little thing he's such a busy man. Same with Bill he's always at the office and when he gets home he's normally on some rant about what happened at work. I try and keep up but I don't really know what he's talking about. It's all legal terminology and people's names, People I haven't met. And he never asks me about my day, because he knows my life's not as important as his is and I agree with that. All I do is shop and keep the house in impeccable order, it's the least I can do if he's bringing the money in and supporting me to have such a lavish lifestyle. That's what real love is.

"Well great we really are the same. All three of us, getting married, coming to terms with the prenup and kind of being alone in it all!" I can tell Sally meant for that to be a positive thing but the ending didn't quiet sound right.

We all look at each other with new found sympathy and even I feel softer somehow. I can't recall a time anyone just looking at me, seeing through my lies and not judging me about it like Anne. Or a time someone could pull so much information out of me in so little time, like Sally.

As we sit in silence coming to terms with each other's predicament, the door opens. Out emerges the man that was once a head of me in line (that feels like a million years ago) he shakes Mr. Hornski's hand and leaves. Mr Hornski looks to our little group and says "Which one of you is Miss Green?"

"Me" I practically whisper, whatever happened to the urgent feeling I had when I first arrived?

"If you'd like to come through" Mr. Hornski starts ushering me into the office and I feel a small wave of panic. Sally's words begin to float around my brain, the minute I stand up. Damn that woman she did it again. Making me think of things I'd rather avoid. *"We really are the same…all three of us getting married…. coming to terms with the prenup…………kind of being alone in it all."*

"Mr. Hornski could….erm… could these two join us?" what the hell am I doing?

"Well yes if you'd like, are these your friends you've brought for moral support?" I can tell he thinks I'm a big baby for needing someone to hold my hand through this meeting, so I set the record straight.

"Erm…no… actually…Sally has just been in with you about the same reason I'm here, and Anne needs the same information as me and I just thought I'd be helpful. I see you're a very busy man and we are very busy women. Wouldn't you prefer to see us all together Mr. Hornski?"

His face is contorted with eyebrows raised to the ceiling. He looks both shocked and impressed, I love my ability to lie on the spot it really is a skill.

"Well yes of course that would be much appreciated if you're ok with that, then so am I. Ladies if you'd like to make your way through to my office. We will get this done with, quickly so it doesn't take up anymore of your time"

Anne and Sally's eyes are wide but neither of them hesitate to come to the office with me. (Thankfully, that could have been really awkward)

I look toward the girls one last time before we go in. I don't think I look nervous but Anne gives me a knowing nod and Sally winks at me and pats me on the shoulder.

"Go on in Jill we're right behind you" Sally's words are comforting and supportive but all I can muster is a look of irritation. I hold my breath and step toward finally getting my questions answered.

"So if he decides he doesn't love me anymore, I'm fucked basically!" I scream in shock.

"Well in layman's terms, yes, pretty much." Jack Hornsky

replies in a definite manner, with a small grin forming on the side of his mouth.

"Ladies just think of marriage as a business, a trade of services if you will. Your husbands will be providing you with a nice lifestyle and you will be providing him with a loving wife to tend to him, cook him dinner, rub his feet and listen to the monotonous drivel about his work that I'm assuming none of you will know of what he's talking about. But you listen and pretend to understand and nod along." can this man read my mind.

"Sometimes that's all men need at the end of the working day, a woman to make him feel good. So let's look at the result of that: you give your husband's love and understanding and in exchange for your service he will provide you with the finer things in life like clothes, jewellery, cars all that sort of thing. But once the marriage is over then you are no longer entitled to that life. You won't be there to give him emotional support so obviously he no longer provides you with nice things. Prenup's have to be fair; well I think in these circumstances this is fair. None of you work, you don't have any money coming in and you rely totally on your partners for financial support. So if you divorce, the business transaction has stopped. He gives, you give. You stop giving, he stops giving and that is what all of your prenup's state. I honestly can't dumb it down any further for you ladies."

Feeling subdued and defeated we finally emerge out of the law firm, feeling the weight of the world resting on our shoulders. One look around at Anne and Sally, tells me that we all need to pick each other up a little before we part ways.

"I know a really great cocktail bar just round the corner. Do you two need a cocktail? I know I do"

"Absolutely YES!" both of them cry in unison

Ok next stop to the cocktail bar.

"We get nothing?" Anne starts the prenup rant.

"What does he mean nothing?" Sally whines.

"Nothing as in what he has now, he will still have even after the divorce." Anne is still trying to dumb it down for her.

"Why do we have to sign a prenup, why are we already talking about divorce we're not even married yet?"

"Because our men want to cover their own backs." I repeat my earlier statement.

"What about us?"

"Look if we get divorced we are screwed, so the only sensible solution is….. DON'T GET DIVORCED!"

"Did you know that a 100% of all divorces start with marriage" Anne tries a pathetic attempt to try and lighten the mood.

Sally's eyes widen as though Anne has just spoken the gospel truth and is shocked by this revelation.

"How can we prevent getting a divorce? What if they fall out of love with us, or they meet some else."

"Someone younger." Great now Anne's panicking what next.

Sally's mouth opens in horror and big piece of muffin falls out.

"Hey where did you get that? We're at a cocktail bar not a café!" I try and hide my horror all Sally has done since we met is eat.

"I keep one in my bag at all times; I call it my emergency muffin. I always comfort eat when I'm stressed"

"Do you find yourself stressed a lot?" I try to hide my sarcasm. (It's no secret that Sally is at least twenty-five pounds overweight. At least.)

"Well I think where heading the right way for divorce seeing as we are freaking out and Sally's stress eating. We deserve to get nothing look at the state of us. Girls we need to get our act together fast."

Sally gulps "you mean go on a diet?"

"YES! We have to. Sally you need to act fast before you get an actual muffin top and Anne and I need to keep in shape too"

Anne hides a smile from my direct words while Sally holds the muffin in disgust and stares it out as though she were seizing up her enemy.

"Kate moss once said "nothing tastes as good as skinny feels." I concluded

"Yeah well poor Kate must never have had a Mcflurry before."

"They're to die for aren't they" Anne joins in to the conversation.

"I know right! My favourite is the Oreo one. You know I was there just the other day when..."

"STOP! Listen to you both. Kate moss is one of the sexiest super models in the world. Clearly she knows what she's talking about. She's famous, beautiful and rich! What have you two got?" I scream sense at them both.

"McDonalds?" Sally looks at me as though that's just as good as stardom and success.

"Well if you're going to keep your McDonalds, you can say hello to your divorce."

Sally's head flops into her hands with a look of anguish.

"You're right, I do love food but I love Allan more"

"Right so we are all going to do something about our figure?" I look to Anne first.

"Agreed" Anne nods to confirm.

"Agreed" Sally adds reluctantly.

"Agreed" I beam (knowing that I'm clearly the leader of the pack)

Great now I have two new sheep to follow me around.

Hey maybe they can help me organize my wedding.

Chapter Three

Muffin Top

"Sally what the hell are you wearing?"

"What's wrong with my outfit?"

"My text clearly instructed lycra! You need clothes that are stretchy and light, not jumper and jeans! How the hell, are you gonna work out in them?" I scream at her.

"But I was cold and the weather man said to dress warmly, I think he knows more about the weather than you do"

God sally baffles me, how can anyone be so dumb?

"I'm not talking about the weather I'm talking about the gym; you'll burn up in that"

"Good I'll burn more calories then!"

REALLY? REALLY! I can't be bothered talking to this delinquent any longer. Let her do what she wants. Where on earth is Anne, I specifically said ten on the dot! I hate when people are late it's so rude to keep people waiting.

Five minutes later and Anne finally makes an appearance. Both Sally and I are waiting quietly at the juice bar; I spot Anne and storm towards her.

"What time do you call this?" I demand.

"Oh I know I'm sorry I'm a little late, washing my gym outfit took longer than I thought"

A glance passes between Sally and I.

"You washed your gym outfit, why didn't you just find something else to where?" Sally asks in shock.

"Well the rest were neatly folded up and this set was a little askew, so obviously I didn't want to disturb my tidy sweats."

I've had just about enough of these two! I need to work off some of my anger; I think an hour on the treadmill is exactly what the doctor ordered.

———⁓〰⌾∽⌾⌾ↀ⌾∽∘⌾ⱽⱽ———

As we make our way into the gym Sally is in awe of everyone she sees.

"Everyone is so fit and muscular even the WOMEN!" she squeaks in shock.

"Close your mouth Sally it's rude to stare" I screech through gritted teeth.

"Haven't you ever been to a gym before?"

Sally just stands there star struck slowly shaking her head.

This is unbelievable I feel like I'm babysitting two idiots. And Anne looks terrified, seriously what's scary about a gym? Do you know what, I haven't got time for this.

"Right you two I think an hour on the treadmill to start. We need the cardio in our exercise plan then we can move on to the spinning class or would you rather do yoga?"

Anne's brows are knit together tight and she's breathing very heavily. How? We haven't done anything yet. Sally looks at me as though I've hit her over the head with a brick, she looks that confused with her brow furrowed in a cringe.

Leading them both over to the treadmills, I jump on and get

to work. Sally cautiously steps on looking frantic about which button to press.

"God's sake Sally just press the start button on the screen"
I'm really starting to lose my patience now.

Right come on Jill just get into the zone, the fat burning zone! Just think of your perfect wedding day with your perfect wedding dress looking stunning. Come on focus.

This feels so good; I can feel all my troubles melting away. The stress of the prenup and my irritation towards dumb and dumber is leaving my body, in this moment none of it matters. My heart's pounding away I'm picking up speed seriously, I'm going so fast it's liberating I feel like I'm actually running away from my problems. I FEEL GREAT! (And I'm only 30 minutes in)

I'm gonna look great in my wedding dress.

Because I am obviously gluten for punishment I take a look around to see if Anne and Sally are breaking a sweat as much as me. And the answer to that question is NO!

I look to my right and Sally is no longer on the treadmill, shocked I start to spin my head frantically in search of where she could have got to.

"She's gone to the juice bar" Anne's delicate normal breathing rate voice comes from my left; I spin my head like an owl and study her with the eyes of a hawk.

"She was red in the face, honestly Jill I don't think Sally is used to too much exercise"

"What are you doing?" I scream.

Man! My anger is back full force.

"I'm cleaning, I'm taking my time. Who knows how many sweaty hands this thing has seen."

"Anne, are you kidding, I've been working out for thirty minutes and you haven't even got on the damn thing yet! And what do you mean Sally's at the juice bar? When did she go?"

"Twenty-eight minutes ago"

"What. That's a bit precise isn't it? Have you been timing her?"

"No I just remember two minutes had gone by on your screen when she left and now it says thirty minutes so....yeah I can do simple math Jill"

I can't believe this. Great. We are here to lose weight, to keep in shape for our husbands or they will divorce us. Why am I the only one that cares about this? I'm not standing for this, time for a reality check.

Jumping of the treadmill I make a clear run for the juice bar, I'm going to give miss bone idle another dose of tough love, it's the only way she'll learn.

"I wouldn't do that if I were you Jill, go slow. You've been on the mill your legs won't be used to the floor!"

What is she talking about course I'm used...to...the...why have my legs turned to jelly? I'm buckling, I'm going down.

"Anne! Anne! What's happening? Help!"

"You silly woman!" she mocks me.

Anne comes rushing to my side and helps me up. Great now the whole gym is filled with sly giggles and sniggers. Fantastic now I'm the laughing stock. Just because I went down faster than a bag of hammers. Well I wouldn't have fallen if it weren't for Sally.

"Get Sally now, we are leaving and never coming back!"

Anne can tell I mean business, I'm shaking, I'm humiliated and I want to go now.

Why doesn't everyone just take a picture, it would last longer. Jesus haven't they seen someone fall over before?

There's this woman, sorry I mean stick insect with long blonde hair that flows all the way down to her ass. She keeps looking back at me and giggling to her friend by her side. Man

I detest bitchy women especially ones that presume to be better than me (Like Farilyn)

"What are you laughing at? I'm not the one with a big hole in my leggings. Yeah that's right you're showing everyone that you're not wearing any underwear."

I love shouting, it really is the best way to release anger (that would be better actually, just have a room where you can shout your head off. Way better than a gym at least you can't get jelly leg from that)

Blondie locks and her friend are fussing over her bottom, her friend covers her with a jacket and they make a quick exit.

I love having the last laugh.

There's a sudden burst of laughter coming from a short stout man, he's kind of muscly with a gruff laugh and big thick calves - almost too thick, his head looks disproportionate to his body.

"Well I guess you got her back" shit is he talking to me?

"Ergh....yeah well she deserved it, tit for tat in my eyes"

"Yeah and you've got lovely eyes"

Woah is this beast actually flirting with me? Please tell me this is a joke surely he can see my canary diamond it's as thick as his calves! Plus even if I wasn't engaged it should be obvious to him that I'm clearly out of his league. Never mind, god loves a trier. Guess I'll just let him down easy.

"I'm sorry sir but I think you'll find your wasting your time" I say flashing my engagement ring his way.

"Should have known, the gorgeous ones are always taken"

Shit, am I blushing?

"Yes well just go about your business, I'm just waiting for my ergh....friends"

That word felt foreign on my tongue.

"That's ok, I don't mind waiting with you, I don't have a client coming in for another hour"

A client? He's a personal trainer? I thought all personal trainers were supposed to be gorgeous. A man that all women want, that's what gets the customers in, just to watch him flex and help position her into the downward facing dog to stretch. No woman would want this....this...short pudgy man. He's laughable.

"Look I don't want you to wait with me, in fact I'm offended that you're even talking to me. Go now before I call the manager over and have you fired. I'm a paying customer and your staff, never forget your place"

His eyes light up with pleasure from my outburst, and he looks rather impressed with me.

"Woah you're a fiery thing aren't ya! Its ok I quite like that. Ok me lady I will remember my place, I apologize if I've offended you" he says in a mockery of an old English accent, just to annoy me.

"Would madam allow me to at least help her off the floor? After all it is my duty as your humble servant" He bows so gracefully I picture him practicing at home, where he lives.... Alone!

"Let me guess, you're single. Am I right?"

I can't help feeling smug. Of course this loser is single look at him.

"Yes me lady I am"

Ha I knew it!

Anne comes dragging a sheepish looking Sally up behind her.

"For god's sake where have you two been?"

"Jill, sorry it took me so long to find her, I've got her now. Are we going?"

"Well yes if you'd both help me up."

"Here let me do that" the beast approaches and scoops me up in one movement before I can protest. He's quite strong for a little man.

Now standing at my full height all "6.2" of me looks down on this peasant. I tower over him, I feel like Gandalf standing next to this hobbit.

"Wow you're an impressive height for a lady" he looks me over from head to toe. Admiring every inch of me with his eyes, just drinking me in. He's making me feel like a giant candy bar and he doesn't know which end to start with first.

P.s I'm totally used to men checking me out like this after all I could have been a model.

"Jill, aren't you going to introduce us to your friend" of course this is Sally putting her nose in, I forgot these two were behind me.

"No I'm not; we are leaving right now, girls."

The girl's halt to attention and follow me as I storm past the hobbit man, well all except Sally.

"Hi I'm Sally, what's your name? Sorry about Jill she's really stressed out at the moment see we are all going through..."

"Sally shut up!" Anne and I shout in unison.

It's getting old how she doesn't care about blabbing her mouth off to total strangers about our personal problems. We both rush back to grab her, Anne's gripping her hand and frog marching her out like a child. And I grab her handbag knowing she has her emergency muffin in there and I'm dangling it in front of her to lure her outside.

Hobbit man looks on at us, smirking finding this whole thing rather amusing. I could hit him, he has no idea how tiring it is to be a full time mother to Sally (Anne and I are just starting to get the picture)

"I'm Burt it was nice to meet you Sally and Jill! And sorry I didn't catch the red heads name"

"Anne Beckety" Sally shouts back to Burt while we are thrusting her out of the building. (Damn why didn't anyone think to cover her mouth?!)

———✦————

We arrive at my apartment, I hardly ever come here because I'm always at Bills lush penthouse suite, but I come here sometimes just to....you know keep a bit of independence as my father say's "nothings final until marriage" and you know that makes a lot of sense. I mean you wouldn't get rid of your own apartment until you knew for sure that you were going to marry and move into a new home with your new husband, so yeah, my dad bought me this place as a safety net, in fact I had this place before I ever met Bill.

It's nice in a small way; nowhere near as lavish as Bill's place but this will do for now and like I said, I won't need it for much longer. The second I say "I do" I'm putting this place on the market, I'm sure dad won't mind me keeping the money, after all he is rich.

"How did you afford this place?" Sally's the first to talk.

Anne and I haven't fully spoken to Sally since the gym incident, I mean we've shouted at her but that's not the same. Actually I'm really annoyed with both of them, neither of them tried to get fit at all, only me. I know Anne was going to, but really this cleaning "problem" really is a problem. She should go to the doctor's and get help, it can't be convenient to live that way (I must remember to mention something to her...you know in a subtle way) but Sally was putting on weight which is the opposite of what we were trying to do. (That reminds me

I never gave her that tough love speech....well better late than never.)

"Never mind how I afforded my apartment, what were you thinking in there? I thought we agreed to get in shape to keep our husbands"

"Jill I tried really I did, I worked out for…"

"Two minutes! I know Anne told me."

"Anne, why are you gossiping about me?" Sally looks hurt and helpless like a little kitten; she can be so pathetic sometimes.

"Don't bring me into this, I only told her what I saw. This is between you two." Anne tries to defend herself.

"I tried, I really tried but I haven't had any breakfast, I was starving. It's not good to overdo yourself on an empty stomach everyone knows that"

Excuses, Excuses.

"I've had enough of you, both of you! My marriage is gonna work out great and I'm gonna be in great shape, and he will love me forever and ever and I'll look AMAZING in my wedding gown. And you two will end up sad, lonely, FAT and Divorced!"

If I wanted a reaction believe me I'm getting one, Sally's blinking back tears and Anne looks outraged. (Well good, they both needed to hear it)

"You know what Jill, size doesn't matter. It doesn't make a marriage last, your too vain and too shallow." (Anne really is a cheeky cow. How dare she call me vain.)

"OH MY GOD! You're hilarious; of course you think I'm shallow because I look good and I actually care about looking good for my man, how you even got a man let alone engaged is a mystery to me. For god's sake Anne your man works all day, every day to provide you with a good life. You do nothing. It's our womanly duty to look good for our men. It's the only thing we can give them other than our time and attention. You should have more pride in yourself."

"I don't need to take advice from a woman who dresses like a Tarted up celebrity. I've got class and an education unlike you." Anne screams at me.

"How dare you, I have style. Just because you look like an old battle axe of a school teacher don't take it out on me."

(I am so hot with anger right now, both of us are red in the face from screaming, in a weird way it feels really good, but then again I've always loved shouting)

Sally interjects "right both of you calm down, to your corners"

In unison Anne and I shout "SHUT UP SALLY"

After our heated argument we settle down with champagne cocktails and pour our hearts out. Sorry let me rephrase that for you, Sally poured her heart out and Anne and I were forced to listen as she gushed on and on about her fiancé and we had to listen to every detail, about the way he pours his coffee, the way he fixes his tie before he goes on the road. The way she stares at him when he's sleeping ok yeah that one was creepy. She very obviously adores him but I couldn't help detect a sort of sadness in her voice, a sort of melancholy. She didn't explain it, maybe I just imagined it.

As flawed as she is, Sally's actually a welcome distraction, because if it had only been Anne and I in the apartment I have a suspicious feeling that Anne would have left already. So again I guess Sally has played the role of our child again, our child that keeps us together.

An hour and a half into the graphic details of Sal's unhealthy love for her fiancé Allan; she drifts off onto the subject that brought us together.

"Do you know what? I'm going to sign that pre-nup thing.

Yes I'm going to do it! What's so scary anyway I mean......it's just a piece of paper and if it's what Allan needs to feel secure entering our marriage then I'll do it. I'm honestly not bothered anymore, and if he loves me the way I love him then I've got nothing to worry about, and neither do either of you."

Here she goes again miss thirteen going on thirty.

I know she's convinced me (well it wasn't so much Sally as more I have no choice) Anne gives me a sly glance out of the corner of her eye and I immediately feel my face redden. We are clearly all thinking the same thing *just sign the pre-nup.*

The room falls silent, each one of us lost in our own thoughts. Sally's not a fan of silence I know this because well......it's Sally.

"I mean if you think about it Jill" here comes the interrogation again.

"It's just like you said, it's not the prenup that's the problem it's divorce, and I'm sure none of us are going to get divorced – we love our fiancés and they love us."

"I know so that's what we are doing now, trying to prevent divorce"

Anne's finally coming to life "look you're both right, Sally we need to sign the prenup because there won't be any weddings to plan. And Jill, I suppose you're right as well...... I mean I don't agree that a man could only love you if you're the perfect size, but I'm sure there are certain things we could do to make our marriages a success"

Sally's beaming at us both, loving the fact that someone's finally agreeing with her.

"Jill, I want us to get on from this moment on, I know you mean well but you come across a bit too bossy for your own good. We are all going through this together and I understand that you're stressed out, we all are. But you need to be a little kinder to me, I'll listen when you're speaking but I expect the same back. If we can get along that would make things easier on all of us. If you give me respect you'll get it back, but not before"

Silence

What do I say to that? I have to give her respect before she gives it back? How dare she speak to me like that! I'm not too bossy. I don't know where to start, I'm just staring at the floor trying to regain my composure......(sort of) I mean I'm definitely not crying. I would never cry in front of people, especially these two.

Blinking back my embarrassment I try not to make eye contact with either of them. Focusing my attention on my Louis Vuitton bag I realise my minds gone blank. I truly have no come back. It's not an argument, it's not hatred it's not even anger she's just asking me to be kind.

"Unless you want to do this on you own?" Sally looks at me as though she's just had an epiphany and this new option has just freshly dawned on her.

"Yeah of course, if we are cramping your style too much we could always just part ways now" it's neither a question nor a threat. Just a statement, a fact. (Which is even worse)

"No" comes a tiny voice.

Sally and Anne glare at me cautiously, studying me intently.

"No, I, I ......you're not cramping my style. I .... I'm sorry I'll stop being so bossy. But in my defence I only say those things because I care and I take charge because.... Because that's who I am ok."

"Look that's fine we understand your personality, we all have quirky flaws that make us different, but your anger needs to stop now, no more arguments"

"Look can I just say one more thing" (I'm cooling down now

a little, I'm trying to look more serious because I really need her to understand)

"He will leave you for another woman, a hot young woman if you don't do something about your image Anne. You've got no sex appeal."

Looking tired and frustrated Anne's shoulders flop in defeat.

"Fine, let's have it your way then. Where can I get sex appeal from?"

Locking eyes with Anne, I smile and say "I know just the place."

Chapter Four

Kinky Couture

O k so this is literally Disney land for adults and everything is super expensive. They actually have solid gold vibrators here, eighteen karat gold! These are the Gucci of sex toys. These sex gadgets are for the rich (the really rich!)

I've only ever passed this place on my way to do some clothes shopping. But word on the grapevine is that this is the go to place for all your boudoir accessories. I've heard that celebrities come here all the time. It's the one place that makes sex sophisticated. I've told the girls all about it through texts and I've also told them to bring their fiancés credit cards because I have a feeling we are going to spend a lot.

I've never bought sex toys before because I've always had a man in my life (even just for sexual purposes) and I've never brought a toy into the bed with a man there, because I've always felt I am more than capable of satisfying him. But I'm willing to expand my sexual horizons for Bill, so bring on the kinky couture.

This whole boutique is lavish. There is pink leather couches scattered throughout the store. Black feathers and silver sequins draping down the walls, and at the door we are served champagne on arrival. God retail therapy feels good. Anne, Sally and I are staring mystified at the sales assistants that are walking around in bondage gear. Black leather corsets, fishnet stockings, maid's outfits. They are carrying solid silver trays ladled with champagne flutes studded with crystals.

The legs on some of these women even put me to shame; I can tell Anne is the most shocked to see women dressed this way. I was totally convinced Anne was a complete prude, so I was beyond shocked when she agreed to come here in the first place. But then again she's the main reason we are here. Time to find Anne's erotic side.

The kinky couture logo is hung above the front desk, we are completely hypnotised by everything. Everything's so strange and intriguing (I guess this is the definition of a guilty pleasure)

"Why is there a phone number on the tag?" Sally's found a feather bower and is inspecting it.

"I think that's the price" Anne corrects her sceptically.

I suppose they're right to be so shocked at some of these prices, but I'd never show my shock. To be high maintenance one has to give the illusion that money isn't an issue, and seeing as we have our partner's cash I don't see why it should be.

(P.S make a mental note to remember to give Anne and Sally a lesson in shopping etiquette if you spend a lot and have an air about you that says your worth a lot, all the right places and people start kissing your ass! They give you special attention and turn you into an instant VIP overnight. If "pretty woman" has taught us anything it's that)

The owner of the store approaches us. You can tell she owns this place because she is dripping with gold jewellery and has a huge ring on every finger. Just the way she walks tells you this woman has money and authority. She has way too much confidence and makes me feel inadequate. The mere look of her is one of sheer arrogance, as though she's in love with herself and everyone else should be as well.

(I guess working with celebrities can give you a pretty big head) well I'll show her I'm a woman with money, she's not the only sophisticated one here you know.

"Hello you must be the owner of Kinky Couture, wonderful place you have here. I've always been meaning to come here; I've heard only the elite shop here. That's why I'm here. I'm Jill green, my father is Mr. Harold Green. He's a top lawyer on Wall Street"

Her eyebrows don't flinch; normally when I drop that line people look really impressed or even frightened. Not this diva though.

"Well hello Jill, I'm Claudette Ginxi. Yes I am the owner of Kinky Couture. It's a pleasure to have new faces here, and who are your friends?"

Oh god Sally please don't embarrass me (again!) my mind is screaming at her but my face is just giving her a meaningful look. I hope she understands subtle messages through eye contact.

Sally comes bouncing over.

"Hi I'm Sally; lovely to meet you everything's so interesting in here. I've never been to an adult store before; to be honest I expected it to be kinda seedy. You know like dirty and unclean, a sticky floor joint with a bit of old school porn music playing in the background. But this is lovely, very glam, ten out of ten in my book Claudette, well done!"

Guess that's a no to the subtle eye contact.

I can tell everyone finds Sally ignorant and foolish because of how they're grinning. I chuckle and try to steer the conversation away from Sally and back onto me. But Claudette isn't paying attention to me; she swerves past me and heads for Anne.

"Hello I'm Claudette Ginxi, CEO of kinky couture if you need anything just ask either myself or one of my staff members. We will be more than happy to help you, whatever your needs" she adds with a wink.

"Why erm...thankyou Claudette, I'm Anne. I'm not really looking for anything in particular. I've just come here for a browse with friends" she flashes me a vicious look, clearly hating this trip.

"Ok ladies please don't be shy with Claudette; I know all women have a daring sexual side to them. Some women put it on show for others to see, that is called being confident. Other women like you three, choose to hide that side of you, and keep it private and that's makes you mysterious. Either is good yes?"

Seriously who talks like that? Claudette is very obviously Russian with a heavy accent, despite her living in New York. I do think it's hilarious how she talks about herself in the third person. Wow she really is in love with herself, but just like daddy says "First you have to love yourself before others can love you"

I love my dad he's a very wise man.

All three of us just stare at each other knowing Claudette is right. Why else would we be here?

"But you!" she points at Anne.

"Are the most mysterious of the group. There is a deep sexual animal urge inside you, but I get the feeling you shun that side of you away even from yourself. Well darling now is the time to get in touch with your dark side; Kinky couture has everything you could ever need in or out of the bedroom. Come with Claudette, Anne! Claudette will teach you, Claudette will show you all you will ever need for good sexy time"

Before Anne has a chance to refuse, Claudette drags her by her wrist and leads her over to the bondage section. Sally covers her mouth in an attempt to smother her piggish snort noises. I feel like this should be funny because Anne looks truly terrified, but I feel slightly concerned like watching a mouse being led away by a lion.

I bet when we meet up with her again she will be a kinky woman with a strong lust for sex, stronger than mine or Sally's put together. Saying that I can't picture Sally as a sexual person, she's too innocent. I couldn't picture her that way and I don't think I'd like it if she changed, she's simple sweet Sally.

As I turn toward Sal I see her bounding toward the vibrator/ sex toy section like a kid in a candy store. She picks up a shiny metal vibrator turns it on and jumps in terror from the power of the vibrations (I was right, she is a ditz, clearly she's never been this close to a sex toy before either) feeling flustered she picks it up from the floor and shoves it deep in to the back hoping no one will notice (but I did) she's looking flushed and shaken but keeps composure and pretends she's idly browsing the shelves, all whilst twiddling her thumbs behind her back (Sally has clearly watched to many comedy shows, that's the opposite of how you look innocent)

I'm gonna forget about them right now and get down to some serious shopping. Right where to start...well seeing as I'm near the sex toys I may as well start here.

Going down the opposite aisle from Sally I find myself in wonderland, everything is so curious and sparkly. First my eyes land on something called Luna beads; I guess kinky couture sells jewellery too! There's also a solid silver handled ostrich feather I have my eye on, it's gorgeous (very burlesque) I turn the tag to see the price and the feather is...... guess how much.....over $600! My word you could break the bank in here, but you would definitely have fun doing so.

———⁓∙∿∘⟨∘⟩∘⟨∘⟩∘∿∙⁓———

Turns out, the feather is the cheapest item in here by a mile. I actually stumbled on a vibrator that must hold the most expensive sex toy record ever, its $24,000! Can you believe that? It's covered in diamonds. I know it sounds incredible but could you imagine if a diamond came loose while you were using it, and it got lost in your womanhood forever! Of course I know the saying is "diamonds are a girl's best friend" but having diamonds stuck in your vagina is taking it a bit too far.

Moving on I find another piece of jewellery. Its name is "the thumb clit ring" it's solid platinum and is worth nearly $70,000 are kidding me? Well that's put the vibrator to shame without a doubt. I can't help grinning to myself it's so ridiculous; I mean there really isn't much to it at all. It's just a plain bent ring, but what do I know it's probably fantastic if it's worth that much...... maybe I should buy two?

Some of these penis shaped things cost millions. The more I find, the more glamorous they're getting and the price tag shows it. They have some with crowns on, dripping with jewels made from the best gold, platinum or silver money can buy. (Totally made for royalty)

I read rich socialites come here often and buy at least one of everything in the store, but my personal favourite is the piece de resistance "The Fantom" it's a silver star covered glass dildo meaning you can look right through it. And laid inside the glass is a blood diamond engagement ring.

I don't want it for sexual reasons; I want it for the precious stone that lay inside. Why don't all sex toys double as a jewellery box? I think more women would be eager to buy them if that were the case. Plus could you imagine how romantic that would be? Your boyfriend surprises you on Valentine's Day with expensive sexories and then you see a ring inside. You look at him and he's already down on one knee and asks for your vagina in marriage.

Come to think of it, it would be an embarrassing story to tell your friends when they ask "so how did he propose?"

Mmmmm maybe a little too modern for my taste, It is a beautiful engagement ring though; I think I'll get it just for the blood diamond. I deserve a treat, after all his money will technically be my money soon.

A scream comes from behind me and I run in panic to Sally's rescue. I panicked for nothing; she's just freaked out at another vibrator. She drops it apologizing frantically and stumbles back and bumps into a beautiful Korean woman, wearing sexy lingerie.

"Oh hunny I'm so sorry I didn't see you there"

Silence

"Did I hurt you...erm I guess I'm just not used to this kind of stuff. I mean that thing is like a power drill. You must be used to it though, working here an all"

Everyone has gathered to watch Sally's apology speech. Anne's returned to the group looking relieved to have a break from Claudette, and none of us can believe this ignorant woman hasn't accepted Sal's apology yet.

All the staff seem to be chuckling to themselves as though they know a joke they refuse to share. They clearly love the show, but Anne and I aren't finding this funny at all.

Anne just has to intervene.

"Excuse me miss, our friend apologized. Why are you so shocked? She hardly touched you."

"Ladies, ladies this is Petina she's our very realistic sex doll costing around $25,000. She's our bestseller." Claudette comes over to inform us. "And girls don't think this is just for men, think how happy it'll make you knowing your man will never leave you for another woman when he has you and patina at home. He can truly have his cake and eat it too, no?"

I'm assuming that's a rhetorical question.

Claudette talks to us in a way that makes you feel like you're the child and she's the woman, very sophisticated if not a little stuck up but she has a right to be. She must easily be a millionaire from the looks of all this, and obviously she's worked with celebrities. I'd quite like to befriend her. Inviting her to my wedding ought to make a splash. Maybe we'll even be in the top magazines; she could bring a date, someone famous. But not too famous (I wouldn't want them to take the attention away from me)

"Wait, wait, hold up" Sally yells looking seriously stressed.

"You're telling me she's a doll!"

"It's ok Sally, it's shocking how many mannequins I've apologized to in shops" Anne tries to reassure her. (No wonder the staff were laughing, it makes sense now)

"I can't believe how life like she is" Sally gets closer to inspect Petina.

No wonder she looks so shocked her face was made that way. She's plastic, I actually can't believe it, she looks so real. I don't understand who picked her mouth to be in the shape of an "O" is that the face men find sexy......? Maybe I should start making that face in bed, I'm way better than a doll. God I thought I was really educated about sex but this place is teaching me a thing or two.

After the initial embarrassment of Sally's mistake, the staff grow silent and get back to just standing quietly looking fantastic. Seriously I've not seen any of them running errands for Claudette or breaking a sweat over any work related task in the shop. I've got a conspiracy theory that their just hired models showing off how amazing their bodies look in Kinky couture lingerie. Fortunately for Claudette her master plan has worked it's magic because I'm definitely not leaving until I have a few naughty pieces to take home with me.

Sally's eyes follow my direction and she attempts to whisper.

"I know they look incredible don't they! Like swimwear models, I wish I looked as good as they do in next to nothing"

I roll my eyes discreetly while my back is turned. Sally's so dumb, you can't complain about your figure when you eat all the time and take no exercise. But I'm not gonna attempt to talk sense into her; I'm going to bite my tongue for a change and be nice just like Anne instructed.

"I'm sure you'll look fab Sal why don't we go and pick some out together?"

Claudette jumps at the chance of showing us around, and takes great delight in showing us every individual piece. Everything here has a top story from which celebrity owns one and in what colour to what material it's made from and where the inspiration for the collection came from and so on and so forth. Claudette really is rather clever I haven't given her enough credit. She makes you fall in love with it, to the point where she knows she's got you under her spell. But due to hygiene reasons we are not allowed to try the lingerie on. We just have to find our size, buy it and hope it fits when we get home. Also she never reveal's the price. The one time I asked how much she just glanced at me as though to say "Why? Do you not have enough?" it was really degrading and I reddened when she looked down on me like that. I told you, you must give the impression money means little or nothing to you it's the only way to impress people. Trust me I know.

To show Claudette just how rich I am. I pick up a matching bra and thong set, a baby doll and something else that had the crotch missing. There I think I've managed to restore my reputation around here.

Sally follows suit as though she could possibly have as much money as me. She goes for the most revealing little blue silk corset, studded with rhinestones and a matching silk thong with jewelled butterflies hanging from the hips. It's really skimpy and beautiful but only a woman half of Sally's size could pull it off.

"I really love this I'm getting it and showing Allan what a sex kitten of a fiancé he has, the lucky devil!"

Sally's all smug and grinning from ear to ear now, like the cat that got the cream. I just hope she has the cash for that thing; I couldn't stand it if she shows me up at the cash register.

Anne's lingering lamely behind, she looks miserable and uncomfortable in her own skin (nothing unusual there then) I glance down to her arm that is ladled with garments, feather bowers, glittery heels, sex toys and a wig.

"A wig?"

"Yeah apparently it's for role-play in the bedroom, it's meant to turn men on when you pretend to someone else"

"Oh....cool"

What else can I say? Why didn't I know that? She's had so much one on one time with Claudette I'm sure Anne knows more about pleasing men than I do now. That's not fair! Right where is that kinky Russian bitch?! I want to know everything and I want to know it now.

"Claudette, tell me all you know about role-play. Pretending to be someone else in the bedroom, do you have anything else apart from wigs for that?"

"Why of course, right this way"

Honestly the more she talks the more she sounds like count Dracula (you know if Dracula was from Russia) She has a very dark dramatic side to her that makes her seem sexy in quite a scary way.

She leads me back to the sex toys and picks up a black leather strap on with different sized attachments. She holds it with both hands out flat, balancing the strap on, on her fingertips as though it were the Holy Grail. Whilst her eyes are greedily worshipping it, I glance at the girls and both are glowing purple with inflated cheeks ready to burst out laughing at any minute (Sally's cheeks have swelled up to the size of two big red balloons. She looks in pain she wants to laugh that badly, even her eyes are watering)

I try and ignore them, what do they know? They're not truly kinky like me and Claudette.

"This is everything you will need to please you man"

Claudette stares confidently into my eyes and without blinking says "this saves marriages; women who are confident with their sexual prowess will always keep a man in tow with this. You see, turning into a new person in sex doesn't just have to be appearance, it comes from your attitude, your confidence, it's you but a whole new side. A side he's never seen before"

Sold!

I snatch the strap on from count Claudette and she doesn't flinch, almost as though she knew how badly I needed it all along.

"All men love a woman to take control in the bedroom. And pegging is just one of the many pleasures you can give a man. Not a lot of men admit to enjoying anal sex…. But all men secretly do. And those who deny it, have not yet tried it. Walk into the bedroom wearing this and he will learn to love seeing such a dominant side to you."

Claudette needn't have bothered saying all that, she had me at marriage saver. Bill seeing me as kinky, I know he will love it.

"Come on girls lets go and splash our cash"

'And get outta here' I almost add, before I end up buying the whole store.

Chapter Five

Cock – Tales

So saying that we over spent is an understatement. I'm not gonna bother telling you how much it was for all three of us in total, but let's just say it would make your eyes water (but I suppose you can't put a price on saving a marriage) I now have complete faith that signing the prenup is not a problem. I'll do it the minute I get back to Bills apartment. No time like the present.

I told the girls instantly what I'm planning to do the minute I get home, and they both agreed on doing the same.

"See I told you we have nothing to fear" Sally declares to the room like she was the oracle all along.

"Yeah it's true we were worrying over nothing. All we can do is our best, they love us they won't leave us" Anne nods to herself.

"And they'll love us even more in these!" Sally holds up her corset and thong like a winner.

"Girls we are going to give our men the night of their lives" Sally squeals with excitement.

"Are you trying it out on him tonight?" Anne looks shocked,

like the shopping was just for fun, and none of us really had any intention of actually using any of this stuff.

"Of course we are. That was the whole point. You heard Claudette she'd outa know it's her job. This stuff will save our marriages and add a bit of spice back into our sex lives. It's good to keep things fresh where sex is concerned. Otherwise it goes stale and the relationship breaks down. You don't want that do you?"

Anne doesn't even bother to reply, she just sits there slowly shaking her head side to side. Anne's been really quite since we left kinky couture. I don't know if she's depressed or just shell shocked by all she's seen. Sally doesn't seem to notice, she's too busy going through her bag of naughty goodies.

"Look at all my gorgeous things. Who ever said 'money doesn't buy you happiness' never heard of retail therapy." Sally declares happily.

"Precisely my point, the more money you have the happier who'll be its just common sense. Why do you think the poor are always so depressed?" Sally suddenly stops unloading her items one by one and stares into thin air, as though to truly contemplate what I've said.

"I mean look at this" I hold the marriage saver, (the plastic talisman of love and lust, the key to happiness, the actual secret that keeps married couples together) delicately in my hands. This is the answer.

When someone asks a couple how long they've been to-gether and they reply with an incredible amount of years, then that person says "Wow what's your secret?" Then the couple always look rather blasé don't you think? They roll they roll their eyes at each other and put it down to love and communi-cation and all that bullshit. Because of course they can't reveal their secret (aka the strap on) otherwise everyone would stay together and no one would be jealous of married couples.

And that would never do.

But finally I'm in with the in crowd. I too now know the secret, and I intend on keeping it to myself. Let the loser single ladies of this world keep guessing, because I'm going to be just fine.

"It looks really weird. Who would ever come up with a plastic penis for men? Think about it, if he likes dick how come he's not gay?"

I roll my eyes at Sally's black and white vision of the world. Nothing is as it seems anymore. Everyone can be into everything and want no labels attached to them at the end of the day. Although I kinda see what she means, it is all quite confusing but hell if this plastic Willy keeps me from being divorced I'm not going to ask any questions.

"I assure you, Bill is absolutely not gay! Anyway haven't you ever heard that a man's G spot is in his…you know?" I indicate with my hands where I'm talking about, and both women are looking at me with eyes the size of saucers.

"I didn't know that but it does make a lot of sense. Allan moans like crazy when I go anywhere near there. So I often massage him there, because that's where he says all his tension is"

I can't help but smile a smile of hilarity at Sally. Of course Allan says that's where his tension is (wink-wink) it's just like Claudette said, not many men admit to enjoying anal but all men do.

"Are you sure that's where his tension is or just where he wants your attention to be?" I give Sally a meaningful look and she looks momentarily stunned and then rolls on the floor laughing, I can't keep a straight face at this. All this time Sal believed him and had been unknowingly causing Allan some serious arousal, anally. Even Anne starts snorting and spluttering her drink everywhere.

"What about you Anne, has your guy ever conned you into touching him there or are you more accommodating than we think" I ask Anne nosily.

"Yeah Anne" Sally picks herself up from the floor and starts dabbing at her watery eyes. "Does your man like you doing anything to his..."

"Arsehole" god's sake, we are adults we might as well say it.

"Arsehole, yes" Sally squeaks between laughs "Yep that's what I mean" Sal says as she laughs/cries her make-up off.

God she's contagious, Anne and I are both biting the corners of our mouths to prevent ourselves from getting to Sally's level of hysteria.

Anne just nods at the question giving no detail and no story, leaving me wanting to know more.

"Well what does he like?" I push for answers.

"I...I...I don't know, Richard likes the same as Sally's man does...you know all men are probably quite similar with that kind of thing" Anne has gone a new shade of red. So the evidence is clear, all men enjoy it up the butt.

Even prudish Mcprude Anne gives it to her man, how come Bill's never asked that from me? Maybe he doesn't think I'm kinky enough? Or maybe he's waiting for me to make the first move. Seriously you'd think after all this time together that we would have experienced this by now.

———— ·ᴍᴏᴀᴇᴛᴏᴏᴛᴇᴏᴏᴍ· ————

I whip up pretty mean champagne cocktails if I do say so myself. The cool liquid hits the back of my throat and the bubbles burst on the back of my tongue, enough of this stuff will make you giddy. Right now all three of us are prime examples of that.

We all take turns showing off our goods from Kinky couture. Weirdly enough I actually seem to have bought less than the others which has got me puzzled, maybe their men are as well off as mine. I'm done showing my pieces, it's now Anne's turn and she cringes as she looks down to her three bags full of sexy surprises. She takes each piece out carefully (Not as though it should be treasured like gold dust but more as something that's contaminated that needs to be held at arm's length.)

Holding every piece of "clothing" between her finger and thumb as though it were filthy, then she brandishes it towards Sally so she can admire it. And then Sally flings it to me so I can inspect it.

Everything is beautiful and sexy, sooo sexy I really can't imagine Anne wearing any of this stuff. The only sexual scenario I can see Anne performing to perfection is head mistress and naughty school boy role-play. (She looks so much like a teacher already she's just missing the cane)

Side note: can you believe the cane was an actual thing! Teachers were allowed to beat children into submission. That would never happen nowadays. The teacher would be thrown into the nearest cell for life and rightly so. It's kinda creepy that adults re-enact those nasty old fashioned days as something sexual in the bedroom isn't it?

Two bottles of Dom Perignon later and we are all laughing about Sally's tales in the bedroom. She can recollect any embarrassing memory with ease, telling us all about the men she's slept with in the past. Anne's gotten really tipsy over the last few hours and seems to be enjoying herself. Sally and I are reminiscing on the best and the worst sex we have ever had. Laughing at the men that had no idea where to put it, and at the ones that thought they were brilliant but in actual fact were terrible. Anne hasn't been telling her stories (I guess even when pissed as a fart she is tight lipped about her love life, SNOB.) but she has been getting involved asking loads and loads of questions which Sally is only too happy to go into graphic (and I mean GRAPHIC) detail about.

(Turns out Sally is a minx and completely confident about her body, she actually doesn't give a shit)

Well today has been a total success, we are all still giggling from the stories and champagne but we know what must be done now.

"God I can't wait to get home. All this talk has turned me on" Sally laughs and stumbles for her coat.

"I know what you mean, let's strike while the irons hot. I feel relaxed and ready for a good time" I feel motivated and eager to get home.

"OOOoowwh you gonna use the cock on him tonight?" Sally smiles up at me with a cheeky grin. (I hate to admit it but I kind of love Sally, a lot. Hell I love Anne too. I don't know why but right now I just feel like I love everyone.)

"You bet your ass I am. I can't wait! I'm excited. He has no idea but he is gonna have the best sex of his life tonight" I chuckle to myself and Sally high five's me.

"Same here, Allan gets home tonight and he doesn't know what he's in for, I'm raring to go" Sally starts witch cackling and I follow suit (I am so drunk right now, but I'm really fine with it)

We turn to Anne waiting to hear her plan of attack.

"Do you know.... I think I am going...to...suddd...uuucce richy tonight. He's earned it, and, and, and I love him..." Okay so Sally and I are relatively sober compared to Anne. She's slurring too much. She's hardly making sense. All I got from that was that she loves someone called richy. She could be talking about her dog for all I know.

"GOD, I LOVVVEEE HIMMM. AND I FEEL SEXY!" Anne is literally shouting her confidence at us and we are startled.

"I WANT IT! And I SHOULD.... I should.... I'm a woman, a SEXY woman" some words are whispers and the others are loud as hell.

"Okay hunny you go and jump on Richard and show him what he's been missing" Sally instructs Anne as we both grab her by the arm to escort her to the door.

Richy...right so that must be short for Richard that makes sense now. I don't think Richard's gonna get much out of Anne tonight from the state of her, but I love her ability to want to give it a try.

We stagger out of my building; I hope to god I remembered to lock up. We're leaning on each other for support and we all keep swaying a little too much. I've smacked into a wall more than twice, and I have a feeling it might have been the same wall.

As we make it out into the cold night air, the full weight of the alcohol hits us and we start swaying and giggling all over again. We put Anne into the first cab we can hail down, we throw her bags in and she gives him the address and drives off. Sally and I run to catch our own cabs and wish each other luck.

"Have a good night Sally, I'll call you tomorrow" I wave at her before getting into the taxi.

"Happy shagging" Sally screams from her taxi window as it flies down the block.

Chapter Six

The Seduction

I let myself into Bill's apartment because the maid has gone home for the day. Just as well I wouldn't want her to witness how drunk I am. I must look a state. Bill's not home so he must still be at the office. Honestly that man work's too damn hard. Well no worry, I'm sure he'll unwind with what I have in store for him. It'll be a way of rewarding him for a hard day's work. My man deserves it.

I slip into our bedroom and look at my reflection in our full length mahogany mirror and sure enough I look wasted. Okay so I need to refresh my look right now. I'll do my hair and makeup and put on one of my new skimpy pieces I got today, and I'll put the marriage saver on the night stand so I can slip it on when the time comes. He doesn't normally come back from the office until about midnight so that gives me plenty of time to doll myself up for him.

At fifteen minutes past midnight Bill's keys jingle in the door lock, I can hear the familiar noises reverberating through the penthouse. All the regular sounds: lets himself in, puts the keys in the bowl, puts his briefcase down, takes his jacket off, then pours himself a double whiskey from his favorite crystal decanter. Sounds like home.

I'm laid on our Chinese black silk chaise long, in a sheer black lace baby doll (I love baby dolls they're so girly and so sexy) I have black leather Jimmy Choo's on with silver killer heels (I bought them ages ago, but they have never been out of the box until tonight) my hair and makeup are flawless and my hair is in thick black curls pinned up in the back for volume. I even have a few ringlets cascading around my face for that sultry vamp look. I've also added a touch of pink champagne behind each ear and down my cleavage (It drives him wild) I've got everything in place and I'm just waiting for him to walk through the door.

Bill comes through the door and looks suddenly startled to find me waiting for him dressed like this.

"Hey baby, had a good day at the office?" I say as huskily as possible.

He puts his whiskey tumbler down and starts taking off his cufflinks.

"Honey the last thing on my mind right now is the office" he gives me a lopsided grin which is code for 'I'm going to ravage you' so I give him a cheeky grin back while thinking 'No honey, tonight I'm going to ravage you.'

He tries his old moves, trying to take control of me. Starts kissing my neck (The key turn on spot for most women, and I'm one of them) peeling away my baby doll, he brings his kisses from round the side of my neck to my throat and slides down.

I know where this is going, but if I allow it I'll totally give in and be completely at his mercy (aka I'll just lay there and enjoy myself)

No I have to take charge aka RELEASE THE FREAK! And give him a show. Give him a night to remember forever.

I push him till he's on his back, jump on top and start kissing, biting, ruffling his hair and pulling at his tie. He makes a gurgling sound, think I got carried away and nearly strangled him because he quickly starts stripping off and the tie goes first. I've never seen a man undress so fast, he's literally out of breath from his efforts and from the bulge protruding out of his boxers I can tell he's also very excited.

Brilliant, this is going to be a piece of cake.

I throw him back onto the bed while he's panting with eager excitement. His excitement is making me excited, I feel dominant, evil and sexy. I touch him in the usual places while he moans and groans.

"Baby I don't know what's gotten into you, but I love it" he pants like a dog in my ear.

Wow Claudette really knows her stuff. Men clearly love a dominant woman.

These are the words I need to hear. That little confidence boost has pushed me over the edge and I am now ready to introduce him to my big fat cock. I nudge him to roll onto his front and he does so with a puzzled expression on his face. He puts his hands under his head as though waiting for a back massage (Which I occasionally do from time to time, but not tonight)

I lean over to the cabinet to collect my toy and instantly I wonder how I'm meant to put it on. Damn I should have practiced before he came home. Never mind it can't be that difficult, it's like a pair of panties with a strap to tighten it. So I stand up on the bed, shimmy it on, tighten and clip it into place.

"What's going on back there?" he questions with suspicion.

Shit he must have heard the click.

"Nothing hunny, just want you to really enjoy yourself

tonight" I lean down and kiss him in his ear, tease his hair with my fingers and stroke his shoulders.

"What's that pressing into my back?"

Shit he can feel it, damn I've ruined the surprise.

"Mmmm you can feel that huh? You like the feel of my rock hard cock mmm? Tell me you like it. Why don't you be a good boy and get on all fours for me" I purr into his ear.

Ok so I literally stole that line from a porno movie but I had to! The woman sounded so sexy when she said it and the man turned into her sex slave. You could tell he had actually fallen in love with her for real at the end of the movie. (And FYI I think I sounded even sexier than she did, I was practicing the whole time before I heard the door open) but let me tell you, the reaction I'm getting is not what I saw in the movie. He's totally freaking out on me. He jumps off the bed and it spins me onto the floor, seriously I've never seen anyone move so fast in all my life. He's stood shaking and shouting at me in the corner of the bedroom.

"What are you crazy? You've gone nuts! I don't want a cock up my ass, that's for faggots! Seriously where the fuck did you get that thing?!"

I honestly don't have a response right now; I'm too busy rubbing my head from being bounced on the floor.

"What the hell is going on here? It needs to stop now, I mean it!"

Shit he's really pissed.

"Honey calm down, give it a chance you might like it" I try and reason with him. Men are men after all; he might just be embarrassed to admit he wants it.

"Baby I'm not going to judge you. What goes on in the bedroom stays in the bedroom. I promise"

Does the expression 'only the dogs can hear you' mean anything to you? Well if not, it means someone shouting and screaming so high from hysteria, that only the dogs can detect the noise. All I could decipher from the screaming is the following: you total bitch something, something, I would never something, something, threaten to my man hood something, throw it in the trash something something. Then he threw a shoe across the room, squealed a final something then shouted

"I'm sleeping in the guest room tonight and in the morning that thing had better be gone!" and then he slams the door shut.

My aim was to excite him......... mission accomplished.

I wonder how Sally is getting on ...

⎯⎯⎯ ᴠᴠᴠᴠᴠᴠᴠᴠ ⎯⎯⎯

I'm gonna look lush for him. His eyes will probably pop out of his head. Allan is a good man; he takes care of me, pays for our home on Amsterdam Avenue (on the upper west side), for us to have nice things and he even funds my infomercial shopping habit. He works on the road constantly, selling house hold appliances door to door. He's also a recruitment manager, he sets up stalls in mall's and persuades youngsters to get on board with his business venture. It's true too; I mean it's so hard for kids to get a job these days much less make a decent wage. The products he sells change all the time, one month it could be kitchenware, the next it could be drapes or vacuum's it all depends on what the company have to sell at the time.

Allan has recruited a team that all work on commission, going door to door in the town they've chosen. Some of the team just have a natural gift for selling, Allan said 'Jimbo is one of my hottest sellers; he goes to an old ladies house and leaves with five sales under his belt. He's a real charmer Jimbo, has great people skills. He could charm the birds off the trees and the older ladies find him adorable.'

I suppose you could say Allan's like the American version of an Avon lady in Britain, only he's a man and his products are far more expensive. He started off not earning half as much as he is now. Every town he goes to, he recruits more teens to help him with selling, making money for him and money for them, everyone wins. Of course anyone can sign up to be a representative, but he prays on the younger ones because he said and I quote 'They have more energy, they can do more leg work. They stay out longer and don't tire as easily as say someone in their 30's or 40's would. Plus kids are money hungry and will work hard to get it.' so I suppose it makes sense, as long as everyone's happy and no one is complaining. Plus everyone gets a decent living from it too.

The only down side is that he hardly ever comes home. I know Allan is faithful till the end; he would never do something like that. He's just very passionate about his work and I'm a very supportive partner (I always have been)

But no more worrying about all that now, he's coming home tonight and staying all weekend. Then he's back on the road on Monday and will be gone for a month (It's fine though I'm used to it)

My corset is just to die for ......or from. My word it's tight, it's a little snug and my every curve and bulge seems to be enhanced dramatically. But on the plus side it makes my boobs look huge! (Can't all be bad then.)

I tie it up as far as it will go (It's even harder when your swaying) Jesus those cocktails at Jill's were pretty strong, never mind we had a good time I'll just have to nurse a hangover tomorrow. Speaking of hangovers the corset's pushed my pudgy belly over the hem of my panties (not a good look I must say) I start repositioning my thong. Should it go under or over my belly? Decisions, decisions, and both ways look awful. Now I know what Jill meant by 'Muffin top' to hell with the underwear, it would have been coming off soon anyway.

I stagger into the bedroom and flop on the bed.

The next thing I know it's two o'clock in the morning. I can't believe I fell asleep. Champagne always knocks me on my ass, I just hope Allan didn't see me and decide to spend the night on the couch so he wouldn't disturb me. I pick my spinning head off the bed and make my way to the living room. No Allan. To the kitchen. No Allan. To the bathroom. No Allan.

Thank god he didn't see me; I haven't even put my face on yet. I have no idea when he'll get in, sometimes it's been as late as five in the morning but I always wait up for him. I see him so rarely I just have too; I get too excited I can hardly sleep.

If absence makes the heart grow stronger then I'm a love sick fool.

It gets to three o'clock and I grab my phone to go on a game in an attempt to keep myself awake. The minute I unlock my phone I see one text and ome missed call, both from Allan.

How on earth did I miss these? I've been here the whole time. I check to see when he tried to make contact and obviously they've both landed on the time that I had accidently fallen asleep (damn it) Disappointment rushes through me as I read the first line of the text message.

'Sally baby, I can't make it back this weekend don't be too disappointed. Got too much on at work, but will hopefully see you soon. Love you baby xx'

For god's sake, why aren't I used to these messages by now. Being on the road is a big part of his job and without it he would be unemployed. And we wouldn't be able to afford this apartment or have nice things.

It still hurts though. Guess I'm in for yet another lonely night again tonight. No bother I'll make do, I always do. I've always got my Ben and Jerry's in the freezer and more than enough infomercial's to watch (they're on practically every channel at this time of night, well technically the morning) it's the perfect nocturnal pass time.

Even though I'd prefer to be doing something else.

I wonder how Anne is getting on …

———⁓⁓•◦℘⋆⊙⊙⋆℘◦•⁓⁓———

My god what a day it's been. I've never drank so much in all my life, but I loved it. I feel carefree and fabulous. I feel liberated like a different woman. Claudette was right you know I bet I do have a sexual animal side to me or whatever the hell she said. I'm gonna do it tonight, I wanna do it tonight! My Richard has been waiting long enough, my poor baby. I haven't been taking care of him as a woman should. I love him and I should show him I love him…….. in a naked way.

Why not? everyone does it, it can't be that bad. And from the sound of some of Sally's stories tonight it sounds like it can either fail or be a wonderful experience, enjoyed by both. I wish Jill luck tonight, I'd be so nervous to try the marriage saber thing or whatever she calls it. I guess tonight's all about firsts. First experience with strange toys and the first experience of feeling this drunk. Neither Jill nor Sally could be half as nervous as I am. At least they've done it before. Well now it's my turn.

I hope Richard takes the lead, hopefully he will, he's done it before. I know he has, not that he's willing to talk about it he's too much of a gentleman for that. Thank god.

Well tonight we are gonna create our own memories and

then I'll have a sex story of my own to tell the girls. I couldn't say anything tonight because I don't have a story and I was more than willing to hear theirs, it's what's giving me courage to act like this tonight. I am scared, but alcohol has dulled my senses and made me feel less uptight then I've ever felt in my life.

I lunge out of the cab and throw him more than what the cab is worth and run into my apartment on Canal Street in Soho. I head straight to the bathroom and quickly change into a mad, sex crazed woman that looks the part. Just like one of the staff members at Kinky couture only a hundred percent less gorgeous. I need to make this transition quick before the alcohol wears off. I don't have any in the house, Richard and I hardly ever drink (only on special occasions) so I better be fast.

I emerge out of the bathroom feeling dangerous and amazing and freakishly confident. Maybe Richard won't have to take the lead now; I think I've got this in the bag. I strut sexily to the bedroom where Richard will be already be in bed waiting for me with a hot cup of camomile tea.

I stand in the doorway waiting for him to look from the TV to me. And there it is, complete eye contact. Neither of us are moving, neither of us saying a word.

I'm saying it all with my eyes ...

His eyes are burning on my face and body, he looks ... horrified? But that can't be right surely he wants this even more than I do. Aren't men sex crazed beasts like everyone says they are? Maybe he's just shy, well I'll take the lead then.

Right so what do I do? Where to start? I'm trying to remember all that I've heard from Jill and Sally tonight. That mixed with everything Claudette said. I don't know what to do or whose right or wrong so I'm gonna do things my way.

I'm just gonna jump on him.

One great leap and I've done it I'm on top of him, only thing is he's holding his cup of camomile and now it's all over both of us. Never mind, aren't wet women one of man's greatest fantasies? I know there are places that do wet T-shirt contests, so I'm trying to look at this as a positive. I'm not put off by his look of horror; I grab him by the hair and bring him closer for a passionate make-out session (tongues and all)

I have a feeling this would be hot if he were participating. His lips are closed and he's struggling to push me off.

Wait! What? I don't get it. I thought being dominant was sexy! Perhaps it's an acquired taste. I pull back for a second to judge his reaction, trying to study his face. (Even though everything right now is a drunken blur) The room has started to spin and for some reason Mr. Invisible has pushed me over. I roll of the bed with all the grace of an elephant.

"What the hell are you doing? You've got liquor on your breath! Where have you been and what the hell are you wearing?"

With every question his voice goes up an octave. What's with all the questions anyway? Take me right now damn it! I want it, I need it now! Why isn't he jumping at the chance? Lord knows he's waited long enough.

"Take me Richard, I feel sexual. Claudette was right, I have buried this side of me for too long and now she's come out to play." I pant trying to peel myself off the floor. Even with Richard's hand guiding me up, I feel like gravity has got me in a headlock.

"Who's Claudette? you haven't mentioned her before. Anne I know you've made some new friends and I was happy for you, until I realized they're clearly bad influences. Anne this isn't you, look at yourself." Richard literally picks me up and I feel like this is my moment. I'm finally being swept off my feet and it's as every bit as good as they say. I hope he devours me, I pray its earth shattering and wonderful (I hope to god I'm good at it)

He puts me down and grabs me from behind. Not sexily, he's quite rough.

"Look! Look! Who is this drunken mess? Wearing something only a hooker would wear. There's no way we are making love like this. You won't remember it in the morning. You want your first time to be special don't you? This is the wrong time; I thought we were going to wait till our wedding night. Hasn't that been your dream since you were a little girl? Your thirty-seven years old, why wait all this time just to ruin it with one drunken night"

I stare at the dizzy bitch in my mirror and I'm filled with embarrassment and shame. How stupid I look, I feel too old to become a sex kitten now. And he's right this really isn't me. I thought it was, but he's right it wouldn't be special on our wedding night. But then again I feel as though I need a little practice or preparation to know what to expect on our honeymoon.

"I know but it would take the pressure off us if we did it now. Then we will be relaxed for our wedding. Seriously I've been having panic attacks at night wondering if I'll be any good or if you will enjoy it, because I honestly don't know how to start it. And I just feel really confident tonight. Can't we just give it a try Richard? Then if it's bad I'll be glad I don't remember anything in the morning." I state my case, at least it's off my chest now, at least I've been heard.

"Babe I haven't bought any condoms. Now we really can't practice without them can we? I mean could you imagine getting pregnant on your first time? And before we are married! What would our parents think? You wouldn't keep it anyway; you always say children are dirty and messy and that they would ruin our home. So let's stop all this craziness and get to bed. You'll need to sleep that hangover off in the morning, so I'll just leave you in bed for the day while I go to work."

Feeling deflated I reluctantly agree and stop trying to persuade him.

Trying to sleep I feel sad but relieved we haven't done the dreaded deed. Anyway I want to be Mrs. Gilbert before we bump uglies, it's only right. Comforted by this thought I fall into a deep sleep with a smile on my lips, I thank god that I've got a good man. Most men would have taken advantage......but not Richard.

Chapter Seven

Signing the prenup

I can't believe what a mess I was in last night. Richard has already gone to work (thank god) I couldn't bear facing him this morning, I'm too embarrassed.

That woman last night was not me, and now I'm paying the price. My head is throbbing, my eyes are not adapting to sunlight and everything around me just feels surreal. I haven't felt this bad before, even after New Year's Eve parties. I hardly ever get hang overs and especially not ones this bad. I'm swearing off drink from now until I die (I think everyone's said that at some point, but I really mean it.)

Every part of me just wants to curl up in the fetal position, but I feel panicked like I need to be acting quickly. I need to get my life together. I desperately want to sign that prenup now, more than ever. I feel undeserving of having Richard in my life. He's too good, too sensible, he literally had the opportunity to take my virginity last night and he didn't! What a perfect man, I'm not letting him go, no way.

What if he leaves me for the way I acted last night? I can't let that happen, the prenup is getting signed today no matter what.

Wow I haven't slept in like this in a long time. I guess I was watching TV till late. I think I made some purchases last night, but god help me I can't remember what. Anyway I like when packages arrive at the apartment all paid for, it's like a surprise every time, and honestly I have the worst memory when it comes to knowing what I bought from infomercials.

It's weird even though I've slept later than usual I still feel so tired, I feel as though I could sleep for a week.

I sit up and rub the sleep out of my eyes and the text of disappointment runs through my mind, reminding me why I feel disheartened at the start of the day. Poor Allan, he was probably really looking forward to being with me just as much as I was with him, but he had to work.

I wander around our apartment aimlessly trying to feel positive and think of other things. Things that make me laugh, I'm suddenly reminded of the state we were in last night. Man we were drunk with a capital D. I wonder if the girls are badly hung over this morning. I'm not, I'm more tired than hung-over but then again I did have a nap then something to eat and then finally after a few hours of shopping I fell asleep (well more like passed out) weirdly I was still holding the phone when I awoke.

I think I'll call them; it'll give me something to do and take my mind off things.

———

I'm telling you I didn't sleep a wink all night. I heard Bill slam the door shut on his way to work (yeah he even works on weekends too) I don't know if he did it so loud to wake me up, or if it was because he was still angry at what I tried to do last night.

Honestly Claudette should be sued, the amount of money

we spent there and none if it went to good use. I felt certain that the strap on was the marriage saver not the break up enhancer she said so herself (False advertising.) Maybe some men are into it, but it turns out Bill definitely isn't. What a waste of money I'd return it but I wouldn't want to make a scene (not in any shop) I'm not gonna throw it out like he demanded, I'll just bury it deep into my lingerie draw, he'll never find it there.

Well I hope the girls at least got good use of their purchases (lord knows I didn't) I'll call them soon and find out. But first things first, I need to secure my marriage to Bill. He's probably more than likely planning to leave me after last night, that's why it's so important for me to sign the prenup today.

Signing the pre-nup will feel great to me now, no fear at all. It'll feel more like I'm signing the deed for keeping a terrific man in my life. And once it's done I'm going to fake ignorance, kinda like nothing happened last night. Trust me I've seen it done before and it works. If you go up to a man and start groveling and apologizing it just makes the man angrier that you've brought it up again. Because if it's so painful or embarrassing (like last night was) he would surely prefer you to pretend it never happened.

I have to call daddy now and ask him to find a notary public who would be willing to fit me in today to sign the prenuptial contract.

One phone call later and he informs me that I need two witnesses to attend the signing with me (seriously what are the odds?) Obviously I know just the two people I'll ask to be my witnesses.

Two phone calls later to Anne and Sally and I've got my witnesses in the bag. They seem just as eager as me to sign it. Guess we have all have had a change of heart (they must have had a lot of fun last night, because they sounded so de-termined about it)

I call my father back and mention that my two witnesses also need their prenup's signed as well. It just makes sense for us all to do it at the same time, that way we can be witnesses for each other.

Chapter Eight

Infomercial Addiction

Did you know over $400 billion is spent each year on items bought from infomercials, and I think maybe half of that is down to me (only kidding, I wish I had that kinda money) but seriously from the look of my kitchen and bedroom and well...... hell every room, you can definitely tell that I've over bought on certain things. I'm not sure I've even got round to using half of them, but I'm sure one day they will all come in handy.

Allan's always been fine with my little night time habit, he's only called me once or twice in the past to complain about what he's seen on his bank statement and then questions why on earth would I need another iron? (Or something as silly as that)

Really how could anyone say that? All these products have different uses, they have different abilities and most importantly they come in all different colours! So if I have a white boring iron am I not allowed to buy a gold iron if I want it? Exactly! That was my point. He shut up pretty quickly and came to terms with what I was saying. So yeah, for the most part he's very understanding.

Plus I feel like celebrating tonight, we've finally signed our prenup's all of us together. If that's not a good enough reason to shop, I don't know what is.

God what a fantastic way to sell to people about amazing gadgets and talk about how they are selling like hot cakes, all while the price is dropping on the screen. I've even tried to sleep with these infomercials on in the background, but if I over-hear of something so great I will sit up and dial in. (what? don't judge me, some opportunities should not be missed)

Anyway, what a brilliant way to get people to buy when we are comatose. (That way we are easy prey) don't get me wrong I love doing this, it fills my nights and then I try and sleep through the day. It's kinda bad though, because if a package comes, a neighbor often takes it in for me and then I have to collect it from him. I'm thankful he does that but on the other hand he is old, creepy and an absolute busy body. He never fails to comment on my shopping habits.

"Been buying again? Little lady you should stop wasting your man's money like that. You go through it like rain water. You should do something productive with your day and go and get a job instead of spending all the time!"

This is the lecture old man Mr. Albert gives me every time I drop by to get my things. On one hand I know he's probably right but I'm not qualified or good at anything. And on the other hand I just feel like telling him to shut up and mind his own business.

Anyway back to the here and now. Shopping!

I'm currently on hold for the most amazing dust buster the world has ever seen. Its hot pink with loads of attachments and I desperately need one. It was originally $400 now on sale at $200. Are you freaking kidding me! That's half off for god's sake why do these call center people take so long to answer the phone? I'm super stressed out, my eyes are blood shot but I refuse to hang up this phone.

I've been on hold for thirty minutes. As I wait in queue, I continue to watch the infomercial. The presenter keeps repeating herself.

"There's not many left, get yours now. This little gadget will make cleaning a breeze and will make your life so much easier" Yes Ok, ok I get it. They'd better not sell out before I get my hands on one.

Another twenty minutes later and I'm ready to throw myself out of the window. Why is the call center always so busy when I phone in? I mean Jesus; I am one of their most loyal customers. I shop with SSS (it stands for Super Sale Shopping) every night. I practically pay the studios rent.

I've heard the same on hold music now for nearly an hour. It started off annoying, but after the 15th time it starts to have a calming effect on me. I'm literally being lulled to sleep. I begin to regain consciousness because I think I've sussed out their little plan. They know how angry I get at being kept on hold that long, so instead of dealing with me I bet they're hoping to make me fall asleep. Well it's not going to work.

I jump off the bed and slap my face several times to keep me awake. I pace around the bed where I have left my phone on loud speaker, I'm trying to keep myself alert for the moment I'm forced to be a moody bitch to whichever unfortunate soul that answers my call.

Jesus! Why aren't they answering, have they cut me off? Do they know I have a problem? Has Allan noticed something bad on his bank statement? Oh god what if he's finally had enough off my shopping? I bet he's called the call center and had them ban me from buying anything ever again.

That's it, I'm being punished.

I can't take it anymore. I need answers.

Just as I was about to hang up my cell so I can call Allan, a loud clear voice comes through the receiver.

"Hello Miss Willow. Your through to Simon from SSS, so sorry about the long wait. My apologies, we have been very busy today. How may I help you?"

It's Simon; he's one of my favourite operators. He has this lovely London accent and he's always so polite. I've discussed many things with Simon before now, everything from shopping, to art, to love, life, to his work and so on. Most of the other call center staff try and rush you off the phone the minute they've taken your card details, but not Simon he's much too nice for that. He talks to me as though we are old friends. Damn all my rage has vanished, how can I get mad with Si? I couldn't, I wouldn't. I think I'll just order this dust buster and have a good long chat with him, he'll understand. He always does.

Its two days after I last saw the girls when there's a buzz on the intercom.

Thank god one of my packages have arrived, I wonder what it is. I love shopping, I do it too often that I completely forget what I bought. So each time a package arrives it's like Christmas all over again because I have no idea what's inside.

I run down and sign for my gift from me to me (well it's more for the house really) and I run up the stairs in excitement.

The label on the box says "Deluxe gold" Oooww is it jewelry?

I rip open the box with strength, scissors and speed. I'm a pro at unboxing parcels; it comes from years of practice. I dig in, in hopes of pulling out a job lot of jewelry I got from a shopping channel, but what I hold in my hand is even more exciting. It's the new top of the line gold deluxe espresso machine! I needed this desperately, I'm so glad I've got one and at a third of the price. I remember I was waiting on hold for a long time to get this bad boy and here it is in the flesh, and even more beautiful than I expected.

The infomercial flaunted all its uses and how quick and simple it is to make all different flavours of espresso in this hi tech glamorous machine. Admittedly I don't drink espresso and I don't know anyone who does but obviously I will be drinking it every day now.

I can just picture it, when Allan comes home for the weekend I can run down to our local deli and pick up some doughnuts and bagels as usual but leave the coffee, come home and make an espresso from our machine. There's loads of flavours to choose from, Allan will have his favourite and I'll have mine (it's so great that they include a month's worth of capsules for the machine. Everything from vanilla, caramel to chocolate. See now you know why I needed this in my life) and then we can curl up with our breakfast and posh coffee's in bed on a Sunday morning. (That mental picture I just described was the main reason for my hasty purchase)

Just as I'm getting ready to try out my latest accessory for the kitchen, my phone rings. My heart jumps into my throat because no one usually calls me, I get the odd text from people but that's about it. I skydive for my cell and pick it up with shaking fingers, it's Jill.

———— ⁓⌇⦿⌇⦿⌇⦿⌇⁓ ————

I'm kinda bored, I haven't heard from the girls since we all went back to Jack Hornski's law firm to sign the prenup's in front of the notary public. Anne texted me once thanking me for getting the job done as quickly as I did (well it wasn't really me with the connections, it was my father) but I told her she was welcome and that was it. I haven't heard a thing from Sally. Maybe she's making up for lost time in the bedroom with her fiancé? I assume that's probably what it is. Well good luck to her, at least some of us are getting some action (the same cannot be said of me)

Since the attempted sodomy session, Bill and I have totally avoided eye contact and the conversation has been limited and to the point. He only talks to me when absolutely necessary. We haven't spoken about that night and I don't intend to. You could cut the tension in the room with a knife. He's been spending more and more time at the office (probably in an attempt to avoid me) which almost, in a way is a blessing. I've tried making a few plans for the wedding, but my hearts not in it at the moment. I want a different type of distraction, I want company. And more importantly how did Anne's night go? Did she let the freak lose? Has she turned into a nymphomaniac? I know Sally will have gotten her money's worth and I also know that she will sing like a bird, when I ask her for the juicy details.

I must have sunk to a new low to crave company, but I don't care anymore.

I'm sick of being proud and waiting for people to need me. If I want something I should just make it happen. I swallow my dignity and pick up my cell. I'll call Sally first; I think her upbeat, excitable voice will work wonders on me right now.

"Hey Jill how are you?" Sally says sounding sleepy.

"Fine, have I just woken you up?" I laugh as I say it, there's no way she could have been in bed it's two-thirty in the afternoon.

"No, no I just haven't been sleeping well lately. But I'm fine how are you?" she asks, for the second time.

"I'm fine I just told you that. Why haven't you been sleeping?

Let me guess, Allan's been keeping you up!" again I fake a laugh so she unleashes the gossip.

"No, Allan isn't here…" she really does sound down. It's more than fatigue in her voice I'm also detecting sorrow.

"He couldn't find the time off work to come home so, no unfortunately I never had the chance to be "kept up" as you put it" Damn! I never saw that coming. I thought for sure that was the reason she hadn't been in touch. I thought she was in a deep sex haze and didn't want to be disturbed.

"Anyway tell me about your night with Bill and the light saber! Did he love it?" I'm not gonna tell her the truth. Well not all of it anyway.

"I think you mean marriage saver, and the answer is NO. Claudette is a con artist, making us buy all that expensive tat and for what? She definitely had the last laugh on that one; we're never shopping there again." I let out a piece of my rage.

"I agree it's not worth the money really. Not when there are so many other products you could be spending on." I hear a light clatter in the background, maybe she's making herself a cup of tea.

"Yeah, so no my night was a bust. Bill didn't enjoy it at all. He even told me to throw it out. I mean I didn't, I couldn't, not for the price I paid for it, and it's brand new. I know I'll never use it, but it's too much of a waste to just throw it away."

"Yeah I understand. What about Anne? How did her night go? Have you spoken to her?" Sally enquires.

"No I thought you would have. I haven't heard from either of you in a couple of days. I wondered if you and Anne would like to come over to my apartment for a catch up, are you free?" I hold my breath waiting for the answer. I feel like the normal upbeat Sally would have jumped into a taxi before I finished the sentence. But this Sally, I don't know. She doesn't sound right. She sounds tired and down.

The line goes quiet while she mulls my invite over. Ok something here is really wrong.

"Sally? Are you still there?" I ask her with panic in my voice.

"Uuummm yeah, I'm just...... kinda...... I don't feel up to leaving the apartment at the moment Jill. I'm really tired and......" I thought so, something's definitely wrong.

"Well I could call Anne, then her and I could get a cab over to yours...you know...if you want some company." I try to flip it round so I don't sound desperate. But in all seriousness, my gut feeling is telling me that Sally could do with a friend right now.

"Really? Well yeah that would be nice. I mean that would be great. I have a new espresso machine! I could try it out on you guys." Thank god, I feel as though I must have said the magic words.

Ding! And simple Sally is back in the room. She sounds slightly more upbeat, for some reason over a coffee machine (but I'm not about to judge) whatever gets her through the day.

"Ok great well text me your address and I'll call Anne and see if she's free"

"Jill, not one of us has a job or a kid of course she's free." oh yeah I've never realized that before.

"That's true, well that's fine then. I'll call her and tell her we are coming over to your place."

"Mmm ok, I mean I didn't have time to clean because I wasn't expecting guests but if you still wanna come over that's fine." how civilized of her to warn me, well I guess I expected Sally's apartment to be a little chaotic, kinda like its tenant.

"Never mind, I'm still coming over."

"Ok great see you then."

A phone call to Anne and a cab ride later, we are at Sally's apartment complex. Her text said its apartment 5C. We buzz her intercom and she opens the door for us to get in. There is no elevator, which is a nuisance and a workout. Sally lives halfway up the building. Still enough cardio for Anne and I to feel the burn in our thighs when we reach her door panting like dogs.

Sally's already at the door staring at us and grinning.

"Come on in, I think I've finally got this coffee machine working"

Anne and I try and regain composer and once we do, we both are overthrown by Sally's wild unkempt look.

"Did you take a nap after I called?"

"Um no, I wish. I'm pretty tired" she's actually saying this, while yawning.

She has a bed head like none I've ever seen before. Her hair resembles a bird's nest. It's like cotton candy mixed with cotton wool mixed with two weeks' worth of knots. How could she get it in this state? Has she been like this for two whole days?

"Sally are you ok hunny, you look a little sleep deprived" Anne's just pointing out the obvious, but seriously I think we are both worried about her by this point.

"Will you two shut up talking in the hall and get in here." Ooowww snappy Sally? I've not met her before.

Anne and I scuttle into the apartment. Sally locks the door behind us and leads us down the hallway. My breath is taken from my lungs, I was expecting a bit of a mess, but not this!

I look towards Anne for a sly 'Her home is a pig sty' kinda look. But Anne's face is contorted into fear and terror. There are actual tears in her eyes and she looks like she's about to jump out the window. Only the windows are hidden behind all these boxes of…of… I don't know what.

There seems to be a least two of everything in here, from what I can see. Everything from mops to irons to smoothie makers to juicers to waffle irons to shower curtains! This place truly makes no sense. Is Sally's home a make shift warehouse? I stare toward Anne once more, just to find beads of sweat on her brow. Oh god I forgot, Anne's a clean freak. This must be killing her.

This level of mess and disorder has even shaken me a little. Poor Anne, I don't know what she must be feeling right now.

"Do you guys want an espresso? Then we can head to the bedroom. That's where I stay most of the time. I know sorry, it's a little cramped everywhere else."

Is she serious? Is she in denial? Do we pretend it's not that big of a deal and just play along? Anne looks at me and I give her a look that says "yep there's an elephant in the room, try to not point it out."

"Mmm… yeah we would love an espresso. Any flavour you have is fine" I take over the talking for Anne because I can see she is lost for words.

"Ok great, I've got all the flavours. I'll surprise you." Sally gets a little excited over her new gadget. I know she said it was new, but I didn't realize she meant brand new. I can tell it is because the box is still on the kitchen floor, and she presses every button before she hits the right one.

As Anne dabs at her brow, we make our way through to Sally's bedroom. The minute we're in, Sally slumps on the bed and curls up in the fetal position. There's a hollow grave dented into the mattress that fits her shape. I'm guessing she spends a lot of time in this position, but doing what? Anne looks around the room desperate to leave; I try and ignore her for now because I'm concerned for Sally.

I watch her in her natural habitat without saying a word. As I watch closely, Sally flicks on the TV and puts on a channel that specializes in infomercials. She is lying on the bed and is immediately glued to the TV set. It's as though Anne and I aren't here (which I'm sure Anne wishes was the case)

Sally already has her hand wrapped around her cell as though that very action gives her comfort.

Call me slow but I'm beginning to join the dots. At first glance of this warehouse, a thought occurred to me. That maybe the reason she has so many new products in her home is because they are hot! And she's storing them for a friend and maybe they were cutting her in on the profits of stolen goods (don't ask, I think I've seen to many gangster movies) but then I realized, that this is Sally we are talking about here.

But seeing this sad little woman slumped on her bed watching infomercials, it all suddenly becomes clear. Sally is a hoarder.

Everything about this place is cluttered and chaotic. Even her bed is strewn with chocolate bar wrappers, half eaten sandwiches; take out boxes and Chinese food. Everything scattered to the four corners of her bed and most of its trickling on to the floor. I would normally lecture her on the reason her figure is the way it is, but every fiber in me is telling me it's the wrong time. Plus (and I'm not proud about this by the way) I too have been binge eating recently. Well ever since the strap on incident, food is the only thing that's comforting me right now. That's why I was desperate for a distraction.

Safe to say, I think I've found one.

Anne edges closer to the exit slowly, but not so slow that I didn't notice. I signal Anne with my hand to stop moving, to hold on a second. I can't take the silence in this room anymore. I honestly don't know why Anne and I are here, Sally hasn't paid the slightest bit of attention since we came into the bedroom. I have no other option than to point directly at the elephant in the room.

Sally picks up her cell ready to dial and buy a set of knives that are being shown on screen. I need to stop her, someone needs to help her. Anne's clearly not willing so it'll have to be me. I lunge onto the bed, in the hope that I can grab the phone from her before it's too late. I underestimate my jump and land on top of Sally, the phone is literally in my face and I quickly end the call.

"What the hell are you doing? You scared the life out of me!" Sally shouts at me.

"I'm sorry, but come on…" I puff out each word.

"This is way too much stuff Sal. You've gotten completely carried away, and I'm cutting you off. How can you or Allan even live in a place like this? There's nowhere to sit except the bed and …… well its hardly convenient" I gesture to all the food and boxes covering the bed spread and she looks at it dismissively.

"Allan doesn't have to deal with it; he's never here it's just me. And buying these things keeps me occupied. And besides a full home is better than an empty home." Sally puts her head in her lap and the full weight of her problem hits me. She's lonely, and filling her house with all this junk makes her feel less empty.

"Sally you need a healthy hobby hunny, not this!" Anne gestures to everything she sees.

"I know but its more than shopping, I've made a friend too. A really great friend, at the call center. Well he's more like a counselor to me, but he really lets me talk out my problems." Sally declares to both of us, hoping to justify her reason.

"What's wrong with telling us your problems?" I shout at her.

"Yeah you can tell us anything, we thought we couldn't stop you from doing anything else." Anne makes a valid point.

"I do tell you them, you two are so great for girl talk and telling me what to do, but I don't know. Simon just listens. It's like he has to agree with what I'm saying and how I'm feeling because I'm a paying customer you know?" Sally looks at us so meekly and pathetically, I snigger. What a crazy woman.

"No Sally we don't know. Why don't you just call a help line or something? At least it's free." Anne suggest helpfully.

"She would but she doesn't get a great new iron for $49.99 with that call." I joke sarcastically and even Anne finds it funny. I can't help but make light of this ridiculous situation it's laughable. Think about it, half of the appeal of buying something to Sally, is knowing she's going to be able to vent her stresses to the poor man that works at the call center. I mean why can't she just ring me? I'm always bored and lonely...I mean you know I could make the time for her, that's all I meant.

Anyway the only person who doesn't find my joke funny is Sally herself, she looks moody and hurt.

"See this kinda stuff. When you guys make me feel stupid, that's one of the things I talk about with Simon. He understands, he always does."

Chapter Nine

Stress Smoking

Sally has really got to me; she's made me feel like a bully. I was only being funny. I have enough on my plate as it is, not just metaphorically but literally. Bill won't talk to me; we can't even discuss the wedding or set a date. And what's worse is that we haven't had sex since I tried to be dominant. Now Sally has made me feel guilty, I've given up on the gym I just can't stay focused long enough to really work up a sweat. But for some reason I have no problem at all, at working up an appetite.

Honestly my clothes are getting tighter and tighter every day. My mother is coming to visit me tomorrow as well and I just know she will comment on my growing size. You'd think it would take ages for you to noticeably gain weight but you're wrong. Apparently it can happen as quickly as overnight, I think that's why a lot of people weigh themselves daily and I used to be one of them. I've even gone as far as avoiding full length mirrors; I prefer doing my make-up in a head and shoulder size mirror. My fear is just the same as heights; everything is fine at eye level but just DON'T LOOK DOWN!

Ok so I'm being a tad dramatic I'm no beached whale yet

but I'm definitely thickening out in a rather unflattering way. Everyone in my family has always been tall and slender but I'm beginning to let them down. I'm so nervous about my mother seeing me this way it's just making me comfort eat even more. I tried to call and cancel, but her response to that was "don't be silly, I need to see the blushing bride to be. I've only seen you once this year and I have back to back plans up until New Year's Eve. Honestly darling I'm going to find it difficult to even turn up to your wedding. I'll try you know I will but let's not change our plans, I'm coming and that's that." So naturally I dived in head first to my stash of chocolate I keep hidden way back in the freezer. Man, I'm turning into Sally, If I start carrying around cakes in my purse, shoot me.

I'm waiting patiently for the woman I refer to as mother (I say that because she left father when I was three years old. I was always a daddy's girl right from the get go. That alone made mum jealous. Apparently everything from daddy's incredible work load to coming home and doting love and attention on me, left mum feeling neglected, and then she ran out on us.)

We only meet up a couple of times a year due to her jet set life. She always has tall tales to tell me when we meet, all about how many fantastic parties she's been to and all the elite society she's met. My mother (Diane Grace) always seems to be rubbing shoulders with celebrities and she always goes out of her way to tell me about it. Kinda though she's trying to rub my nose in it, but I know this is just a character trait, she has a very showing personality.

I know you think I'm jealous of mum but I'm really not. To me she's nothing more than a rich, spoilt cougar! It's true you know, she always has some young boy in tow. I don't know what they see in her (other than her incredible amount of plastic surgery and her wad of cash)

Daddy was really generous with my mother when they divorced, he said in his own words that "She did nothing wrong, we just fell out of love with each other. She wanted more attention than I could give. Your mother was always one of the most attractive beauties at any social gathering and I was always a little more than aware of some of the glances she received. Your mother's a handsome woman; I knew she could have any man she wanted. So I set her free. Admittedly she was never mother of the year, and even in the short time we were married she was never the best wife I could have asked for. But biologically she is still your mother, and I could never hate anyone that gave me something as precious as you."

Can you believe how amazing my dad is?

He's my absolute hero, I could never love anyone more than him.

Even when on the few times we have discussed mother he has always been fair when referring to her. I mean he could definitely speak ill of her, anyone would. She's a spoilt woman that craves attention off men that my father was too busy to give her so she ran out on her family, leaving my father a single parent. If a man did that we would hate him.

I've tried more than once to rattle his cage about her but to no avail. He is ever respectful of her to the end. That's why he gave her as much money as he did. He said he wanted to do right by her in respect for the life and child they briefly shared. There is literally no greater man than my father, that's why my standards are so high for a husband. Thank god daddy handpicked Bill for me, that's why I trust our marriage will work because my father knows best.

———∼∽∾⌒⌒⌒⌒∾∽∼———

Sure enough my mother walks into 'The garden' restaurant looking like she owns the place. Dripping head to toe in Gucci, diamonds and the latest Rolex (No wonder I'm high maintenance, I must have got it from her) we greet with a Paris style kiss, but only hovering from cheek to cheek, then we take our seats. Before our butts touch the fabric she is already gushing about her trip to Bora Bora with Frankie, her twenty-five year old lover.

Pathetic.

The sordid details my mother divulges in even the most elegant of restaurants is disgraceful. (Yes the irony is not lost on me that her maiden name is Grace) Our relationship has never felt like mother and daughter, to her I'm sure it feels more like we are old college friends or even sisters as she likes to fool everyone that we are not that far apart in age.

"Frankie is absolutely gorgeous Jill; I can't wait for you to meet him. We are kindred spirits two halves of a whole. I'll bring him as my date to your wedding darling, if I can make it. Have you set a date yet?" mum finally asks me something for a change instead of talking about herself all the time.

"No actually I haven't gotten round to it yet. I've got other things on my mind" I try and steer the conversation away from the wedding and Bill, or anything to do with our relationship. I can't be bothered opening up to a woman I only see twice a year, and the occasional post card. I prefer to stick to small talk where Diane is concerned (she normally steers the conversation back to herself anyway)

"I know what you mean hunny, lots of things to plan and prepare for. Like the honeymoon for example and moving all your stuff into his place. I recommend Bora Bora for your honeymoon dear; it's the most romantic place in the world! I should know. We were there for six weeks and it grew more glorious by the day. It's hard to describe that kind of crystal blue waters if you've never seen it. You should go."

Mother is persistent about Bora Bora so I'll agree just to shut her up. She was like this when she came back from the Alps, skiing with friends. She talked so long and hard about it, I agreed to go there sometime just so she'd change the subject but all it did was land me with two plane tickets to get there. Mothers treat for Bill and me, but Bill couldn't get the time of work so I got a refund and had to fake to mum that we went and we had a brilliant time. This was many months ago by the way, she said it was our wedding present from her. So whenever she refers to the Alps she looks at me for agreement. I just have to nod along and smile brightly (it works every time)

Our food arrives and I finish mine in record time. Mum looks amazed "Darling, I just realized it but I do believe your becoming quite chubby. Well more than a little Jill it's really quite noticeable. Please don't tell me I'm going to be a grandmother soon?" she looks terrified as she lights up her third cigarette since her arrival.

(That's why we dine outside; she's such a heavy chain smoker. She always picks little quaint bistro's and restaurants with an outside dining area so she can get her nicotine fix)

"NO! Absolutely not! No, no. Bill and I want to be married for at least four years before we start planning a family." I shoot back at her. I just knew she'd bring up my figure, but I never expected her to think I'm pregnant.

"Thank god for that, you gave me quite a scare. Well at least you're being sensible about when the right time is to start a family. But I can't say the same about your weight Jill. I know planning a wedding is a stressful time darling but you mustn't turn to food for comfort. Keep concentrating on how fabulous you'll look in your bridal gown." Mum beams her pearly whites at me and her eyes light up in delight. As though she's more excited about it than I am (Which is true at the moment)

"I know mum your right, I'm trying to watch what I eat, but I think I'm just going through a phase at the moment. Don't worry; I won't even attempt to walk down the aisle until I'm a size 2......again"

Ok so I've never been a size 2, I've been a size 4 all my life but my mother doesn't need to know that. It's hard to keep up appearances with a woman who's had more Botox than hot dinners (literally) she's so well put together. Her figure (at the moment) is better than mine. She used to say we were always in competition with each other about who looks the best. I'll willingly back down and admit defeat on this occasion.

"Good girl, I'm glad to hear it. You know many celebrities have the same problem as you. They eat their way into a crisis. It's as though the very motion of putting something in your mouth momentarily distracts the brain. It keeps your mind occupied, that's why I smoke dear and many Hollywood types do the same. You know in Paris it's considered stylish to smoke. At least that way you're not taking in empty calories. I really think you should consider it Jill, before we have to roll you down the aisle." mother chuckles nastily at her own joke. Her point is not lost on me, I know celebrities and models take up smoking to appear sophisticated and to stay slim, but I've never enjoyed the smell of them so I'm not too eager to find out how they taste.

"Honey laugh, I thought you could take a joke. Jill dear in all honesty you must do something about this soon, today in fact. It'll only get worse. After all its not considered desirable for the bride to be as wide as the church." she actually snorts at this one. I feel like this shitty visit is over now. I'm not in the mood to hear lame jokes about my body coming from a woman who is 90% plastic. Her forehead should read 'made in china' and her breasts may as well still have the price tag on. At least I can fix my problems the natural way; I'm not stooping to surgery even though it has become a fetish for some.

Why couldn't my mother be a Mary Poppins type?

After I've cleaned my plate with my tongue (only joking) I make the motion to leave.

"Well mother it's been wonderful seeing you again. I have to go, I'm running late meeting a friend." I try and scurry out of 'The garden' whilst throwing my leaving speech over customer's heads to reach mother.

"Ok dear, have a nice time. I hope to see you at the wedding, just not so much of you." Diane the comic throws back my way.

I really hope I don't see her at the wedding.

———~~∞∾∾✿∾∿∾~~———

I decide to walk back to Bill's apartment, it's only a few blocks away and after the conversation I've just had, I feel as though I need the exercise.

I over estimated this walk in heels, my feet feel like they're rubbing down to nubs and my heels are wearing down to flats. Two blocks in and I stumble upon a newspaper stand, I linger around mainly to rest my weight on one foot and then do the same to the other. I browse casually pretending to be interested in the newspapers, magazines and cigarettes that are for sale.

My interest peeks when a bridal magazine catches my eye. I suppose buying a couple of mags might give me some inspiration for my big day. After I grab a hand full of magazines varying from bridal to celeb gossip, I pay the man who asks me "anything else you need?" my mother's words ring in my mind about my starting smoking to avoid gaining more weight. I glance at the star studded magazines and sure enough more than half of them on the front page have a cigarette hanging out their mouths. Everything in me says I'm crazy for listening to her but I suppose it can't hurt to just buy some. I don't necessarily have to smoke them; I'll just keep them with me as my last option if everything else fails.

I buy twenty cigarettes and stuff them into my purse. I feel like a rebel from this action, I feel guilty like a criminal. I know it's wrong and totally not like me, my cheeks flush. I can't look the street merchant in the eyes. Cigarettes are legal but I still feel like a crook on the run and that's exactly what I do. RUN. Partly from my new reckless feeling and partly because smoking is the last thing I want to turn to. If I can just get back into my fat burning zone through cardio then I won't need these smelly things. I lose my breath before I start to feel the burn in my thighs. The only thing I feel are my lungs fighting for breath (God I really need to get back to the gym.) the phrase "running before you can walk" applies perfectly right now. I need to take baby steps, back to my normal routine.

I finally make it back home and all I want is a cool bath with chardonnay, chocolate and Michael Bublé serenading me through the surround sound system we have installed all over the apartment.

I slip into our hot tub and crank the bubbles up to the highest power and I do the same with Bublé. That man could charm the birds off the trees. His voice melts on my skin like hot butter. Damn now I'm hungry again. I brought the chocolate in as a reflex, totally forgetting I'm meant to be doing something about my weight. I know I need to watch my figure before Bill doesn't want too anymore.

I throw the chocolate to the floor and try to drift away into the atmosphere. The silence from my phone has unnerved me; Sally hasn't spoken to me since we discovered her hoarding obsession. I don't know what to do about it and I don't think I said anything particularly awful (Anne was joking on too) I've been in touch with Anne and she said the same that she hasn't heard from Sally either. I am worried about her, her condition isn't healthy. It also doesn't look new either, seems as though she's been doing it for years there is no other explanation as to why she has so much stuff. You can't acquire that much junk in a few weeks.

I wonder how long it's been going on for, and what the trigger was to start it off in the first place. My mind is wandering and spinning off into all directions, which is preventing me from having a relaxing bath.

I pull myself out of my romantic setting and settle for a curl up on the couch with my new Danielle Steel novel.

I leave the T.V off so I can enjoy my book, but before I get past the first page thoughts of the candy bar are playing on my mind. At this moment in time I no longer care about weight, I'm home alone trying to enjoy a little relaxation. Every woman indulges herself from time to time; I might as well have a little binge tonight and then start fresh tomorrow.

I bring in all the goodies I'd been hoping for, chips, dip, chocolate, a left over sandwich and a brand new tub of Ben and Jerry's. I stuff my face more than read; the food seems to have caught my full attention.

Why does fattening food taste better than healthy food? It makes no sense!

Anyway I digress, as I'm stuffing my face like someone entering a pie eating contest (and winning) I catch my own reflection in the blackened T.V set. Holy hell, what a sight. That's mortifying, I'm literally unrecognizable. If I saw someone in a restaurant eating that much, that fast, I'd pull a face and talk about them bitchily to my companion.

I have literally turned into my opposite, what has become of me? And how can I fix it?

I look away from the set embarrassed and mortified at what I see. My eyes wander to my coffee table where all the junk food is and just behind them are the trashy glam and bridal mags I forgot about.

The answer is being spelled out for me here. A picture of a celebrity smoking, a title underneath reading "How Gerry lost 5 stone" Tiny celebrities in tiny bikinis being shown with a picture of what they looked like before. Then of course the bridal magazines, need I say more. We both know they have and will never print a picture of a fat bride in one of these things. They're all just models wearing a different dress for a photo shoot; they're not really getting married at all. But even knowing this is not helping me. I know what the universe is telling me and I know I have to do it (I'm just scared)

As I mull this over I slump to my feet, I cautiously step toward my purse and remove the pack of twenty I bought from the news stand earlier. I forgot to get a lighter; thankfully I know where we keep the matches in Bill's apartment. I strike the match and freak out a little as I bring the cigarette to my lips. I swallow my fear after taking one more look at the stunning model smiling up at me wearing a vintage bridal gown, and I take the plunge.

I suck hard on the tip and that's it, I'm smoking. It takes me several attempts to fully inhale it (I know I'm such a wimp) but when I do I'm not disappointed. It's the most revolting thing I've ever tasted. This is what sucking on exhaust fumes must taste like. Why would anyone do this for fun or pleasure? It's so disgusting I'm baffled at how many people in the world smoke. I mean how can anyone become addicted to this?

Relief washes over me as I realize I have nothing to fear about becoming addicted to smoking. I'm purely going to continue to smoke to lose weight. Cigarettes to me are just like when you were ill as a child, your parent would feed you the nastiest tasting cough syrup and you'd cringe but it did help cure you. So that's how I'm looking at cigarettes now, they're my gross way of getting rid of binge eating.

I feel better about all this now. I feel as though I've got control back of my life. Feeling new and empowered I realize the other thing that's bothering me (apart from Bill avoiding me and me now having no sex life) is Sally. I'm gonna call and apologize. I'll force her to let me come round and I'll bring all this junk food with me as a peace offering (I know she'll eat it and it'll remove temptation from me)

Goal list

Mission one: make up with Sally

Mission two: lose weight/get in shape

Mission three: once in shape go and surprise Bill at the office, wearing nothing but a flash mac and a smile.

Chapter Ten

Bedroom Blues

So apparently the horrendous taste of cigarettes wears off after a while, then it doesn't taste of anything much. But on top of that you keep finding that you have one in your hand at all times, even when you have just stumped one out. I'm not saying it's become a crutch in life but I'll admit I am a little worried.

Sally says she hates the smell of them, apparently its everywhere in her apartment now. I can't help it, I can't tell where the smoke to go, I have no control over it. Plus if she wants my company she's just going to have to accept that the cigarettes will always be coming with me.

Her constant complaining about it has started to upset me. I mean I'm getting really paranoid with the way I smell. If it's all around her apartment then it's got to be in my hair and on my clothes too. My bathing routine has gone from once daily to two showers a day and a bath on the night, but it's no use.

My father has scolded me and I told him it was all moms' fault, she talked me into it. He called her and complained, calling her a 'bad influence'. It's the first time I've ever heard him telling her off about anything and he said her reply was laughable, that she giggled with delight and congratulated me on such a sensible decision and wished me well.

(Dad was not impressed by her flippant attitude; she didn't even try and hide her pleasure. That's mother for you)

My worry about my new...hobby (smoking) has not fixed my eating habit at all. (The stress of my new *habit* feeds my old *habit* even more. The more I worry and question if maybe I'm becoming addicted after all, the more the need to comfort eat kicks in (BIG TIME) I've been stuffing my face for weeks and it really shows. I can't believe I've nearly out grown all of my clothes, I've just been living in my gym outfits like sweatpants, hoodies, lycra, and such. Regardless to say I haven't been to the gym in them, I just curl up on Sally's bed and pig out on junk food with her.

We've basically turned into each other's feeders. (Look it up it's a fetish) Only there's nothing sexy about how Sally and I do it. We've even cut Anne off (a little) we haven't seen her in person recently; don't get me wrong we still talk to her all the time. I often call Anne myself and put her on loud speaker so we can have a three way conversation.

She's asked several times if we can meet up at my apartment (because she can't breathe in Sal's place) but I can't bring myself to go back there just yet.

So mortified am I, I've took sanctuary in Sally's apartment so Bill doesn't see me like this, I've even stopped going back to his apartment at night, he's been working later and later these days anyway.

I've quit waiting for him to forgive me and swoop me in his arms and have his way with me (to be honest I don't think he could lift me now) he hardly comes home anymore and when he does I'm already in bed asleep, well half asleep. The other half I'm laid there awake waiting for him to put his arms around me, which never happens. I don't know what's going on be-tween us or when the problem will fix itself but at the moment I'm finding comfort in mourning my sex life at Sal's place. I've practically moved in. We sleep in her bed then get up and talk and eat all day.

I think Sally finds this as comforting as I do. From what I've gathered from all of our talking is that Allan doesn't really live here. He lives on the road; he lives for his work (sounds familiar) and I've told Sally as much. I'm no longer snobbish round Sal, we've seen each other with messy hair, no make-up on with the remains of Dorito crumbs round our mouths. Keeping up appearances is over when it comes to Sally.

All Allan seems to do is give Sally full reign of his credit card (which is always a bonus, but is it enough to keep a relationship together? Can it hold you at night? Can it make love to you? Can it talk to you when you're lonely?) I know Bill is a worka-holic too but at least he comes home every night. We'd have dinner, talk and then have short but satisfying sex before we'd melt into each other's arms and slip into our peaceful dreams. Sally doesn't have any of that. All she has is her love for her man and the comfort of his credit cards and that's it. So I know my constantly being here is just what she and I need.

I can tell Anne feels left out; she's constantly blowing up our phones. I can't be bothered to make the effort to look decent and go out. We're messy slobs stuck in a rut and I've told Anne as much.

Speaking of the devil my phone lights up and vibrates.

"Jill, Anne's calling should I answer it?" Sally leans back on the headboard getting comfortable for another T.V shopping session P.S I kinda get the whole addiction thing now. Before I thought she was crazy but I've actually bought a couple of things for mine and Bill's kitchen at really quite a reasonable price.

"No It's ok, I'll get it" The very movement of bending forward to reach my phone reminds me how bloated I've become being Sally's roommate.

"Hey, how are you?" I ask caringly.

"I'm ok, really bored though. What are you two doing?"

"Same old, same as every day. What about you?"

"Nothing just bored watching the T.V. God Jill I don't know how you can sit in that apartment all day. The place is nothing but clutter. I'd offer to come round if I could handle the claustrophobic feeling I get in there. I damn near fainted. I wasn't expecting her to live like that." this is Anne's favourite topic: to talk shit about Sally's home. Whenever I put her on loud speaker the first thing I say is "Anne, I'm putting you on loud speaker now, Sally wants a word" which is code for 'stop bitching about the state of her place now' thankfully Anne is far more perceptive of my hidden meanings than Sally, but hell everyone is.

"I know, I know hunny. We wish you didn't have to do that thing-" I say, again in code for Sal's sake.

"Then you would have time to come and see us." We are used to talking like this every day because Sally is always sat beside me and she might over hear. Thankfully the T.V takes up most of her concentration, I do belief she maybe the only woman in the world who can't multi-task.

"Well I know but…I want to come round. I'm so isolated round here, at least you two have each other to talk to I've got no one. Richard's working overtime to raise more money toward the wedding, which is sweet of him but that leaves me all on my lonesome as usual. I don't know how I used to put up with this feeling before I met you two. I always used to feel I had my days filled…with cleaning. But I still clean every day, but now it just doesn't occupy me for long, there's only so many times you can vacuum, you know?"

She always brings up cleaning, she should come clean Sal's place. Lord only knows when it last saw a vacuum in here which is ironic considering Sally has four of them in different brands (I counted one day I was bored)

"I know hunny but if you can you know...get over that thing, then why don't you come over" just as the words come out, Sally rips the phone from me and screams.

"Anne! Yes come on, come on over. We'd love to have you I just bought a new shaker, we can have cocktails. I'll make anything you want. Come on it'll be fun; we haven't seen you in ages." Sal's come back to life with all the excitement of a child.

I loom in and press my head on to Sally's so we can both hear. I wonder how Anne's gonna get out of this one?

"Erm...errh...I want to Sal I just have too much on at the moment. I need to finish some stuff. I miss you too, both of you. I'm feeling quite lonely to be honest."

"Look don't say another word!-"Sally jumps in with complete conversation control "leave whatever you're doing and come round, I'm not taking no for an answer. There's plenty of Chinese for everybody, I'll get making drinks right now. I'll see you soon." Sally darts out the room with a new zest for life, in fact I don't think I've ever seen her move that fast before.

Anne is still on the line so I pick up where Sally left off.

"Anne, please tell me you're gonna face your fears and come round! Sally is too excited you can't let her down. This is the first time in weeks I've seen her get off the bed for a reason other than to use the bathroom, please tell me you're on your way." I plead with frustration. I'm putting pressure on her I know I am, but I think Anne will be a breath of fresh air for both of us.

"God's sake, ok, yeah. I can do this, no problem. I want to

see you two so I will. I won't let her mess get the better of me, I'll take control. Jill if you could just do me a favor and clean the couch area before I get there that would be great. I'm not lying on that smelly stained rag she calls a bed. I know I'm being cold hearted but I can only push myself so far. If you can just clear a bit of space in the living room, move some boxes into a pile and make the couch acceptable then fine, I'll agree to this." Anne sounds breathless.

"Yeah no problem, I'll try and clear away as much as possible just in the living room though. I can't do the whole apartment it's too much of a challenge. Give me an hour to straighten things out and we'll see you then."

"Ok thank you Jill, oh and give it a quick vacuum it'll need it desperately. I'm worried you two have been breathing in all sorts of dirt and dust. Open the windows, while you're at it you might as well dust around a little. I'll tell you a great trick for getting rid of dust easily, all you do is-" *CLICK*

I'm sorry but I had to hang up, she was boring me to tears.

─── ༄༅˚◦◦˚༄ ───

An hour later and I've done all I can. I'm completely exhausted. I don't know how Anne cleans all the time, its hard work.

I've moved loads of boxes (believe me it was heavy lifting) and the more boxes I moved the more dust and filth I unearthed. If anything it felt like I was doubling the work load. I was able to do most of it while Sally was in the kitchen fixing up only what I can describe as a full menu of drinks. Lugging boxes and unpacking a few as I went along, seeing as most of the items in the boxes are cleaning products. I thought it made sense to finally get some use out of them. I pulled out a brand new vacuum, some dusters, room deodorizer's, a box of new cushions, a broom and a full box of funny looking hats.

Ok so the hats are not needed right now, but I was able to work wonders with the rest. Needless to say Sally heard all the commotion and rushed in looking frazzled.

(From the looks of this place I assume it's because she's never heard a vacuum going before)

"Why are you doing that Jill? You don't have to clean my apartment silly, you're my guest." Sally scolds cheerily as she heads over to remove me from the room.

"No honey its ok, I want to do this." I try and reassure her, but between my panting for air and my beetroot face, I wouldn't be surprised if she didn't believe me (Hell I don't believe me)

Sally stops dead to inspect my face and says slowly "Ooookkkayyy...whatever you want." She looks frightened as though she's cautiously tip toeing around an insane person, desperately trying not to make any sudden movements in case she tips me over the edge.

I suppose I must look a little crazy, no one has seen me clean before. Actually I don't think I have cleaned before. Actually come to think of it, no I haven't. I've never had to, daddy always had a cleaner come to my child hood home, and now Bill has a cleaner.

I remember as a child I'd watch Madeline for hours (she was our French maid turned into a cleaner in New York) I used to love her accent though, the French are so sophisticated. In fact Madeline used to make cleaning look fancy, she'd potter about delicately taking her time on each chore making sure never to rush.

Madeline never broke a sweat, so why do I feel like I've had an hour at the gym? I suppose Madeline never had this kind of challenge to tackle and with a deadline of an hour. Now that's what I call pressure.

I realize Sally is still in the room and I come to.

"Uuumm I want to do this, it's like a workout to me. You know I want to do a bit of exercise so I feel I've earned those cocktails." I nod emphatically at Sally, just wanting to be finished already.

"Cocktails! Damn I almost forgot, there's lots of calories in them isn't there! Never mind we deserve to treat ourselves once in a while." Sally giggles naughtily and scampers out of the room. She really is all the bad influence I need. I'm very easily led these days.

'Treat ourselves' I think to myself as I clear the rest of the couch, pat the dust off and replace the old cushions with the new. All we've been doing is treating ourselves. Every time I notice what's in my hands I always find a cigarette in one hand and a tub of Chinese food in the other, there's no stopping me, I'm out of control.

Just as I stand back to feel the satisfaction of a job well done the intercom buzzes and I know Anne's on her way up. I'm sweating like a hog roasting on a camp fire; I wish I had time to shower. I have a feeling I may repulse Anne; I just hope she knows I'm only in this state because of her. Anyway there's no time to worry about that now, I need a well-deserved Manhattan.

Sally and I open the door to Anne, only to find her holding a cloth over her mouth and her eyes are tight shut.

"Anne honey, what are you doing you look crazy." Sally chuckles thinking this is some kind of game, but only I know how Anne feels about this.

I grab Anne and lead her to the clean sanctuary I've created for her (Ok so it's no palace but I did the best I could, at least there's somewhere to sit) I race her to the living room and tell her to open her eyes.

"You can open your eyes now-"

"Ta da!" I exclaim knowing for a fact it's a vast improvement from before.

"I...I...well I suppose it's better than before. At least you can see the couch now. It's still a little erm-"

"Small?" Sally suggests, emerging from behind the door. Shit I forgot she was here; Anne needs to shut up now.

"Ergh... I ...erm yes it is a little cramped in here Sal, but its fine." Anne tries to make good knowing she's being offensive.

"I know exactly what you mean. I keep telling Allan about the limited space in here. Honestly it must be bad if you've noticed it Anne, I thought it was just me because I see this place every day but I guess it really is small huh? Jill you didn't mention it. I guess Anne and I just notice things more than you do." I bite my lip on this occasion. I know all too well why this place feels so small but I'm keeping my trap shut.

"I'll have to get back to Allan and do something about it Anne, I feel as though I haven't got anywhere to put anything." Sally tells Anne, but Anne isn't looking sympathetic, she looks stupefied.

"Never mind. Jill why don't you sit next to Anne and I'll sit on the floor. Look what I've got ladies, I've made manhattans and we've got loads of snacks. I've got chips, toblerone's, Oreo's, pretzels-"

"Wow Sally this is too much for just for the three of us." Anne says shocked at the quantity of treats. Meanwhile Sally and I have already helped ourselves to popcorn and Oreo's. (God why can't Anne get into the spirit of things? She's such a party pooper.)

"Jill I'm not being mean here but you reek of cigarette smoke, where have you been today?" That's right Anne doesn't know I'm a chain smoker yet does she. Actually speaking of cigs I've needed one since blitzing this room. I think I'll have one with my cocktail.

I dump my snacks on a napkin and pull out a packet of full tar cigarettes.

"I haven't been anywhere Anne; I started smoking a while ago. Well actually the reason I started was to lose weight, it was my mother's suggestion but as of yet it hasn't worked."

Just from my small speech it's made me feel sad and disappointed in myself. Anne stares on at me then to Sally, with worry in her eyes.

"Well you two seem to be in a sorrier state than me at the moment." Says Anne concerned.

"What's that meant to mean?" Sally looks perplexed at the notion of her having a problem.

"I mean every time I call the pair of you, you're both eating constantly. I can hear you crunching when you're on the phone, you don't even hide it." Anne's words are making me suck harder on the tip for a more satisfying nicotine fix.

"Sally we've always known you like a bit of junk food now and then but it's never been as bad as this has it? And Jill what about you? You've changed your tune. You were a fitness freak, you were the one trying to force us into shape, now look at you!" I knew this was coming, I knew she'd tell us off as if she were our mother. I know I need to hear this but the more words that fall out of her mouth the more toblerone I want to put in mine. (Life's so hard)

"Jill I hate to say it hunny but you don't look like the same woman. You haven't got make-up on and your hairs not done, you're wearing sweats to relax in and now you've picked up that horrible habit. You know smoking makes you feel sluggish too, when did you last go to the gym?" Man, send in the Spanish inquisition! I think I'd prefer them to Anne's interrogation.

"I haven't been feeling up to it, besides that gym we went to is the best in New York and I can't ever go there again after the way you two embarrassed me."

"Oh come off it Jill there's plenty of other gyms." Anne knows I'm just looking for an excuse.

"Why not go back" Sally jumps in "that personal trainer guy was cute, he seemed to like you Jill."

Like me? Who likes me? I'm getting married anyway. Who's she talking about; I didn't see any trainer...a personal trainer? You mean that hobbit guy with the square head?!

"Sally what the hell, that guy was a creep another reason not to go back. Thank you for that Sally, I completely forgot about him. See Anne I can't go back because I was sexually harassed by the staff there." Nice save.

"Forget that gym we can work out from home. All exercise is free anyway. We only pay money at gyms to use their machines and god knows you'll never get me on those things again. Sweaty and germy, we could have caught a disease from them. No we can work out here. Well no actually not here. But we can go for a jog or a walk or anything you like. I have a few yoga mats at my place you two are more than welcome to come and practice yoga with me."

"Do you know I think I have yoga mats round here somewhere. I've been meaning to get into it. I went through a phase once of wanting to be someone that eats only organically, does sun salutations in the morning and is very flexible. Plus you know I heard yoga gives you a better sex life, it makes you more supple and bendy."

I don't need a BETTER sex life.

I just need A sex life.

Ordinarily I would be the first person to insist we take up yoga but all I want to do is get drunk, stuff my face and chain smoke until my lungs are content.

"Instead of being all active and shit, we should just bring Anne over to the dark side with us Sally." Ice cream dribbles from Sally's mouth as she giggles and gurgles.

"Yeah Anne we should just treat ourselves, women are always dieting anyway, give it a break for tonight. Allow yourself to eat whatever you want." Sally adds supportively like a helpful professional but I take it one step further. I pick up the tray of candy and hold it before her

"Go on take it, take something Anne. You won't regret it." I must look like the devil tempting her. I really mean it I want her to be on our side for a while, so I feel less guilty. I can't be bothered with healthy right now.

"Yeah Anne have a bite, the Oreo's are so good." We've both turned into bad influences.

"Well maybe just one of these candies. But this doesn't mean anything; first thing tomorrow we are all doing yoga at my apartment."

Feeling victorious I watch her pick a piece of hard boiled candy, and I feel like her dealer. I put down the tray feeling a sense of achievement, until I hear- "AARGH! OOWW! HELP!" (Oh shit)

"You're not meant to bite into it!" Sally screams from the top of her lungs.

"You're meant to suck it!" I shout so loud I put the fear of god in us all, even I jump.

"It's a little late for that, her mouths pouring with blood." Sally freaks out in a panic.

109

Anne's head is down near her lap, both hands cupping her mouth in hopes of catching the cascading crimson river. This shit is a straight up horror scene. Sally's flapping and panicking and I'm breathless. This really is the dark side of eating junk food, and it's enough to put me off it for life.

"Right everyone get your coats we have to get her an emergency appointment at the nearest dentist." I command and everyone follows my orders.

Coats and scarfs swirl around us in a flurry of utter chaos, emotions running high mixed with two women sobbing their hearts out and I'll be damned if there is a third. I gotta keep it together and keep cool, but I can't help feeling guilty as fuck. It was me that talked her into it.

But on the other hand everyone knows to *suck* not *crunch*.

Chapter Eleven

Dentist Drama

Tugging, pulling, screaming and crying- and that's just coming from Sally!

There's blood everywhere and the other half of the tooth's not budging. The other half was in Anne's hand before we left the apartment but the other piece is being a stubborn little shit. It turns out the broken tooth was riddled with decay (which Anne never knew about till now) that's why it crumpled so easily over the hard boiled sugar piece of candy.

Anne's laid in the dentist chair with tears streaming down her face, grimacing and cringing every time the dentist takes a tug. It's painful just to watch. I hate being at the dentist, I don't think anyone would choose to spend their spare time here. This is the house of pain and torture and that's just how the adults feel. I think if anything it's easier when you're a child, the dentist is normally a pleasant old man with a great bedside manner that says things like "ok so we are just having a little checkup, nothing to worry about. Now open wide."

He'd usually take a small mirror to see way back to your baby teeth and if you were lucky and didn't need any fillings he'd give you a sugar free lollipop and a sticker.

So why as adults when we go through something as traumatic as a root canal do we not get given a trophy? We don't even get offered the sticker any more. If anything I think we need them more now than we ever did.

Anne's brow is covered with beads of sweat and her screams of agony are enough to leave everyone shaking, even the dentist himself. Her gory, horror movie screams become too much to bare, at last I shout.

"Anne the local anesthetic isn't working because your adrenaline is too high, ask for a breather." seriously I can't handle the noise anymore. The dentist has given her three numbing injections now and clearly none have taken effect.

"Yes she needs a break!" Sally chimes in sounding hysterical "just let her get her breathing steady. I think she's gonna pass out."

The man playing the role of the dentist is looking panic stricken. I think he's used to dealing with just one difficult woman......not three.

Although saying that I have calmed down considerably after taking several hits from the laughing gass (don't judge me I needed it) this day has turned into a nightmare for all of us. I just hope this will all be over and done with soon.

The dentist relents, his brow is glistening with beads of sweat from his effort to remove the remaining piece of Anne's tooth and from the obvious stress we're putting him through. Anne gets up slowly and staggers to the door, Sally and I run to her aid but she pushes us off.

"I'm fine I can do it myself!"

"Ok, ok we are only helping."

"Well I don't need your help; you two got me into this mess!"

Mine and Sally's heads are hung down in shame knowing that Anne is right. But being riddled with guilt won't help anyone now; we just need to get through this. After a few minutes I take it upon myself to see where Anne's got to, all to find her not two steps away from the operating room, laughing her head off.

"Oh my god Anne what's happened to you? Why are you laughing? Did you take a hit from the laughing gas too?" Sally emerges with tears streaming down her face, she's been laughing her knickers off she actually looks in pain over it, doubled over giggling holding her enormous tummy. This site affects me; my laughter comes back in no time and seeing Sally in such a pant wetting state makes me chuckle hysterically. The next thing we know we are all rolling on the ground doubled over laughing harder and harder with every breath, I don't know how to stop and not really sure if I want to.

Who knew a trip to the dentist could be so much fun?

Chapter Twelve

You Don't Know How To Cook?!

While we were all still chuckling the dentist removed the rest of the tooth. It proved to be rather difficult for the dentist, but I think he preferred us laughing than crying and shouting.

The effects of the laughing gas finally disappeared when we got to my place. I tell you what, laughing like that was a real workout. It felt good while it lasted, I've never laughed so hard for so long that my cheeks hurt.

Considering everything Anne's been through today I didn't want to put her through going back to her private hell aka Sal's place, also I didn't think any of us could face going back to the scene of the crime. Unfortunately now the laughing gas has worn off us and we all just feel a little depressed about everything now.

Three women, two of which got fat and one of them started smoking. And now the third one has had her tooth pulled out. Fantastic, just fantastic, I can just see the wedding pictures now.

Sally in the background, stuffing cupcakes into her clutch, Anne grinning a toothless smile over the champagne toast. And me crying into my wedding cake with a cigarette in hand, sucking on it hard because I know how terrible I look in my XXL gown.

Yep that sounds about the gist of it.

We all look to each other with a glum expression, as if they've also just predicated the future and they're unhappy with the outcome too.

I don't know what to do, so I head for the alcohol and pour everyone a drink.

"I'm really sorry about forcing candy on you Anne. But you're the daft one for biting into it." I know I started off nice and then it turned into a back handed apology, but she had to know.

"I know, don't worry about it. It's my own fault." Anne says while rubbing her cheek.

"Still sore?" Sally enquires.

"That's a stupid question Sally. She's just been through a traumatic experience at the dentist." I say, exasperated with Sally's stupidity.

"I guess eating can be bad for you after all." Sally says looking thoughtful.

"No Sally it's not bad at all, if you eat the right foods. Instead of loading up on sugar and nibbles we should all be eating healthy balanced meals. I'm no chef but even I can make the most basic healthy dishes. I wouldn't mind taking a class to learn more about the art of cooking actually." says Anne, only slightly parting her lips to speak because she's still in pain from the surgery.

"I think that sounds fun" Sally interjects. "I've always wanted to be able to cook like Nigella. Ya know? They always make it look so much fun on T.V."

"Yeah I love her, she always makes it look very glamorous doesn't she." Anne agrees wholeheartedly.

I can see what they're saying; although I've never really wanted to do any domestic labour before but what the hell. I've been a cleaner recently why not try to be a cook too? My life's spiraling downhill anyway, what harm could it do?

"Come on Jill it'll be fun. We'll learn a new skill" Anne throws at me. I think she saw the look on my face and could tell I'm not exactly jumping up and down at the idea.

"I mean haven't you ever wanted to cook Bill breakfast in bed? You know they say the way to a man's heart is through his stomach." Anne concludes.

Actually I have wanted to do that, not that I'd know how. To be honest I've tried to cook a little when I've been bored (not that I've admitted to it but every time I try I either burn myself or the food, more than often both. So I stopped trying.)

"Yeah they do say that don't they!" Sally beams. "Maybe there's something to it. Men love it when they come home from work and their wife has slaved away all day to prepare a lovely meal for them. I think it would be nice to be able to do that for Allan when he gets back. He's never had a home cooked meal before because I've never took the time to learn. Well now I will, I'll start buying recipe books and practicing from home. Actually I think I may have a few mixers, tins, baking trays and stuff I've bought before but not yet used. I'm sure I bought quite a lot of cooking equipment before, because I had the urge to learn how. I guess I just forgot all about it."

"Well actually I was thinking more about attending a class. I know of this little community center not too far from here, that holds classes like that all the time. What do you think guys, Shall we go? I want to improve on my culinary skills and you two both need to know how to cook, even if it's just the easy stuff."

"Look, I did want to learn once but every time I tried to cook I'd walk away with third degree burns." Anne and Sally let out a giggle. "Yeah you can laugh but you don't know how painful it is. I'm telling you my oven is demonic."

DING! a text comes through on Anne's phone.

"It's from Richard; he just said he hopes I'm feeling alright since the whole dentist thing." Her head is down, eyes on the phone.

"How did he know you were there?" Sally asks.

"I called him on our way there, he never answered so I just text him letting him know what happened and where I was going. I was really shaken and I wanted him there but obviously he was at work and busy so...... I didn't expect him to drop everything and come with me."

Yeah right, that's exactly what she had been hoping. It would never happen. Everyone knows work comes first but it is a nice dream though.

"What does he do for a living?" Sally asks intrigued.

"It's really long winded and complicated. It revolves around computers. He's a technical engineer and a website designer. Richard installs software on people's devices and updates programs and all sorts. It's a difficult and boring job from the sounds of it." says Anne in admiration for her man. "That's why I try and make his life as easy and relaxing as possible at home." She says in a mocking tone, looking directly at me.

"I see what you're getting at Anne. You don't think I'm a real woman because I haven't yet made a meal for Bill?" I accuse her, I'm offended.

"For god's sake Jill, you're a fully grown woman! You should be able to cook a simple meal by now."

"What so if you're born with breasts you're just supposed to know how to cook and clean and look after a man?!" I raise my voice with my words dripping with sarcasm.

"Well yeah, your mother should have taught you." Anne says sensibly.

"Absolutely, in a perfect world my mother would never have walked out on me, and every weekend mother and I would migrate to the kitchen and make chocolate chip cookies with the secret family recipe! Of course I wish that had happened. But it didn't!"

Oops I never intended on spilling my life story but … never mind, now they know.

Sally and Anne look at each other with pity in their eyes over me.

God I hate pity.

"Look Jill I'm sorry. I didn't know. I shouldn't have assumed you have a mother, not everyone does. You only ever talk about your dad. That should have given me a clue. I'm sorry, I guess I didn't think." Anne looks at me with remorse written on her face.

I really don't want to get emotional over this so I blink so fast I feel like my false eyelashes may act as wings and lift me off the couch.

"Yeah Jilly, I'm sorry your mom did that to you. But didn't you tell me you had lunch with her the other week?" Sally says looking confused.

"Yes I do see her once or twice a year for dinner and that's all. She's more like a distant relative or even a glamorous acquaintance than a mom. I just pray she doesn't have time to show up on my wedding day."

Both women look at me and nod with understanding. I'd like to get off the subject now; it's starting to bother me.

"Never mind Jill, it doesn't matter now. Forget her; it's never too late to do something new. You said yourself you wanted to learn once, so why don't we all do it together?" Anne asks, trying to turn this into a positive.

"Just like the three musketeers!" Sally jumps in all hyped up.

Even Anne tries to smile but it's still a little lopsided from the local anesthetic.

I look at the two new additions to my life and realize these freaks of nature are the closest people in the world to me right now. Bill and my father are workaholics, as are Allan and Richard. I can tell all three of us have started to need and lean on one another more than any of us could have anticipated (especially me) so Sally's joke of us being the female version of the musketeers isn't actually that far away from the truth.

So is the way to a man's heart really through his stomach? I'm not sure but I think we will try just about anything to make our relationships work.

Chapter Thirteen

Behind Closed Doors

Anne has been in touch with the details about a cookery course found in Hell's Kitchen (I know, the irony) she's promised it's quite a successful class too. It's apparently run by a once famous (ish) chef, so it's almost always fully booked and we were lucky she had enough slots available for us.

Anne seems really excited about the course but I'm a little skeptical as to my culinary abilities. I suppose if anyone can teach me how to cook it'll be this highly accomplished chef. I'm kinda stumped as to why this well-known cook doesn't have her own TV show instead of a low key class being held in a rundown community centre in Hell's kitchen of all places.

Never mind I'm sure it'll be great. At least now I have plans for Saturday evening.

I'm going back to Bill's apartment tonight, I've moved out of Sally's place because I knew I was in hiding. Nothing will ever get better if I don't make an effort for Bill. Plus Sally and I equal disaster. We are too comfortable with each other and I have known for a while that we both need a kick up the ass! So

I took the plunge and left the familiar surroundings of Sally's cluttered world. Back to civilization and then back to the gym for me.

Just me though, I'm not going to mention it to Anne and Sally because I'm going back to the one I humiliated myself in. I know that there are so many gyms in New York and maybe even better ones than "The Burn" gym and juice bar, but in all honesty I am starved for male attention. Even just a compliment or two from that hobbit man, would make me feel like an attractive woman again. (Not that I'll let him know that) but to be blunt I'll settle for any nice words from any man at the moment.

Things are still no better with Bill, and I'm really going to work on it, I mean it I'm going to pull out all the stops.

When he comes in tonight I'll run him a bubble bath and pour him a tall flute of champagne. Then when he gets out of the tub I'll give him a hot oil foot massage. I bet his feet are killing him being at the office all day.

I'll make it up to him; I'll make him fall in love with me all over again. Not that he called off the wedding or anything; I'm just concerned over his silence. He didn't text me or call me once, the whole time I lived at Sally's. Which made me more depressed, so I ate more, then I got bigger, then I buried myself a little deeper into Sally's bed. I won't let that discourage me, I'm back now. He'll be surprised when he comes home tonight, I haven't told him I'm coming back I want to see the look of relief on his face when he first sees me. Perhaps my being away will have been a blessing in disguise, maybe when he sees me he'll realize just how much he's missed me and can't bear to live without me.

Yes that's what'll happen. We will be stronger than ever!

I've heard about Bill through daddy. When we are on the phone I just ask how Bill's doing at work, which doesn't sound odd to my father, he just sees it as my way of showing my capability of being a lovable, doting wife. I'd never tell him I wasn't staying with Bill at the time; I wouldn't want to worry him.

Anyway daddy reassured me that he had seen Bill recently and Bill had told him that he's working on a hard case. He also mentioned how Bill took the news of my smoking. Father was the first to tell him without knowing it; he assumed Bill knew from living me that I smoke like a chimney. Dad said Bill looked perplexed when he brought it up to complain to Bill how upset he was, now that I'm a smoker like my mother.

Apparently Bill responded by saying that smoking has never really bothered him and that a lot of his work colleagues smoke.

Father made no more comments on my new "filthy habit" which I'm relieved about and I'm especially pleased that Bill doesn't care that I smoke. I have been worried what his reaction might be but now I longer have to worry.

I unpack my bags, take a shower then set out to make the place more inviting. Candle light, slow music, and maybe I'll put some perfume in the air. I take my time because I know he usually strolls in past midnight.

I potter around the apartment at my leisure, making the place smell amazing. This isn't about seduction you understand. I'm not about to pressure him for sex. I'll wait until he's ready to give it. Nope, this is purely about reconnecting and spending a little time together.

One o'clock comes and there is no sign of him.

Two o'clock comes and there's no sign of him.

Three o'clock comes and I'm so exhausted I can't stay

awake any longer; I have to go to bed. I'm sure when he comes in he'll be able to pour his own wine, everything's laid out for him. Unfortunately the bath I drew for him will now have gone cold but I'll leave it in the tub as proof that I've made an effort for him. And as the old saying goes "It's the thought that counts". I desperately wanted to spend some time with him but if I sleep now hopefully I can wake up before he heads back out to the office.

I set my alarm for six thirty in the morning, admittedly I'll still be half asleep but at least we can share a couple of hours together over breakfast.

I curl up on my side of the bed and feel the cold crisp sheets hang loosely over my body. I want to say I've missed my bed and designer sheets, it's a far cry from Sally's unkempt bedroom, but honestly I haven't. I think it's just the company I miss, anyone's company. Everything will be better when Bill gets home.

I can't imagine why Richard wants such a big wedding. It'll cost far more than just a simple, small, tasteful ceremony that I had in mind. Richard and I have been discussing ideas for the wedding, but it seems our vision of the perfect wedding, are as different as black and white. I want tiny and intimate and he wants everything with bells and glitter on!

"Anne my god, why are you thinking on such a small scale? This is our wedding day and I want a big traditional wedding. I want everything to be grand and white and sparkling! You're going to have the most amazing dress ever. I already know what type of style it's gonna be. Same as the centre pieces, I know a guy who runs his own little florist shop on the side of his regular job and he's shown me some amazing arrangements he's done for weddings. He wants to be a florist full time, so I think it's important we give him our business.

Anne I'm telling you the things this man can do with a pot of glitter, white roses with diamanté's and pearls is just exquisite. Honey our wedding is going to be sensational." Richard is literally breathless with excitement. He's looking past me into the distance as he makes this speech, with misty eyes that are imagining the most glamorous affair of the decade. The kind that put celebrities to shame.

"But darling think of the cost. It sounds like you want to spend an absolute fortune. Why can't we have just us two, a vicar and I have a few people in mind I would like to invite as witness's." yes I am thinking of Jill and Sally. The girls and I haven't discussed it yet but I hope we are all intending on inviting each other to our weddings.

"I was thinking maybe in a nice little chapel somewhere. You're wearing your best suit with a small rose in your lapel and me with a simple white dress. No frills no glitter just a clean white silk dress with straps. I don't want a gown with a hundred layers with a matching tiara; I'll feel like a fool. Can't you please get excited over an elegantly put together service?" I'm begging for my life here. All I want is for the main focus of the wedding to be on me and my husband and the vows we've written for each other. I don't want the main attraction to be bejeweled flowers or how many crystals are on my gown.

Just nothing but the love should be on display. Or at least that's how I feel, but it's clear Richard doesn't agree.

"Anne, have you heard yourself! An elegant service? Service! Just listen to yourself. We are planning on getting married only the once, we should do the big, high gloss, over the top wedding. It should be a huge deal! I want our wedding day to be like a show, something for everyone to enjoy. Both our families are gonna be there, my mum is so excited she's already bought her hat and dress with matching kid gloves. And believe me her outfit is very fancy, more so than yours sounds. You can't have your mother in law upstage you on your own wedding day.

What's wrong with you? Forget about the money, I've got it covered. I'm working overtime and my parents have given me a big fat cheque to go towards the wedding, so everything's fine. Will you stop worrying. Look everyone is so excited about this, but aren't you meant to be the most excited of all? Isn't it every girls dream to have THE wedding, the kind that fairytales are made of?" Richard gawks at me like I'm a complete weirdo and in a way I guess he's right.

What should I care of cost when it's not me paying for it? I know traditionally its meant to be my dad that pays for this and he did offer but Richards parents have been saving up for this moment since he was twelve year's old, so they refused my dad's cheque which he was hardly upset about. My father always was a tight fisted man but it's helped me understand the meaning of being wasteful.

Also Richard's passion for this is adorable. He only wants the best for us, what's wrong with that? Most women have to plan the whole thing themselves and just tell the guy where and when to show up. I should be thankful it's not like that with Richard.

He's so actively involved in this, it's me who's being the bore, as usual. As my mother always says "Marriage is about compromise" so it looks like I'll have to start now.

"Ok" I say, feeling a little at a loss but determined to try and look happy about it "let's do it, let's have a wedding that will put the Kardashian's to shame." Richard puts a hand over his mouth and gasps with delight "Go on Richard write all your crazy and wonderful ideas down. We're going to do it; we are going to have the wedding of your dreams."

—–⁓⁓ᴏᴏᴇᴛᴏᴏᴇᴛᴇᴏᴏᴍ⁓—–

Another three packages arrived today; I'm just trying to figure out where to store them.

As per usual on my way up the stairs from collecting my parcels, old man Mr. Albert took a nosey look at me scuttling down the hall. I saw his door slowly open so I quickened my pace. My physical fitness obviously let me down and his voice bellowed after me.

"Miss willows! Shopping again are we? I see you haven't taken my advice to do something meaningful with your life." It's more like judgment than an observation.

So what anyway. What's he doing with his life? I've never noticed him having visitors (not that I would know because I rarely leave my apartment) but it's not as though he lives the high life with his millions of dollars, skydiving, owning a business or helping the needy. All he's good for is prying into other people's business. I hate know-it-all busy bodies!

"Well actually yes Mr. Albert I am. I'm taking a cooking course this weekend so I'm just buying equipment to prepare my kitchen for all the homemade cuisines I plan on making. Good day to you." that's as firm as I can get. Well I know not everything in these boxes are kitchen appliances, but it was partly true.

I let myself into our apartment with urgency, glad to have avoided an essay length speech on how I'm a waste of space from the gray complexioned Mr. Albert.

My shopping habit had slowed down a bit, but since Jill left I've become reckless again.

I loved how we would discuss new items and swap feelings on what was being advertised. Jill really got into the spirit of the game. We could talk about one product for an hour before making a decision to buy it or not. She was also particularly helpful on some of the more expensive ones that cost thousands, she would talk to me sensibly and ask me if it was "something I desperately needed" and "was I sure I didn't already have one." (Which it turns out, half the time I did)

Normally I don't think like that, I'm just caught up in the moment and excitement. That's when I tend to make hasty decisions. Unfortunately now I don't have anyone to monitor me or anyone to talk to. Not just about teleshopping, but about anything. Life, love, marriage, sex (Jill wasn't as open mouthed about that as I thought she would be) and all sorts of other stuff.

We still constantly call each other but it just isn't the same as someone being here. Since her departure I've become more and more aware that I hate living alone. It was such a pleasure having someone to wake up to, and spend time with but now I just feel as though I'm going cold turkey again.

Every purchase I make seems to take me through to Simon at the call centre, he's so lovely to speak to honestly I feel as though he's in the wrong profession he could have been a psychiatrist. So I still talk to him every day and Jill and Anne. I've tried to call Allan hundreds of times but I know he's busy working hard and he can't answer, so I'm texting him instead. So far I've received three texts back from the twenty-five that I've sent. It's really no company at all; a text.

I feel as lonely as ever but I'll get by. I'll just look forward to seeing the girls at the cooking class this weekend. I hope we get to bring our own aprons; I've got a box full of them. I'll bring three with me just in case they aren't as prepared as I am.

———〰ᴏᴏᴄᴛᴏᴏᴛᴏᴏᴍ———

My alarm went off predictably at six thirty. After a startled lunge to turn off my alarm, I lay back with a groan. I feel like one of the undead. I feel desperate for extra sleep, just a few hours more and then realize why I was so adamant of getting up at this hour: for Bill.

I roll over to give him a good morning kiss, only to find his half of the bed is still made without as much as an indentation of his lying head on the pillow. He didn't come home last night, I know he didn't, I didn't get to sleep till late and I've only been in here for three and half hours. I wonder where he is and why he never came home. I also wonder how long this has been going on for. Since I left probably.

Bless him. Oh god I feel awful. I bet he was distraught when I left, but his manly pride prevented him from calling me and telling me to come home. I bet he spent the entire night in the office. Partly working, partly napping on the couch he had installed near his desk for intense cases that take a lot out of him. He's slept at the office a couple of times before, whenever he has extreme cases and files to work on, that normally keep him up all night anyway. So his staying there just makes sense to him and I never dispute that but this time he's been sleeping at the office because of me! That makes me feel terrible.

He probably couldn't bear to come back to this place knowing I wouldn't be here to greet him when he came home from work. This whole apartment probably seemed meek and desolate in my absence. Right that's it I'll never leave his side again I mean it; I swear it to the old gods and the new (where have I heard that before?)

I'm just gonna have a few more hours sleep before I get up properly, then I'll call him to let him know the good news.

Honey, I'm home!

Bill was so happy to hear from me – *and kind of shocked* – but mostly I'd say he was relieved. He didn't really have much to say to me, he sounded busy and under pressure. Most probably work related so I didn't keep him on the phone long. You see it's a wife's duty to pick up these subtle things and know when to leave your man alone when he's busy.

He said he's coming back to the apartment tonight and that he'll see me then. I told him I loved him before we ended the call, and he said "I'll see you soon."

You see that's how hectic and rushed he felt, he couldn't even get his words out right. Never mind I'll just wait patiently for him to come home.

Its 4pm and the hours have gone by so slowly. Usually I'm used to having the days to myself and then enjoy Bill's company on the night. I think it's because lately I have felt there has been some kind of silent war between us these days that I feel completely impatient.

How does Sally do this every day? Only her guy doesn't come home at the end of the day like mine and Anne's do. Sally has to wait months and months. Truly that woman has the patience of a Saint.

I've been on the phone with both of them, they're fine (or so they say) apparently Anne and Richard are already underway making plans for their wedding, where as I haven't even been given the chance to talk to Bill about them. This is gonna be the first time we have spoken since before I signed the pre-nup. Which feels like a million years ago.

Anyway it sounds as though Anne and Richard are going

BIG for their wedding and Anne mentioned how much he's enjoying himself, planning and organizing everything. I suspect she'll have an easier time of it, if she has a partner to help her with every detail. Plus I think it would make a nice bonding exercise between future man and wife.

Yeah I mean why not? Both parties should be hands on with an event as huge in magnitude as their wedding day. I know normally it's the bride that sorts it all out but I don't know ...... I'm starting to see things in a new light. Bill should have as much of a say in our day as I do. Brilliant, actually this gives me a topic in mind to start a conversation when he gets in.

I don't know why, but I have a suspicious feeling our first few words to each other will be a little awkward, I'm sure after that though we will be fine.

I make the same effort I did last night, and that too all went to waste. Bill didn't come home until 2 o'clock in the morning. I stayed awake hoping he hadn't forgotten I was here. A part of me was bursting at the seams to text him and ask what time he was intending on leaving the office, but from out previous conversation I assumed that would have been a bad idea.

The moment I hear the door open my heart skips a beat, I don't know whether that's due to excitement or nerves. The minute we see each other we just stand staring at one another face to face.

Ok so this isn't the romantic scene I had played out in my head but at least he's here. I have prepared my monologue to get us talking.

"Hey honey, how was work?" I ask, still a little flustered.

"Don't remind me of work Jill, I've had a lot on and I just want something to eat and get some sleep. I have an early meeting in the morning." Man he's in a bad mood. Now I'm doubting if I should try and tackle the subject of planning the wedding together, he doesn't look in the mood to talk at all.

"Ok honey, no problem. The cook left dinner in the kitchen." I'm sure after several glasses of wine he'll start to unwind.

We migrate to the kitchen in silence.

The cook always tends to every detail in the kitchen after she's prepared a meal. She lays out the table to perfection and display's the silverware in an orderly fashion. Sometimes I like to wander into our kitchen just to stare at everything in admiration. This is why I don't mind that often when Bill doesn't take me to high end restaurants (due to his working schedule) because my kitchen looks just like one. I wish he'd let us entertain here from time to time; I'd love to really show this place off. What with Bill's paranoia about letting people he doesn't know well in here, he believes everyone who doesn't have his lifestyle would be jealous and would try to steal expensive items like our jewelry and ornaments. I agree with him actually so I've never forced the issue.

We take our seats and I pour him a very good chardonnay from "1967" and he practically inhales it, so I pour him another.

My mind is trying to conjure up another question and all I keep getting is "how was work" but I've done that one. Come on! Think of something, anything. It's so unbearably quiet in here; I can hear my hair grow.

"How's the wine? It's lovely isn't it?" *don't judge me it's a question isn't it.*

"Yes its great wine, I need a large one after the day I've had." immediately I grab the wine bottle to give him a decent refill. After the comment he just made I feel it's my duty to enquire further about his day, almost like he can read my mind he looks at me and shakes his head.

That bad huh? Fine I won't go there, but what else can I do?

Bill is happily picking at his food and slurping his wine when it finally dawns on me. We have never had a decent, heartfelt, real conversation. Ever. You know the ones I mean: the kind of talk, where you spill your guts to each other, completely exposing yourself with no shame because you know the person so well. You assume they won't think less of you because they know who you are; they understand you as a person.

It strikes me as odd that I've only just noticed this but now that I'm aware of it, it's bothering me. Suddenly my appetite has gone and I instantly switch to autopilot, I light up a cigarette at the dinner table.

"That's right; I forgot you've started smoking. Your father mentioned it the other day." I jump up as though I've been burnt only when realization hits me that I'm literally blowing smoke in his face while he's eating. My bad.

I back up all the way to the other end of the kitchen to leave him eat his dinner in peace, but he pulls me back in with his words.

"Never mind all that. I'm not particularly hungry now anyway. Give me a cigarette Jill. And pour me a whiskey will you, I need something a little stronger than this wine."

Bill wants a cigarette?!

"What! When did you start smoking? I've never seen you smoke before!" I ask in shock, which is rather like the pot calling the kettle black.

Side note: I've heard that expression all my life and still I'm clueless as to its meaning but either way I'm sure it applies here.

"Well I don't know what you're so angry about. Can't a grown man smoke in his own home if he wants to? I'm a casual smoker, I always have been." Well this is news to me. I'm not angry I'm just gob-smacked. I never knew that about him until now. No wonder he took the news of my smoking so well, why should he care when he occasionally smokes himself?

I adjust to this newly found information and he lights up. I take another one out the pack to calm me down. Bill's really not in a social mood tonight at all, trying to become the best of friends in one night just isn't possible. Hopefully he will feel better after he's slept; he polishes off the rest of the wine that had been laid out for the two of us and we take ourselves off to bed in what feels like forever.

There is an awkward sort of tension between us when we first lay down next to each other, but he obviously doesn't feel it for long as I can hear him gently snoring beside me only a few minutes later. The comfort of having someone breathing and snoring peacefully in bed with me has always made me feel safe and cozy, so I join him there.

In the land of nod.

I awake to utter panic and chaos.

"For Christ sake it's 8 o'clock already! I've over slept, I'm late. Jill get up help me get things in order. Get me a new suit out of the wardrobe while I take a quick shower. I'll call the office let them know I'm running a little late." He's flapping around like a headless chicken.

I'm laid in bed trying to figure where to start first as I rub the sleep from my eyes.

"Jill, get up now! Fix me a coffee in my travel mug and throw some fruit in my briefcase. I don't have time to go to Starbucks this morning, got I hate sleeping past the alarm" he's borderline screaming now so I jump to and get going.

On the odd occasion Bill is late he's never cute with it like the rabbit out of Alice in wonderland "I'm late; I'm late for a very important date." I'd prefer to wake up to a funny rhyme than a sergeant's drill and I'd still get the message.

As I pick up the pace and perform these small errands for him it hits me that we're never gonna have quality time together. Due to his career we have never really had quality time together, so why suddenly do I need it now? It's always been like this, nothing has changed. Have I changed?

I throw these silly thoughts out of my head and put them down to lack of sleep. This is fine. This is married life. I'm being very wifely right now, helping my future husband get ready for work. I'm sure he realizes what a good woman he's got, he clearly needs me.

And he'll need me even more when I know how to cook. He can fire the chef and I can make our meals just like a proper housewife should.

Already I have images of me in a tiny-waisted apron with frilly edges, pink and white I think it is. I'm holding matching mixing bowl with a whisk, and my hair is done to perfection. In my head I look like the girl next door, unfortunately in real life I don't. I'm currently making plans to change that; I'm sneaking off down to the gym on my own later. I will not be a size 26 for my wedding day. Of this I am certain.

Feeling more upbeat and positive than I have in weeks I finish my chores without delay. Bill runs off full steam ahead charging past me, picking up everything along the way. Apartment keys, car keys, briefcase and coffee, all while holding his cell between his ear and shoulder apologizing frantically to the person on the other end. I manage to give him a peck on the cheek while he's blustering around like a whirl wind. The response from my kiss was not well received. His reaction was of someone being stung by nettles. He backs up several steps to give me a wide birth. I notice the crease in his forehead deepen with annoyance and impatience as he makes a gesture with his hands for me to get the door for him.

As he gets into the elevator I stand there frantically waving him off, but he doesn't notice. He doesn't even look up, clearly too focused to think about anything other than work right now. And as an understanding fiancé I get that and try not to be hurt by it.

Now that I'm awake I'm gonna keep it that way and head to the gym A.S.A.P. It's pointless my dilly dallying around here with nothing to do, I've got to put the time in to getting my figure back. Also should I happen to get a compliment or two to feed what little I have left of my ego, well so be it.

After all, a compliment never hurt anyone.

Chapter Fourteen

Working My Ass Off!

(Literally)

After I arrive at 'The Burn' I start to wonder if 'Bilbo' or whatever his name is might not be in today. I should have called in advance and booked a session with him. He's not the main reason why I'm here but he does add a little something to this particular gym.

I stroll to the reception desk and ask if I can have a personal trainer for the day. I know you can sample different trainers before you take up a contract with a particular person. You have to know if the chemistry is right for you to work together, after all it is a working relationship of sorts.

"Yes of course, we have a few free today at different times. Were you looking for anyone in particular?" the bright eyed, athletic looking receptionist asks me.

She looks more as though she should be teaching a yoga class than stuck in admin work, but whatever floats her boat.

"Um...yes...is Bilbo free this morning?" I ask without thinking.

"Bilbo?" the receptionist asks looking baffled.

Damn it! Damn him! I've totally forgotten his name.

"Sorry not Bilbo" I laugh awkwardly. "His name is...something...it begins with a B. I think. Hang on I'll remember in a moment. It was...Bob...Billy...Bernard...Burny...b...b" I look like a stuttering fool trying to remember.

"Burt?" the receptionist jumps in, lending me a hand.

"BURT! That's right. God I felt like I was losing my mind for a minute there." Still trying to make light of my stupidity, but the face behind the desk doesn't find me funny.

"Well you're in luck; he's quite often free these days so I expect he'll have a slot for you. I'll just go and find him then I'll take the payment before you start training today." She says all teeth and smiles.

"Sorry before you find him can you tell me why he's often free these days? Is he not very good at his job?" or is he unprofessional and flirts with every woman he sees? Obviously I don't ask her this, but the thought of him being a weird flirty creep with just anyone kind of bothers me. So much so I think I'd rather take my business elsewhere.

I know it sounds strange because I've only had one encounter with him but I'd like to believe he's only a weird flirty creep with me.

"Oh no, no! It's nothing like that I assure you. Burt is a qualified professional. 'The Burn' only has THE best staff here I promise you. He's free most of the time because he doesn't have enough clients to fill his time here." the woman leans in toward me as though we are lifelong pals just having a girly catch up.

"Actually I've heard they may be putting Burt on a part time contract because he's basically being paid to just stand around all day doing nothing. Which isn't his fault but it happens to the best of them." The receptionist with a name tag that reads

'Becky' gets up and scurries away to fetch the soon to be out of work Burt.

Who knows then, maybe my coming by and giving him my business will help him keep his job. I just can't help but wonder why no one wants him as a trainer. Has he pushed his luck with a woman and she was so appalled with him that she never came back. Not just that but she spread the word far and wide to all of her friends and family and told them never to take him on as a personal trainer because he sexually harasses women? Surely everyone knows the power of gossip. The word of mouth can shut down entire companies; maybe that's why his career is in the toilet.

I have to find out the truth before I sign a full contract with him.

Becky comes back with a big grin on her face, holding Burt by his arm as though she were his mother letting him know there's a friend at the door wanting to know if he can play out.

"Here we are" Becky says looking triumphant "Burt this is your new client for the day" Burt approaches me with caution as if he's seeing things and just can't believe it.

"You" he mouths silently at me, a wide grin spreading over his face spilling over onto mine.

He's in front of me with his hand out ready to play the role of a professional. Just from our one introduction I feel like we are already past the point of civilized pleasantries.

"Hello, I'm Burt Laurel. I'll be your trainer today." What a bad actor, he can't look me in the eye and the corners of his mouth are twitching. I can feel mine starting to do the same.

"Hello, I'm Jill Green. I'll be your client today." I see Becky from the corner of my eye looking pleased as punch, probably hoping Burt will keep his full time position after all.

"Ok Miss Green, if you'd like to fill out the paperwork so

we can take the payment, then you and Burt can get to work." My word, that's the second time bossy Becky has mentioned payment, what does she think I'm gonna do? Steal exercise?

She hands me a small stack of papers to sign, which I take from her and take a seat. Burt looks on at me impatiently, clearly wanting to get started and can't possibly wait for me to complete all these documents.

"I'll just wait for you over near the dumbbells, and then we can begin with some upper body exercises." He tells me, still smiling.

I nod in response feeling my cheeks flush with colour. What a strange reaction to have just because he's looking at me. Have I been so neglected of attention that I get excited over the smallest thing?

God I need help!

As I approach the weight lifting bench, I feel all my fat jiggle as I sashay toward him in what I'm hoping to be a slightly seductive manner. The way my ass is bouncing just reminds me why I'm really here, to apply myself to a hardcore workout. Not just to flirt with Burt.

"Right so; let's get you set up with a few stretches to warm up. We don't want you to pull anything now do we?" He looks at me as though I'm fragile.

Hey buddy before the weight gain I was pretty damn strong. I was as fit as a fiddle. I'm still strong even though I've thickened out a little but I dare say he has too from the looks of things. But he's the supposed professional so I just smile politely and follow his lead.

Just from these few simple stretches I feel the heat creep into my face, and my face and my heart rate has increased just from the slightest bit of exercise. I try and waft myself to cool down while his back is turned to fetch me the lightest weights imaginable.

Pre, pre nup Jill would have laughed at him and gone for a bigger weight and looked like a pro doing it. Today's Jill is mortified by her lack of energy. And this is just a warm up! I take the doll sized version of dumbbells without any hesitation and echo all of his movements.

Grunting, panting and sweating all the way, I no longer feel like a sexy woman I just feel like a sweaty red faced beast. No wonder he hasn't made any advances. As I glance in the wall mirror facing us, I figure 'Who would.' I really don't blame him. Suddenly it occurs to me that I gave him that whole awful speech before about us being in different classes. And that he should learn his place.

It all comes flooding back to me, every word. My god I can't believe how self-loving I was then, I wouldn't dare say something like that now. I feel like a completely different person these days, and not necessarily for the better. At least I can safely say my head has deflated a considerable amount.

Burt tells me "Let's take five."

"Thank you" I say as he lets me sit down and hands me a bottle of Evian.

"For you, me lady" I look up in shock. I can't believe it I totally forgot he's a loser. A loser that plays around with his already English accent, and now has morphed back into my butler all because of what I said last time.

I inwardly cringe.

Looking up I see Burt's face looking amused as hell. Ok so if he can laugh about it than I might as well.

"Would Madame like a towel?" Burt the butler asks me, treating me like royalty.

I figure I'll continue the fun and play along with this little charade. I think it'll break the ice.

"Yes Burt, go fetch me a towel at once! Do you expect me to fetch my own things?!" I put on the voice of a posh old snob woman and I must admit, it comes all too easy to me. That can't be a good sign.

I glance again in his direction just to see the response I'm getting, praying he's enjoying it.

And boy oh boy is he ever! His face lights up as if we are finally playing his favourite game. His cheeks are so high they're burying half his eyes. He's a funny little man come to look at him clearly. His eyes are a nice shade of blue, extremely short blondey brown hair just a touch of white appearing at the temples, but there is nothing old about him. I'd estimate him to be anywhere between late 30's to early 40's. One thing I will say about Burt is he's got HUGE arms. Muscle's for days, they really look disproportionate to his body. Short legs, hairy thick calves, a short stout build to his frame, topped off with a round button nose.

It's true what they say you know, looks really are deceiving. If I were to have seen this man on the street I would have assumed he was a rough around the edges boxer. But after a couple of hours of our to and fro aristocratic role play, he just seems to me like a silly man, an over grown boy trapped in a man's body, a teddy bear dressed up (hoping) to look like a grizzly, but failing.

Burt's laughter is contagious and I feel as though we've done more laughing and talking than exercising. He put me on the treadmill and kept increasing my speed but at the same time he was still pretending to be my butler, wanting me to respond in my 'Dowager' accent. He was the one that labelled it 'Dowager' I quite like it. With the speed I was going I was breathless anyway, so talking was out of the question.

"Do beg your pardon marm but is this contraption going too fast for you?"

Pant. Nod. Pant.

I couldn't answer. He laughed so hard at this, knowing he had control over the speed button. I would have jumped off but I didn't dare risk making a fool out of myself again in here after the whole 'Jelly leg' incident. I persevered through and I tell you what, they don't call it 'The Burn' for nothing. It was just the push I needed into the right direction and even better that I got to watch a grown man giggle like a little girl the whole time.

But you better believe I made him pay for it when I finally got off.

"What the ... your trying to kill me ...I'll get you ...for this" I'm panting like a dog in the sun and after Burt's insane chuckling and wheezing he snaps back into being my servant.

"Oh my Dowager, how ghastly. Did the mechanical floor get the better of you? Dear, well I'll have to do something about that pesky machine Madame."

He keeps talking all this gibberish as he pats my forehead with a damp cloth and then feeds me bottled water like I'm his newborn baby. Pulling me back he lays me down in his arms. I'm protesting all the way with my legs kicking in the air. He doesn't loosen his grip and grabs my wrists in his one giant hand.

"Now, now Dowager, not to worry. I won't let that despicable robot near you again!" his accent never falters. My protests fade as does my energy and I lose the fight. I'm completely laid in Burt's arms with a flannel on my head being force fed water. The ridiculousness of the situation makes me spray the remaining water in my mouth all over the both of us. I'm half witch cackling, half drowning and as I expected, Burt pulls me into the sitting position and starts rubbing and patting my back just like burping a baby.

Naturally a few people in the gym look over to us to see what all the commotion is about, but thankfully the majority of everyone here comes equipped with their favourite music and headphones so they can remain in a world of their own.

Eventually I stop spluttering and coughing.

"Well Madame I'm afraid we may have to go a little lighter on your workouts" I think real Burt's voice is gone for good but I don't mind, today has been a lot of fun for me. This whole session has been like therapy, for so long I've been depressed and down, barely smiling and often lonely. Even round the girls, none of us have been laughing much recently, I was hoping we'll have a few laughs on Saturday but today has been just what I needed.

Admittedly the flirtatious side of things hasn't really come into it but I figure he's stopped for good after I told him I was engaged. I noticed several times when he had his hands on me during stretches that sometimes he actually grazed my ass and seemed to linger. Obviously I wanted to read into this but as I looked around at the other trainers with their clients I saw they were all doing the same thing.

Never the less today has still been great fun and it really was just the right amount of male attention I needed. Nothing sexual was going to happen, I'd never cheat on Bill. It's just that every woman needs male attention, so this has been just what the doctor ordered.

I keep thinking about how much my cheeks hurt, more than that my legs and arms and every inch of me is throbbing in agony. Clearly he has worked my body to the core, so in his way he is a good instructor (maybe a tad unprofessional but in a fun way of course) but I can't see everyone playing along with him as I have.

Wondering why he's losing business proves to be too much for me, so I let my curiosity get the better of me.

"Why is it you don't have a lot of clients? Is it because you behave like this all the time?" I ask, only half joking.

"What? No my lady. This is just special treatment for you." Burt's real voice is coming back slowly but he hasn't yet managed to drop the full character.

My eyes penetrate his, probing for a further explanation.

"To be honest this all started to happen around the time 'The Burn' hired Jason. He's the newest addition to the gym and he's rapidly becoming the star personal trainer. All because of his good looks, he's a former model-" It's just Burt now, all jokes and accents are gone completely. He looks serious and a little defeated over this Jason guy, but continues with his story as I listen quietly.

"He's six foot six with enormous shoulders, pecks, calves the works. So the minute he walked in here all the women started to swoon. A few of my regulars cancelled their contracts with me so they could sign up with him. I should mention that some of these were men. I think Jason was a swim wear model or something I'm not sure but all I know is he seems to attract everyone. I'm not the only one it's happened to; many of the other trainers in here have experienced the same thing as me. He's bad for our jobs but he's great for the company. How did you know I don't have many clients left?"

"Just a hunch, considering you were free last minute. Normally you have to book an appointment with trainers in advance." Burt looks mildly embarrassed by this so I quickly add "Obviously it's not your fault. It's this Jason's fault. Don't let it get you down after all how many people can he cater to? He's bound to run out of time to train with everybody, then these other people will have to come to you." I think I may be the worst person in the world to try and make someone feel better about themselves. I really need to work on that.

"Guess you're right. Although I have overheard that the company maybe giving us all part time contracts, but give Jason over time. It's clear that they wish they had another twenty just like him. Jason's crafty though, I've seen him walk up to women while they're working out and he'll flirt mercilessly with them. Even with the married ones, obviously it's all an act. He just wants to steal clients from under our noses and it works every time. Like I said, the men go to him too, I guess it's because they wanna look just like him. I once saw him approach a guy, and they were talking. I just happened to be passing by when I heard him tell a man that if he works with him he can guarantee he will have a six pack just like his, by next summer!"

"So what's wrong with that?" I ask, not completely sure what's so shocking about it.

"The man was heavily obese, he could barely walk! Next summer? Is he for real? That's only a year from now, there's no way he can get that man in shape by then." I see. I get it now.

"Jason's list of clientele is growing longer and longer every day. There's actually a waiting list to train with him now. All the guys want to be him and all the girls want to be with him. It's incredible how fast he's taken over the place. I've only been here for two years but still I've never seen anything like this before. I'm actually thinking of starting to look for work in another gym. That's why I was so shocked to hear someone was at reception for me. I nearly fell off my seat. Why did you ask for me by the way? After all from our first meeting you hardly seemed taken with me."

Errmm...shit, I wasn't expecting this.

What can I say? I wanted some attention? No. I was hoping you'd flirt with me because I'm not feeling too sexy at the moment? Definitely not.

"Well actually I knew all about Jason so I felt sorry for you. Clearly you need all the business you can get, so I thought I'd come down and give you mine. Plus you're the only trainer whose name I knew so it was just convenient really." God I'm a quick thinker, I surprise myself all the time. Anyway I think he bought it, it seems reasonable enough.

"I see, I thought it was because you had a crush on me." I look up in shock and see a sarcastic expression written all over his face.

"Only joking Jill. You made it quite clear that you're getting married, so I promise to be on my best behavior." I don't know what to say. I can tell he means it but a part of me wants to take it all back. I regret telling him now. There's no chance he's willing to push the boundaries, especially knowing that without me as a paying customer he may be more likely to lose his job. Great going Jill, you've really stuck your foot in it this time.

He stares at me as I mull this over and from the corner of my eye I see him do the "scouts honor" sign. He really is on his best behavior; just as well really after all I am almost a married lady.

"Great then" I try and fake enthusiasm. "Well that's all settled then. Erm, when can we arrange to do this again?"

"Pretty much anytime, here I'll give you my number then you can call me the day before you plan on coming down. It'll save you a wasted trip that way." I log his number into my cell and he walks with me to the entrance carrying my bag for me.

"Here you are me' lady, I do so hope you've had a pleasant stay." He's back in a funny mood and I want to pick up where we left off but Becky the receptionist is looking on at us in bewilderment. I don't feel brave enough to test the waters of her sense of humor so I settle on thanking him, I'm sure he understands why.

"I've had fun today, thankyou Burt. I'll see you soon."

And I really mean it.

Chapter Fifteen

Hell's Kitchen

A nne sent me yet another text confirming the time and address of the cooking course, held in Hell's Kitchen. It starts in about an hour's time, but I'm planning to be early seeing as I've got nothing else to do today. As I apply the finishing touches of make-up, I throw my sling backs on and immediately feel like a girl again (a pretty girl. I don't know how heels make you feel that way but I am a strong believer that heels make the woman)

Whirling out of the elevator I hail the nearest cab with urgency. I think the driver stopped so suddenly because the way I screamed "STOP!" kinda made it sound like an emergency.

We screech to a halt at the side of the curb and I throw him a wad of cash for getting me here in record breaking time. One glance at my white gold watch tells me I'm here too early. I've not really thought this through. I assumed getting out of the house would prove to be more entertaining but as I look this run down community centre over, I wonder why I was in such a rush.

The whole area has a smell in the air of ash and soot, possibly there has been a fire nearby or this is just the natural aroma of Hell's Kitchen. Dark grey clouds are forming in the sky and I pray it doesn't rain. Not wanting to take any chances I head toward the paint faded building to get a good seat, as a gay couple walk by me hand in hand. They seem like they're in no rush and have all the time in the world, they also look blissfully in love and I immediately envy everything they have in their relationship. Never mind Bill and I will have that soon enough, just wait until I become a top chef. Hell's kitchen is notorious for its gay scene, and no doubt many of them will be attending this class today, I can hardly wait.

Making my way into the room, who do you suppose beat me to be the first person in the class? Anne.

Yes Anne is here in all her splendor, sitting there at the ready with full focus on the front of the room. So in the zone is Anne she doesn't even hear me walking up to her.

"Well aren't you the teachers pet." She jumps a mile with my lips practically touching her ears. I think she also suffers a short, mini heart attack.

"Jill, my god, you scared the life out of me." Anne pants after each syllable.

"Hey come here-" she stands up displaying her arms offering me a big hug. "What time is it? Is the chef late?" I love how my turning up should mean everyone's late. When have I ever been late around Anne? Never.

"Yey, I'm so glad we all got here early. Thought I'd be the only one here." Sally's head pops round the door. "I knew it! I just knew you two wouldn't bring any cooking accessories. Thankfully I've brought more than enough for all of us." Sally's arms are ladened with bags. She pulls out aprons, hairnets and ......Chef Hats?!

Is she serious? There's no way I'm wearing that!

Sally hands us one of each item. I can see Anne is just as

gob smacked as I but Sally's too happy to notice. I stare open mouthed at this tall white and shake my head from side to side as Sally tries to put it on me.

Anne chuckles as I fling the silly thing off my head, because it's totally ruining my hair.

"Don't be stupid Sal. Nobody will be wearing those in here, not even the chef. This isn't a bloody cartoon ya know, it's just gonna be some middle aged woman teaching us how to make a decent cake. Right Anne?" Anne nods at Sally and pats her on the back.

Cake! That reminds me, I must work out tomorrow. I'll text Burt and see if he can fit me in first thing in the morning. I'll need to burn off whatever we make today. I have a feeling I will be eating a lot.

Burt replies back within an instant, and tells me we start at 8 o'clock in the morning and that he looks forward to seeing me then. Great at least I'll be able to enjoy myself tonight and not feel too guilty about it.

"Nice thought though honey, but if we wear them I think we may get laughed out of here." Anne backs me up on the silly hats idea.

"You two do what you want. I'm wearing mine. I've had this stuff ages, I'm just glad to finally get some use out of it." Sally's hell bent on looking the fool but neither of us has the strength to tell her no. Why ruin her fun?

I'm just not looking forward to sitting next to her throughout the session; we all know everyone ties you in association to the person your with.

After I make my peace with our loveable idiot I finally look around and take in the setting of this place. There are eight mini kitchens that are compacted into small work stations. Each of these special table things have an oven, a chopping board and all kinds of tools on them laid out before us.

While we are chatting and catching up on what we've been up to (which sums up to not much) the rest of the class come through the door two by two, sometimes even three of four come in at a time. A few short minutes go by before we notice the whole room is filled to the rafters. Everyone has taken to a station in their groups, I over hear different pieces of conversation here and there. From what I can gather everyone in the room is crazy passionate about cooking. I even heard one man compare a chocolate gateaux recipe with a woman on the next bench, already making new friends for they know they all share the same interest. I feel like a virgin, stumbling upon a new experience and feeling totally out of place. If this is a class for beginners why does it sound like everyone knows what they're talking about?

The three of us share a look that says 'maybe we should leave' but considering how much we have all been looking forward to this we decide to stay. I mean how bad can it be?

A quick head count tells me there are twenty five people here, with only one table left available in the front facing us. I check my watch for the time, only to find we are a mere minute or two away until we are supposed to start. The chef can't be as excited as us; it doesn't seem she cares at all if she chooses to walk in last minute.

Taking in the scenery for a final time for lack of something better to do, it strikes me as odd at how many people have brought in a cook book. Why would they do that? Were we supposed to do that? Did we have to research a recipe or something? Did we already have homework? Why didn't Anne tell us?

As I spin round to ask Anne what the hell is going on quiet descends across the room within a heartbeat. One minute everyone can't get their words out fast enough, the next minute you can hear a pin drop. I peer in the direction where the drama seems to be coming from and see a petite plain looking woman enter and take to her stage.

"Good evening everyone. I'm Ingrid Butler." That's all she says to get one of the biggest reactions I've ever seen. The whole room breaks out into applause and cheering, I even heard a wolf whistle. The girls and I give a halfhearted attempt of a clap but we aren't really giving it our all. Who the hell is this woman? Clearly she's a huge deal to these people. She's at her alter and we are supposed to worship her. All I can think is if she is such a celebrity in the cooking world maybe I could have a word with her later and see if I can get her to make a great big banquet for my wedding.

The applause finally dies and the room grows tense and serious.

"Now firstly let me say hello and welcome to my culinary expertise class for the advanced-" at this I freak out. Feeling Sally and Anne's glares burning holes into my face, I swallow nervously and slowly feel the panic rise.

"I'll tell you a little bit about myself. I'm sixty-three years old and have been cooking since my mother began to teach me at the age of ten. I have worked in several famous restaurants and the most notable of which is the 'Four Seasons' in Budapest. In which I served a long career of just over thirty-three years. My favourite dish to make is my legendary holiday feast of the classic Turducken, and my favourite desert to make is baked Alaska. I'm also an author of six bestselling cook books. And now I am retired and live in the Hamptons with my husband and our two dogs, Jasper and Fondue. Now for the ice breaker.

I want everyone to introduce themselves. So I want your name, your favourite dish to prepare and what restaurant you have or are currently working in. I think we will start with this station first." Ingrid points at the first bench on our side of the room, we are literally the third lot of people she will interrogate with her questions and I know none of us are prepared for this.

I notice Sally and Anne twitching in their seats beside me and I'm ready to take off in a sprint, but we can't. We are trapped, with only moments to go before we are asked to introduce ourselves. Trying to clear my throat I sense a scream working its way up, or is it vomit? Either way I swallow and try to put on my game face.

There truly is no getting out of this, quick Jill use your talent of lying on the spot. I'm brilliant at that but my brains blocked, my minds drawing up a complete blank. Come on! Think, think!

"Hello Mrs. Butler my names Carl and can I just say I'm a huge fan. I have all your books and I've actually brought your latest one- I was hoping maybe you could sign it, if it's not too much trouble."

"Actually I've brought my copy too"

"And me-"

The next thing we know more than half the class are heckling Ingrid and holding up their copies of one of her best sellers, in hopes of getting the famous chef's autograph except us.

This is not looking good.

"Ladies and gentleman will all quieten down and take to your seats. I will sign any book of mine at the end of today's session but not before. We have an awful lot of work to do. Carl if we can get back to you, tell me what your favourite meal is to cook please." Ingrid takes full control over the room and you can tell from the instant silence that she has everyone's respect.

"Of course, my favourite meal to prepare is a hog roast for special occasions with all the trimmings and my top dessert is a dark chocolate mirror glaze cake. I'm currently working in Fabro's restaurant and I'm hoping to have my own restaurant one day." at this everyone applauds, even Ingrid.

She doesn't look like a woman you can please easily, there's nothing loving or warm about her, but she does look impressed by what Carl just said. I pray I can come up with a clever answer for all of us. If I can introduce them myself then I will. Actually that doesn't sound like a bad idea; I could say we all work in the same restaurant.

Ok so what's the name of the place? I look around for inspiration, a spark to light the fire of my imagination. I see a whisk then a fork then I turn to my right and I'm staring at the side of Sally's silly head. She's still wearing the chef's hat! Ingrid will think Sally's the real deal; she'll wonder why she's never heard of her before! Right calm down, let's not panic, just use this to your advantage. I can get us through this with our reputations undamaged.

How about Sally is the head chef and we are her assistants? I think that could work, as long as Sally never speaks. If she does the game is over, the cats out of the bag and all the other sayings that basically mean the same thing. So that's the story and I'm sticking to it but I need to think of what the name is for the restaurant. It's so hard to concentrate when there's a giant white hat looming in the corner of my eye.

Hat … white hat … cat in the hat … chef hat … man hat ten … top hat? None of these sound right; anyway looking at Sally, Top hat is pushing it a bit. More like Mad Hatter!

That's it *'The Mad Hatter'* restaurant in Manhattan. We will definitely get away with that. There are too many places to dine in New York; no one could possibly know it doesn't exist. Plus

I can say it is a very small establishment and brand new, that'll cover up the tracks.

Man I'm a genius.

Finally the moment of truth (lies) is on us and it's time for my lies to shine.

"So let's come over to this bench. Ladies it's your turn to introduce yourselves." Ingrid looks over to Sally expecting her to be the first to speak but I take over.

"Hello Ingrid I'm Jill and this is Sally and this here is Anne. We all work at *'The Mad Hatter'* which is a very new and small bistro." I nod emphatically hoping this is enough information for her to move on to the next group.

"Well thank you for that Jill, but I'm sure Sally and Anne are more than capable of speaking for themselves." Mrs. Butler's full attention flies back to Sal and I know it's all because of that dumb hat; I just want to rip it off her head.

"So Sally, tell us, is *'The Mad Hatter'* your restaurant?" Sally looks at me for the answers but that's just making us look more suspicious.

After what feels like an eternity goes by Sal realizes she's gonna have to think on the spot like I did.

"Erm… yes … *'The Mad Hatter'* is mine. I'm head chef, I'm sure you can see … you know … because of the hat-" god bless her she's stuttering like a fool and Anne's looking at her feet, probably dreading her turn.

"Very good-" Ingrid says, not sure whether to believe her or not. "So tell me Jill what's your favourite dish to cook or bake. You never told us." Her intense beady eyes are locked onto my retinas but without missing a beat, I simply say 'Crème Brule' it sounds fancy and I've had it several times at home when the cook prepares it for Bill and I. Actually I often used to watch cooking programs during the day so I have enough knowledge to know it's just burnt cream. And for my main I tell her I love to cook pizzas. I know it's lame but it's all I could think of.

The famous chef nods her approval and asks the same question to Sal.

"And yours?" In typical Sally fashion she takes forever to answer but finally blurts out an answer.

"Cornflakes"

Half of the room chuckle under their breath, the others are unsure of her sense of humor.

Is she serious right now? The only lie she could come up with right now is a bowl of cereal. I could kill her sometimes I really could.

Ingrid looks as though she's getting annoyed and rightly so. I can see impatience written all over her face she clearly wants to move on to the next bench, but out of politeness has to ask Anne her favourite meal to make.

"So Anne, what about you? And please spare the jokes unlike your friend here." she gives Sal a shady look.

"Um … mine … the dish I like making the most is … beef wellington." Wow Anne nice save, I'm really quite impressed by Anne's quick thinking. Far better than Sally's.

"My, my … isn't that a surprise. This should make for a very easy day for you, because beef wellington is the savory assignment I had prepared for us today." Ingrid winks at Anne and inwardly I can tell she wants to cower behind our cooking bench. And honestly I don't blame her.

Mrs. Butler carries on getting to know people around the room while the three of us are doing our utmost to communicate through facial expressions. Anne's face says panic and embarrassment (in fact I see her slyly trying to google a beef wellington recipe under the table just so she can brush up on some info in case she gets quizzed or is asked to help with a demonstration. Could you imagine if that happened? I'd have to fake a heart attack or something to get her out of it)

Sally's face is saying she finally feels silly in the hat. Thankfully she takes it off and immediately I feel more at ease than before. There was just something about that hat that felt like a lit beacon in the dark bringing us unwanted attention. Kinda like a neon sign above our heads, thank god it's gone.

My face is saying "let's run for the hills!"

"Listen up everyone, and pay attention. I have made a beef wellington previous to my coming here, and I've brought it with me. I will hand out a copy of my recipe to each of you. All the ingredients you need are in the pantry in the back of the room. I want everyone to taste my beef wellington and pay attention to the detail, the craftsmanship, the colour, the texture and the taste before you try and make your own. I will come round to inspect your work and I will be keeping an eye on all of you. Also I will mention that you are being timed, after all this is only a three hour session today but that is more than enough time for this dish. So use this time wisely and don't waste a minute of it."

What! Three hours?! Anne never mentioned that. I'm shocked at how little information Anne has divulged to us about this cooking class. Surely she must have known how long we were gonna be here, after all she was the one that made the call and paid for the three of us to get in last minute. She told me this cost $500 and I wired her the money without question, I figured it was because the cook used to be a big deal but I didn't think for a second it was due to this being a severe boot camp for advanced chefs.

Don't get me wrong I'm not complaining, it's not like I have anywhere else to be. Anyway on the bright side at least with several hours of cooking I will surely get my money's worth.

We are told to begin and that our time starts now. Ingrid's wasted thirty minutes of this time just by going round the room talking to everyone. We read through the instructions and instantly we are all stumped. Just completely lost for words.

How do you sear? It says sear the beef fillets. And what's a duxelle? A tool? A vegetable? Are these instructions in English?

Before we all start flapping round like headless chickens I suggest we fetch all the ingredients first and go from there. The instructions are for beef wellington and red wine sauce. From what I've read, the sauce alone takes an hour to make according to this sheet.

We are left scratching our heads and trying to figure out where to start. I can't help but look around and observe what everyone else is doing.

Everyone here (except us) is off to a flying to start, with little or no fuss they each take their individual jobs and get going. Ingrid catches my eye and I can see something shifty flash across her face,

"Girls, what's happening? Why are you wasting time?" we each grunt a small "we're fine" or "we are just starting now" and "it's all under control" I think we are all in agreement that we don't really want her over here. Once she witnesses our lack of skills she'll know us for the frauds that we are.

As I maneuver about (making it look as though I know what I'm doing) I pass a bench with one of Ingrid's cook books laid on top. The title on the front reads "Dinner is served" and underneath in bold is her name in thick silver on a black background.

"INGRID BUTLER"

Butler ... it reminds me of Burt.

Burt as a butler.

I'm not sure why but the mental image of him in my head puts a small secret grin on my lips. I have a feeling that Burt wouldn't like Ingrid much. In fact I don't like Ingrid much. He would probably be a little frightened of her.

"What are you smiling about Jill? I need you to focus." In a whispered tone Anne comes closer to my ear.

"Now I know the instructions aren't helping us much so I've found bits of info on YouTube. I think I can handle it and I'll have Sally as my assistant." clearly we wouldn't give her a job of her own, it would be disastrous. "So I'll need you to be the head sauce maker." Anne is taking this so seriously, as if this is a competition between us and the other groups (yeah right, like we have a chance of winning. Never in a million years!)

Admittedly I shouldn't be scared, honestly how hard could it be to make red wine sauce? The name if it alone sounds pretty self-explanatory, it's probably just red wine and sauce that fuse together for an hour in a pan.

Cool, great, got it.

I've lost my god damn mind! What's a shallot when it's at home? I've already underrated this task and I haven't even begun. This mission is definitely for the advanced and I'm barely a novice.

I go in search for the four large shallots required in the pantry. Turns out, the pantry is more of a mini room full of food rather than a large cupboard. The shelves are sky high, they touch the ceiling. There must be thousands of different types of ingredients in here. Where to begin? It's just like trying to find a needle in a haystack especially if you don't know what the needle looks like. That's what I'm going through right now. There's also an incredible amount of wine too, it's like part cellar, part pantry in here. I'm sure no one would know if we use more than one bottle.

I need red wine vinegar but I can't see any. Surely just regular vinegar and a bottle of Shiraz would equal to the same thing. I hear a yelp come from the prep room and everything in me tells me its Sally and that she's burnt herself, I want to run to her rescue but I know she has Anne for help and my main priority right now is to find the shallots.

The only problem is I don't know what a shallot is or what they look like. I'm searching and searching but whatever they are they are definitely not labelled in the pantry. Typical.

I'm looking at everything from fruit to white wine. Seriously what does a shallot look like? I tried to gain insight by taking note of everyone's work station's but there's too much going on, on their tables to figure out which is the mysterious shallot.

I have heard of *'The lady of shallot'* poem by Tennyson. Could it possibly have something to do with that? Let me recap on parts of the poem I can remember. So there's the boat she goes in, there's the knight and the river. None of this makes sense.

Was shallot the town she lived in? And how do I get four big ones? All this tells me is that shallots come in different sizes.

My gut instinct is telling me shallots are actually pieces of bark. I think this is purely because the bark is staring me in the face, but come to think of it as I said earlier one of the main elements to the poem is the boat she uses to take her away from the tower to get her to the knight.

Here's my train of thought; boats are made from wood, and bark is wood! I think I've worked this little riddle out. Maybe this was Ingrid's test and I've just passed.

I pick up the packet of bark and decide these are shallots. It's not as though we are going to be crunching on them, I'm going to use it to merely add a woody flavour to my red sauce. Look at me talking like a pro. All I have to do now is find out how to do that. I grab all the other ingredients that are on the list and get to work.

Arriving back to our bench all I see is Sally holding her arm with a look of pain on her face.

"Help me if you can the kitchen's burning down" Sally sings in the rhythm of the Beatles hit song "Help!"

"And I do apologize for this awful sound; help me get my melted skin back off the ground"

"Shut up Sally!" Anne demands through clenched teeth.

"Won't you pleease, pleeeease help me." obviously Sally's burnt herself and has to make a song and dance about it.

"Anne, mind that flesh coloured puddle in the middle of the kitchen" Sally's such a drama queen.

"What?" says Anne, clearly not in the mood for sarcasm.

"My wrist has been signed off. I tell you that frying pan is lethal." Sally exaggerates by rubbing her miniature wound.

With all the chaos Sally's creating, Ingrid takes action and fetches the first aid kit. A bit of cream and a band aid after, Sally's finally quietens down again. I can see Ingrid losing her patience with our table; she keeps a close eye on us at all times and watches us with a look of curiosity.

I tackle the sauce situation full steam ahead and pay full attention to the instructions at hand. Anne's blustering around me like a speedy tornado, that mixed with Ingrid keeping a watchful eye on us suddenly feels like too much pressure. I need to get this done and fast.

Wine will take the edge off. I have faith in wine, I'm sure we can have a sneaky glass or two while we work.

Olive oil, beef trimmings, red wine (three bottles instead of one), vinegar and beef stock. These are all the ingredients I am dead sure about. Now when it comes to the following ingredients, I've just taken a wild guess at. Shallots, peppercorns, bay leaf and thyme sprig. I'm frying, stirring, simmering, bubbling and boiling. Feeling like the pro that I am I feel an air of confidence surround me. It's actually really quite simple once you have all the ingredients in the pan. Now I just leave it for an hour and I should have an incredible sauce at the end.

The extra bottle of Shiraz is eyeing me up, several huffs and the occasional swear word float over from Anne and Sal and I know they too are in need of a stiff drink.

I sneakily pour us a few glasses when I see Ingrid isn't looking, I feel like a naughty kid in school which is strange because I never was a naughty child, I was a straight A student. The girls down it without a second thought as do I, so I just keep filling them up. After all I do have an hour to kill.

―――――~∞∽∽∞∽∞∽∞∞~―――――

Now I'm not sure if it's the alcohol making me see things in a different way but to me it seems that everyone here has created the most scrumptious looking beef wellington and we have just made a pig's ear out of it.

Not only have we botched up the meal but we also have botched up our bodies. We all pitched in with the wellington while my completely fabulous sauce was cooking. The wellington came out looking like charcoal and we are all covered in small burns on our hands and arms. Ingrid made the first two trips to the first aid box, when the next several times arose she would just point at it and tell us to get it ourselves.

Anne is devastated over the end result of all our hard work. Bless her I can't believe she thought we could pull this level of cooking off! With both of us fussing over Anne's hysterical tears and Sally's vain attempt of scraping off the thick black crust that has engulfed our 'wannabe master piece' I notice a different kind of smell. Definitely something burning but its more than the cremated beef before us, it's something else.

Immediately I perk up in delight, at last someone else has cocked up. We are not the only people in here that suck. Thank god. This ought to take the attention away from us now.

Whilst feeling smug the fire alarm goes off. The whole place turns into total pandemonium.

"FIRE, FIRE!" people are gasping, others are getting water to throw over … oh god, it's MY SAUCE! My beautiful sauce has set a light and has spread to the open bag of bark and then onto Sally's stupid chef hat which just so happened to be laid out near the pan. I knew it, I just knew that hat was gonna get us into trouble but not like this. It's not just Sally though it was me, I've made the ultimate fuck up. I put WAAAY to much wine in the pan. I have no idea whether it was the amount of alcohol I put in or the fact that I accidentally neglected it to focus on the wellington, or was it because I put actual bits of tree in it. Either way I've never seen a blacker smoke in all my life.

Honestly you can't see your hand in front of your face. In mere moments the entire room has disappeared into plumes of smoke. I feel someone reach for my hand, my vision is so impaired I have no clue whether it's Anne or Sally. Hell it could be Ingrid come to kick my ass! I hear many people choking and coughing.

Sally screams "Jill, Anne! Where are you? I can't see anything! Where are you? Reach for my hand I'm scared."

Anne shouts in the direction of her voice "Sally, follow my voice, grab my hand." It's clearly Anne's hand I'm holding for her shouting is still ringing in my ears.

I interject "Sally we are over here!"

The clap of hands and the texture of soft, chubby fingers fills me with relief.

"Everyone, evacuate the building NOW!" comes the voice of a livid Ingrid. The sound of feet stampeding in a hurried fashion gives us a clue where the door is.

"AND YOU THREE!" we can't see her but we know we are being addressed by the teacher. "Never show your faces in my class AGAIN!" YOU'R BANNED FOR LIFE!"

Gasping for breath we suck in as much clean air as possible, as we stumble upon the streets of Hell's Kitchen. Never have I fought so hard to breathe in all my life. I feel as though I've smoked a pack of forty in five minutes flat and I know the girls feel same.

Sally is the first to speak, shaking with anxiety "Please can we just go home. I just want to lie on a couch and chill out."

I jump into action I hail a cab by putting my entire body into the middle of the road. That's one way to stop a cab, that way they know you mean business (although I don't encourage you to do it, you see it could work or it could kill you. Don't take the risk, I just feel reckless at the moment) luckily for me it worked.

Both Sal and I drag Anne to the car, she's speechless and completely beside herself as are we.

We leave behind us a smoky building with everyone on the curb cursing at us and flicking us the 'V' sign. Charming. As our eyes glisten with tears, swaying from the incredible amount of wine consumed I look down to our arms and see an array of band aids, cream and remnants of food splattered all over the three of us.

A thought crosses my mind that maybe

Just maybe

We won't be master chefs after all.

Chapter Sixteen

Jerry Springer

S etting in to our (now frequent) hide away aka my apartment, I make us a pot of coffee in hopes of sobering us up after a hellish evening. We are all so drained I let the silence surround us. I potter from mug to mug, pouring my Italian roast.

The girls have taken to the couch and have chosen opposite ends, leaving me the middle. Instead of letting them stare into space, I turn on the TV, only to find my favourite show playing: Jerry Springer. And it looks like a good one too.

After I order us a large pepperoni pizza to share I take to my middle bit of couch. Sinking into the thick velvet cushion with my steaming posh coffee in hand, I finally start to mellow.

This episode of Jerry Springer is on men that aren't stepping up to fatherhood, only the real title is "Oops ..... I slept with a tranny!" A "Wigs to the wall" special. I'm completely enthralled, it's all about a woman who slept with a transvestite man and he has never been to see his child. Firstly they seem to be mostly talking about why he's a transvestite and how he declares "all lips look more kissable with lipstick" but then the conversation turns and matters start to escalate, I love it when it escalates. Chairs flying, hair pulling, and many a beep over curse words.

Sometimes I love it when there is a series of beeps in a single sentence, that's when you know the person is MAD!

As the couple fight over their offspring, A thought comes to me.

"Do you think when we have their kids it'll prevent divorce? I know you'll still have arguments but I bet they wouldn't leave us. After all you'd be a family." They both really reflect on this for a moment before answering.

"I suppose so" Sal's the first to offer her opinion. "I mean either way if you have a boy, your husband will then have an air, someone to carry on his name." she adds cleverly.

"Also should they divorce us after having their boy I've read that you can get a bigger settlement. But only if it's a boy not a girl." I'm surprised Anne has heard of this. Of course I knew this, my father told me all about it years ago, that a lot of men put that on their prenup's and I was shocked even then, I still am.

"Why are boys so special anyway?" Sal enquires "Why are boys better than girls?" this has left us all dumbfounded. The only thing I can think of as some form of explanation is the name sake thing.

This leads to a full discussion whether we should have children or not. I know I do, eventually, one day but not right now. Anne says she'd love to once she's married but honestly I can't imagine her handling the amount of mess kids make. Then Sally announces a shocking fantasy of her wanting three boys and two girls.

What on earth? Could you picture Sally with five children? It would be hell on earth. It would literally feel like a child raising five children.

A complete nightmare.

As we are in mid conversation our attention becomes divided between each other and the TV. The words that are coming out of the woman's mouth are slowly turning us off the idea. She's screaming and crying over the lack of interest the dad has had in the past fourteen years of their son's life. Her words are ringing in all of our ears. Evidently from the state of this 'family', having a child doesn't cement people together after all. Obviously men can turn their backs on their families, leave you to look after the children while he's off with a pretty young thing that's fun and has no responsibilities.

The conversation of possible motherhood leaves as abruptly as it came.

"There's no point going down that route unless he wants to be a father, because apparently that shit's optional." Says Sally with more anger than I've ever seen her possess.

"Yeah why do men get the option to be fathers?" Anne joins in with the man bashing.

"Well women seem to get the same option, if they actually want to be mothers" I know I'm uprooting my sore spot about my own mother, but I can't help it.

Sally doesn't see the link to my last statement to my life and continues on her feminist rant.

"Not really, all it takes is for one little rip in the condom and BOOM! You're a mother. Was it the woman's fault? No. was it the man's fault? No. But the woman doesn't have a choice; she is going to give birth either way. Either to have an abortion, give birth then give it up for adoption, or to keep it and become a mother. That is beyond traumatic that we have to decide and give birth no matter what, whether it passes through as a heavy period or by coming out as an actual baby. Why do men get a choice to be involved? Or even just to be supportive or to be a shoulder to cry on?" Sally is seriously passionate about this.

I agree, she's totally convinced me. "Yeah your right! Now you mention it, both people did the shagging so both people should handle the consequences."

"Exactly and it's not like it's happening to the man's bodies, either way they have it easier than we do!" Anne adds with outrage.

"Amen! Amen!" we are all completely irate at no one in particular, just mankind as a whole.

I think we've just become celibate... forever.

Chapter Seventeen

If I Only Had A Brain

The following afternoon, I finally wake with a mild pounding in my head. I can't believe how long I've slept; the clock tells me its 1.20pm and I'm the first up. I'm in my bedroom which feels completely foreign to me as I physically can't remember the last time I spent a night here. It must have been years ago. Attempting to roll out of the bed I happen to bump into a body. Freaking out I jump up, my brain has yet to calculate what I'm doing here. My mouth is as dry as Gandhi's flip flop; I must have drunk my own body weight in wine last night.

"You're getting up already? What time is it?" says the lump.

Jeez it's Sally. She must have crawled into my bed last night without my knowing it. Not that I mind, I now recall bits of Jerry Springer and an awful amount of red wine at the cooking course. Oh man the cooking course! I'm not ready to relive that memory just yet, I need to get my baring's and several strong coffees. The coffee I made last night didn't help sober me up at all.

Making my way into the living room, I pass Anne on the couch and she's still in a deep sleep. Not wanting to disturb the lazy ass women I have in my apartment I head to the kitchen to fill myself with caffeine.

Waking up slowly is the best thing in the world if you ask me. I hate when someone wakes you and pesters you for something or worse yet: The Alarm Clock. Don't you despise having to set your alarm for whatever reason, maybe you have an early appointment and a huge noise comes from the alarm not only waking you up instantly but starting your day off with pure panic, then you're put in a bad mood for the rest of the day.

I love waking naturally and not being in a rush, left to your own devices to just potter around, taking your time and soaking up the luxury of curling up on the couch. Sipping on your third cappuccino or latte, I think all mornings should start like that. That's why I feel bad for the likes of Bill and my father; actually I have it easy compared to every working person on the planet. As I start to wallow between feeling self-pity and spoilt, a series of noises come through my phone alerting me that I have received a text. I become hopeful, assuming it might be a message of concern about my whereabouts from Bill. I did text him last night when we came back from the class that I was staying with the girls in my old apartment but I never heard anything back from him.

Opening the message my hopes dash to the winds when I see it isn't from Bill. It's from Burt. Burt! Oh god, oh shit, I've missed my session with him. Suddenly I become frantic in my disappointing Burt and for being so forgetful. Reading the text over and over till the words have lost all meaning I both smile and feel worse than ever. It says "Did we forget about our appointment today Madam?" I want to reply with a barrage of apologies and a bit of insight into what happened last night but instead I stick to the game and all I put is "Clumsy me Mr.

Burt would you mind terribly if we reschedule for tomorrow morning? That is if you're free?" Send.

Now reading it back to myself I know I was trying to maintain the role of the grand lady dowager, but now I'm starting to think maybe the last line may have come across as slightly bitchy. I hope that's not what he thinks. Even if I had set an alarm for the gym I'm in no shape to undergo an intense work out today, I'm far too hung over.

He replied with a simple "Yeah, no problem" and I become calm again.

At last the girls get up under their own steam (Naturally, I refuse to be anyone's alarm) and they in turn congregate around my small kitchen table each of us with our favourite morning beverage in hand. Anne has a cup of herbal tea, I'm on my second dark sugary coffee and Sally predictably goes for the only drink with chocolate in. A thick white hot chocolate, that has been in my cupboard for years, which amazingly still smells creamy and delicious.

Discussing the state of fatigue we are all still in, how we slept then the conversation leads to out hellish experience in a different kitchen only so many hours before.

"I can't believe we nearly burnt the place down!" exclaims Sally "I'm never gonna cook again."

"It's not our fault; it was a class for the advanced. I should have paid closer attention to the description" Anne says trying to take her share of the blame. "I think I was just too excited seeing it was being held by a famous chef. I was too eager to just buy our places because I knew how quickly things like that sell out. Even though it didn't exactly go our way last night and I have no wish to do it again, I still think it's a fantastic thing to say we met and cooked with THE Ingrid Butler." I had no idea that Anne would be the optimist in this; I thought that was Sally's job.

My head is down in embarrassment as I know the cause of the fire was me. "No, no I'm sorry ladies but we all know I was to blame. I didn't exactly stick to the ingredients as well as I should …"

"What do you mean?" they ask in unison.

"I overdosed the sauce with more than twice the wine that was needed. And I'm still not sure if this had anything to do with it, but for the shallots I put in pieces of broken bark."

"Into the sauce?" Sally asks then leaves her mouth hanging open.

"What!? Why on earth would you do that! Why didn't you just put the shallots in?" well that's a turn for the books, now Anne is full of aggression, where did the optimist go?

"I didn't know what a shallot looked like and practically nothing was labelled in the pantry." All my frustration comes out in one fell swoop. How can they not remember how baffled we were with everything? I wasn't the only one who was flustered.

"If you knew what a shallot looked like why didn't you tell me. I asked you both twice."

Sally looks to Anne and I know they are just as clueless as I am. For future reference I'm googling 'Shallot' and then 'The lady of shallot'

"Well it's true we have no idea what it is either. I'd say you should have asked Ingrid but I'm thankful you didn't." Anne finally tells the truth and I'm no longer embarrassed that I didn't know because now I do.

Turns out, a shallot is a weird shaped onion, or at least it is part of the onion family. What the hell? Why not just say an onion on the instructions. Also onion in a red wine sauce sounds awful. I'm sure if all had gone well with my bark fla-vored sauce it would have tasted even better than Ingrid's recipe. Unfortunately all it proved was that I am the fire starter.

The search on the poem shows me that '**Shallot**' and 'The lady of **shalott**' are spelt differently (well anyone could have made that mistake) if only I had known that at the time I'm sure everything would have turned out for the better. I tell the girls and they are as shocked as I am. Guess we have all learnt something new. At least I know now, and should someone ask me one day what a shallot is, I'll be able to provide them with the answer.

A row of sighs surround the table and I know how we are all feeling. Deflated, tired and sick of all our feeble attempts.

"We are no good at this are we" it's not a question it's the truth, coming from me.

"Why should we try anymore. Why do we care. I don't think they do." Comes an irritated Sally.

"They probably do they're just busy men." I tell her and I mean it. "We just need some kind of fall back plan-" I'm not sure Bill cares much; I know he's busy but he hasn't text me once. He knows I'm safe; it's just the thought that counts. Anne's fiancé Richard seems to care about her a lot. He text her last night asking if she was coming home or not. See, that's the kind of concern and love I'd like to have with Bill. Just moments ago Sally got a text from Allan reporting from the road. Just a simple message telling her he's super busy but that he loves her and hopes she's ok. I'll admit that stung my heart when she read that out loud and I'm not too proud to admit it but it made me extremely jealous.

Instead of silently wishing Bill to get in touch, I decide to reach out first.

"Hey baby. What time should I expect you home tonight?

I'll ask the cook to rustle us up something special. Maybe we can have a romantic meal together. Xoxo" that should get his attention. I bet you think I'm so ignorant calling her the cook. Yes I know her name it's Susan but once when I referred to her by name to Bill, he snapped at me. Bill said it's not proper to get personal with the staff. Should there come a time we need to fire her, it will be harder if you know her personally. So therefore if we are discussing her, we call her 'the cook' and if we are speaking to her then we can call her by her name.

He's text back! That was quick. Needing to announce it to the room to see the look on their faces that Bill does care. Only I know for sure that I care far more than they do, it's written all over their faces. A look that says "we never doubted his love for you" then why did I?

"Doesn't look like I'll be coming home at all tonight. I have to stay at the office; I'm dealing with a huge merger of two giant corporations right now. I've got back to back conferences for the next few weeks to. My hands are full right now Jill, so don't worry if you don't see much of me. Just have her prepare a meal for one. Sorry."

Stumped. I look like a fool for having read that aloud.

"Never mind Jilly" Sal tries to comfort me. "He's busy like you said. All our men are busy."

"Yeah Jill, we should be used to it by now. Anyway what were you saying about a fall back plan?" in my head I'm thanking Anne for the change of topic.

"A fall back plan is obviously money." I say snappy and to the point, not really wanting to talk animatedly just now.

"Your right, financial security is the only reason why we are scared of divorce. It's not that we are afraid to be alone or that we will have no one to take care of us, because we take care of them." Sally the suffragette is back ladies and gentlemen "When they are ill, tired, stressed, hungry, moody and......"

"HORNY!" I interject. Well it's true.

"Yes exactly. We do all that emotional and physical stuff. We are capable of more than we give ourselves credit for."

Anne and I just stare at each other completely dumbfounded. How can soft simple Sally be so right? How hadn't we seen it before, Sally has a brain.

"So wait you knew all this in the beginning and didn't tell us?!" Anne asks in disbelief.

"And when did you become Oprah Winfrey?" I ask completely wowed.

"Well I thought it was common sense, but you both shoot me down the minute I try to talk so what's the point?"

Full of shame we put our heads down in shame.

"Sorry Sal" we each apologize in turn.

"It's ok I forgive you......so how are we going to make us some money?" Sally asks getting straight to the point.

I tell her I have no clue and Anne says she doesn't know either.

In unison we ask the master for her plans.

"Sally? Have you got any ideas?"

Chapter Eighteen

Sisters Are Doing It For Themselves

"Divorce will be hard either way. You'll be heart broken and sad but to add salt to the wound we will also be poor and maybe even homeless for some of us. The plan is to create a safety net just in case." I recap over the basics of everything Sally has said and we are still racking our brains for a definite plan. We are all in an agreement that we probably have nothing to worry about; it's just us taking extra precautions just to be on the safe side.

"I was thinking we need to work, ya know. Like maybe get a job." Sally's bright idea is starting to hatch: a job. I could totally do a job. I know I just made that speech about alarm clocks but come on if the majority of the world can do it, then so can I.

Also I think it would be cool to own your own money, and have somewhere to be every day. As I start day dreaming about my becoming a serious business woman in fashionable, tailor made suits with killer Louboutin's, strutting around the office Anne bursts my bubble.

"Don't we need qualifications and experience? I don't think

I'm qualified to do anything." Anne tries a dry laugh "What about you two, Am I the only one that feels unemployable?" Damn, she's got it in one. This is our only drawback, never having worked a day in our lives. Admittedly it's a huge draw-back but I'm sure if we put our heads together we can think of something.

"I don't think there is any job I could do." Sally complains. "Just wish I hadn't spent so much on teleshopping. If I'd saved all the money I've wasted on Teleshopping I bet I would be rich by now." Sally says only half joking.

This gives me an idea.

"Why don't we sell all your unopened items?" I ask with excitement. I've had a complete brain wave. Maybe it's not the best idea but at least it's something.

"That's a brilliant idea Jill" Anne chirps up "and while we are at it, the less chaotic it becomes I can start cleaning around the empty spaces. Slowly we can sort your apartment out." This is a huge project for the three of us to get our teeth stuck into and also it will put our skills into perspective.

"Whatever is new that you can part with, I'll sell it online for as close to top price as possible because it's never been used before. We should be able to get a very decent price for them. And Anne can be the cleaner, in a short time you will have a clean spacious apartment and hopefully have kicked your shopping habit, and don't forget the money that we'll be bringing in. I know it's all your stuff but I think you'll need our help to get these jobs done." Sally looks so unenthusiastic about this but finally pipes up.

"This sounds like hard work but I suppose it'll give us some-thing to do, and I'm sure Allan will be thrilled coming home to a clean home." She seems to be coming round.

"We will all be thrilled you have a clean home." Anne says sarcastically.

"Come on now, no more jokes. This is a big challenge but the point of the exercise is to see if we can work and get something done, and it'll prove to us what we are capable of doing. You know, if I'm any good at online selling I could have my own online business. Loads of people make a good living that way you know. We can just treat this like work experience."

At this Sally smiles, she's already finding this fun. Either way it's an excuse we need to spend more time together, rather than be left alone in our otherwise empty lives ... I mean empty apartments.

———⁓⚬⚬⚬⚬⚬⚬⚬⚬⚬⚬⚬⚬⚬⚬⚬———

Work, work, work. There is no rest for the wicked. It's amazing though; this place is coming on leaps and bounds. At first I'll admit I didn't have a clue how to go about selling things online but freakishly I have always been an expert when it comes to shopping online. After much research into online selling and virtual shops and such, I stumbled upon eBay. If you are unfamiliar with eBay (which I'm sure you're not unless you live under a rock) it's a huge website that sells literally everything from clothes, jewelry, old records, second hand this and brand new that. To cars and designer handbags and real diamonds; which is my kind of place.

I have heard of eBay before but I suppose the snob in me wouldn't let myself wander onto the site to have a good old browse. I believed it was like an online goodwill store that only sold second or even third hand items that cost a whole dollar. Stuff that should clearly never be resold and should probably have been burnt and thrown into the trash. How wrong I was; the variety on this thing is incredible! There are so many things that I have bought (accidently, I know I'm meant to be helping Sally with her hoarding, I'm not meaning to start my own clutter problems) but only because the price was so ridiculously low. Justified. God I am starting to sound like her now.

Another site I've found very effective is Facebook. All of us are on Facebook but what I didn't know is that you can create a page on there to sell whatever you like. And the price to start a page on there costs $0. It's absolutely FREE! Which is ideal, as it's been helping our ambition of selling as much stuff as we possibly can. Within a short time the difference in this place is incredible. Already we can begin to see bits of carpet and hidden wardrobes that even Sally herself no longer knew she had.

It's tiring work though. Packing, shipping, cleaning and even just the admin part is stressful. Taking pictures of different products and adding a full description about how this utensil works and how many batteries this device needs, so on and so forth, it's a nightmare. All Three of us are wiped at the end of the day, it has literally turned into a full ... no actually it's an overtime job. I can't complain though, I've never slept more soundly. Nowadays I sleep long and hard without disturbances through the night. Normally I'm such a restless sleeper trying with all my might to drift off but half of the time I'm just lying there for hours, willing myself to sleep. Trust me counting sheep doesn't work, It's a myth.

Our exhaustion is overwhelming, after a great day's work and a good job well done we begin to yawn. Stretching, rubbing our eyes, massaging the lower of our backs and sometimes with aching feet and a banging headache.

I've never been happier.

You probably think I'm crazy but I can't believe how satisfying it feels. As I moisturize my hands and feet before bed and all my bones are screaming for me to lay down and rest, all that comes to mind is "You've earned this, you have worked for this pain." I can't help but get the sensation of complete and utter pride and self-worth. I'm not sure if it's normal to have these thoughts but it's almost as if the more it hurts, the happier I am. To really work your ass off has amazing results, and once you start to see all your hard work paying off you've never felt more content in your life. It's just like the gym; I'm in the same mood after a hefty workout. Well I'm in twice as much pain when I come back from 'The Burn' because of how hard I laugh with Burt. I hate to admit it but I've missed more sessions than I've attended, only this time it isn't because I've slept in and I'm lazy, it's completely the opposite. Thankfully he knows it, I told him all about my new business and I've really made it sound high end and glamorous even though it's really not. He seemed really impressed and again I swelled with pride.

He's always so interested in me, asking me tons of questions about how it works and if the business is still going strong. He's actually very supportive and understanding when I do lose track of time and miss our appointment. Burt commented on my figure the other day and I almost blushed. He correctly assumed that I've been working out even when I'm not with him. He then made a daft joke about my secretly going to his rival, Jason for extra exercise. I laughed it off and assured him I would never do that to him and I meant it. I've since seen that Jason guy swanning around the place in the skimpiest semi outfits I've ever seen. I have never looked at a gorgeous male model and then just as quickly looked away before; I had to before I fainted. Let's just say, Jason is extremely ... well packaged? ... Physically defined? ... Mmm ... he'sss ... LOOK, he's got one of the BIGGEST cocks I've ever seen in my life OK!

I was embarrassed to stare longer than half a second, I felt like a pervert only it's his fault for putting it all out there on show. Jason's no idiot though just like Burt said before, men wanna be him and women wanna be with him for obvious reasons. I hate to say it but I do see the appeal, Jason is gorgeous. Unfortunately he knows it, he walks like he knows it and to me that's off putting.

Burt told me he's still looking for somewhere else; if and when that time comes he said he will text me with the details of his new place so we can continue to work together.

Following the next few weeks I keep noticing Anne constantly bringing up Richard's wedding plans. Richard wants this and Richard wants that, almost daily it seems as though she has a new comment to make on her big day. I'm happy for her, I AM! I'm ecstatic, truly if not a little jealous. Rambling on and on about all these elaborate detailed ideas and the excitement in her voice always manages to rear the green eyed monster within me. I've started making a list as long as my arm about what I envision for our wedding. I haven't yet been able to approach this with Bill as he comes in later and later these days. And like I said more often than not I'm already asleep by the time he gets in, then he's straight back out before I get up.

The enormity of this merger is taking up so much of his time, we've barely spoken in weeks (well actually closer to a couple of months) so I have been incapable of having the "let's make plans for our wedding" chat that I so desperately want but I can't seem to keep Bill still for a second.

He's so busy that we haven't even set the date yet! Normally I would mind much more than I do, but thankfully I've got my hands full now. I often forget to be bothered which in its way is a blessing. Trying to become what I hope to be is "the perfect wife" I refuse to pester him (for now)

Working at full steam one day, Sally gets the text of her dreams. Miraculously she hears from the mysterious Allan (of whom Anne and I have still never met, come to think of it none of us have ever met each other's partners) that being said he's written to her to let her know he's finally flying back for only one night to see her. Forgive me, but at this I got so choked up. She's so ecstatic, she's literally over the moon; jumping up and down like an excitable little girl, come Christmas morning. Before Sal loses her mind she replies rapidly with eagerness making what I suspect to be a million spelling mistakes.

She tells me that she's text him back saying that's she's getting new carpets installed so he can't come back to the apartment at the moment. Why that should prevent him from coming back to his own home I have no idea, but it seems to have worked. Apparently he's making reservations at a semi respectable hotel I've heard of here in New York City. I mean it's not The Plaza but I'm sure they will have a pleasant stay.

Have you ever said something, or pulled a certain face and you're immediately reminded of someone. Kind of like you turned into that person, I feel as though I say this often but just now talking about the hotel I turned into my mother. I always feel like my mother when I say something really snobbish or high maintenance. Not my most attractive quality I will say, I just wish I didn't occasionally turn into her from time and time.

Anyway the reason Sal lied to Allan is because she doesn't want him to see the progress we've made in their home. By the next time he comes to visit this place should have had a full face lift, so she intends on keeping it a surprise until completion.

On the day of his arrival she was of no use to anyone (not that she does as much as Anne and I anyway) so we were quite happy to let her go and enjoy the day with her fiancé. In fact no one was routing for her as much as I was, that's why I got choked up when she said he was coming, I know only too well how much it means to her. Only I know the full depth of Sally's feelings when he's away, after all I did sort of live with her for a short time. If anything the work we managed to achieve that day seemed more than usual and in between Anne sweating and panting like a dog, and me constantly rubbing at my temples from the stress of organizing the shipping to the right places; my mind often wandered back to Sally, silently praying she's experiencing what must feel like her honeymoon come early.

At random times throughout the day, Anne and I would receive the odd message from her, letting us know how perfect everything was in her world and how desperate she is for us to meet him. Ordinarily I would have suggested we all have dinner together but I wouldn't have cared to get in the way of the few short, precious hours they had together. Sally's next message informs us that we are all to have coffee the following morning at brunch. In brackets she told me that she will be having him for breakfast with a wink face at the end. I wanted to text back saying "too much information Sal!" but something in me said "don't dampen her mood, not today." Agreeing with my brain I reply with a "no problem. Can't wait to meet him" smiley face and I get back to work.

The following morning we're eating bagels and drinking coffee in a small quaint bistro called 'Coffee cake' we are all chatting and laughing at Allan's stories. It's a though the four of us have been friends for years. Seeing Sally and Allan together for the first time is bizarre, we have heard so much about him that it feels a relief to put a face to the name at last. You can tell Anne likes him; he has a way of including all of us into his conversation in a way we can't ignore. It's no wonder his line of work is in sales, he's such a chatter box and a people person with incredible enthusiasm when he talks you can't help but become totally transfixed with him.

His eyes light up with expression while he's talking a mile a minute which leaves you completely captivated, you feel as if your there with him living out this scenario he's painting with his words. He's sort of a vocal magician, no wonder he's successful at what he does. If he approached me with whatever he was selling at the time; I'd be bankrupt!

Well Bill would be bankrupt but either way anyone listening to him doesn't have a chance, his looks don't hurt either. Allan Rodgers isn't a stunning man but he's definitely handsome in his own way: average height, with short dark brown hair with a natural curl to the ends. In this case it isn't so much his looks that makes him attractive, it's his personality and sense of humor.

Needless to say they make a very good match in my eyes, it's just a shame he works all the time. His work has currently led him to Texas; that's where he's just flown from yesterday, and where he will be going back to in just a couple of hours.

I look over to Sally only to see how mesmerized she is by her one true love. She's glowing and it's written all over her face how much in love with him she is. Her cheeks are tinted with rouge; on first glance I think "gosh, has she's made an effort to wear makeup" but on closer inspection I realize it's a beautifully rare shade by "Natural" titled "Happiness". As I gesture to Anne that we'd better leave the love birds alone on their final hours together, we say our goodbyes and head back to work. Allan being the lovely soul he clearly is insists on kissing Anne and I on the cheek twice (and hard) and then giving us the biggest squeeze I've ever been given in my life.

We discuss what our impressions are of him, as we make

our way up Sally's never ending stairwell. Aside from the dizziness and the bruising he left behind, I think I like Allan and Anne agrees with me.

The naughty minx finally comes back later the same day, looking like a woman in love and floating on cloud nine. From her behavior I can only imagine they must have made love constantly, making up for lost time and the smile on her face says it was the best sex of her life. Green really doesn't suit me (even though it is my last name), I need to remember that.

Sally; playing a game of dizzy ducks in her own bedroom just because she can now that she has the space, declares to the room in a dramatic fashion. "Look at us guys! We are working. Anne's a cleaner and Jill is a kick ass business woman. We are a great team." I lock eyes with Anne and we both notice she didn't mention her part in all of this, because she doesn't have a major role like we do.

"Guys I've decided, whatever we make I want to share it three ways. I couldn't have done this without you-" well this much is true. "And the boxes seem to get less and less every single day. Look at how big my apartment is, I never knew I lived in a palace!" we all laugh at this because at the moment Sally's high on life and it's contagious.

"You don't have to do that Sal. We are happy to help." Anne tells her and I agree.

"And I think it's helped us realize just how capable we are of work. We might not be great chefs, but as god as my witness I do believe we may very well be business women." I can't stress the fact enough, I really do love to work and be kept busy.

"No I insist. I want us all to profit from the work we are doing here and besides it never was my money to start with." That's true too; it's Allan that has provided Sally with the funds she needed to get herself into this state in the first place. Perhaps now we know that, I don't think we will have as much of a problem taking the money from her. After much debate we all finally agree to take our fair share of the profit; after all it's mostly down to Anne and I ... or so I thought.

As my bladder begs me to stop working so I can take a bathroom break, I run as fast as I can. My cell has been ringing off the hook for some of the latest gear Sally has bought not so long ago. They are so new that some of this stuff sells almost immediately, after I've posted the ad on Facebook or eBay.

Dashing back to my post to be near my phone in case someone calls (I never take my phone to the bathroom, it's not like I'd dare answer it when I'm peeing) only to find Sally talking to someone on my cell. Shit! I was too slow, she's answered it and she's probably gonna put the customer off buying. To answer the business line aka my personal cell phone (I know now that I think about it I should have bought a separate phone) you need to have a professional telephone manner and be helpful by answering any questions the customer has. Can she sell it to them or will she scare them off?

Listening closely to monitor how she's dealing with the business call, I'm amazed at how confident she is. She's talking in depth, being descriptive and even going further than that by telling them what they can use it for. I can't believe how cool, calm and collected she's being; I really didn't need to worry.

Taking a seat to swallow what's left of my cold cup of tea I've had on the go for hours today, I sit back to watch Sally doing some work for a change as she starts to wrap up the call. Resting my head on the comfortable head rest, I close my eyes just for a minute and this is when I get the full effect of Sally's sales pitch. She sounds exactly like an infomercial! She has watched so many she's got the patter down. And of course she must have watched all of them that described each product she has, otherwise she never would have bought them in the first place.

In all honesty she's better than me on the phone, I tend to get impatient when people start asking the same questions over and over again, as I can tell this customer is doing to Sal as she's had to repeat herself multiple times already. She never loses her cool, then it dawns on me again. Sally is on the phone buying this stuff every day and I know she's even made a friend at the call centre; she calls in that often he knows her by name! It's all the proof I need to know she lives on the phone. She is very informed on every item and she's a friendly, bubbly chatterbox; much like her fiancé Allan. They have more in common than they know, and I'm sure Anne will be only too happy to learn that Sally now has a major role to play in this project. Sally is the telesales advisor and after this is all done I think she could definitely get a full time job in a call centre, maybe that friend of hers can give her some pointers on how to go about getting a job in that line of work.

I'm so happy I have found Sally's calling in life! *Pun intended.*

Chapter Nineteen

Till Death, Do Us Part?

They say it takes two to tango, and I couldn't agree more. Instead of wondering when he's getting home; asking myself why we never see much of each other, I'm taking matters into my own hands. I'm not going to speculate, calculate or over analyze what I'm doing. Life should be all about the here and now so I've decided to surprise Bill at the office. Ordinarily I would never have thought to do such a thing for fear of getting under his feet, but as I figure I'm going to be Mrs. Swanson I have as much right as anyone to see him at work.

I'm not doing this out of rebellion; I'm doing this as a loving act, a kind gesture. If he can't come to me then I'll go to him bringing a box of his favourite chocolates in tow. He'll never say no to that. While I'm there and he's munching on his candy, I'm gonna tell him out right all the ideas I have for the wedding and I'll purposely leave as many gaps in the conversation, so he knows I'm not turning into bridezilla and that in fact I want his imput on it.

I want everything Anne's got with Richard.

In truth I envy her; having a fiancé on board and he's dedicated on making it an amazing day. Because of Anne I've since realized I don't want to do this alone, besides it shouldn't be just my big day, it should be our big day.

I put on my smartest tailor made suit so I don't stand out in a bad way in his office. I bet there are loads of lawyers milling around the place. They'll be scrambling around from office to meeting room, to meet up with clients in a blind panic; so I want to look my best.

My smart sexy suit is pure black velvet and it fits like a glove, making me look professional and sexy. I admire myself in the mirror before heading out, even I'm impressed. I've only worn this suit maybe once or twice before. My father told me any wife of a lawyer on Wall Street needs to look the part at a moment's notice in case she needs to put on airs and graces, to impress clients and the like.

I'm confident he's going to be thrilled to see me, as long as I don't make a habit out of it I'm sure everything will run smoothly. Should he disapprove of my turning up to his place of work, that's when the chocolates come in to play. He orders them in from Italy and it's the darkest chocolate I've ever seen. Some people love dark chocolate, the darker the better, but for me it's the other way around. I love milk and white chocolate; I love the creaminess in a milky chocolate and to me a black colored chocolate is too bitter and sharp in taste. Where's the pleasure in that? Even in Galaxy commercials they always por-tray the woman dressing in her finest silk night dress, strewn across her chaise lounge with the lights dimmed. She puts on candles and shuts the world out so she can properly seduce herself. And the she pulls out a shiny, posh looking box where she keeps her secret pleasure and out emerges a full bar of her favourite Galaxy chocolate.

Mmmm that's what chocolate is all about isn't it. I'm actually getting chocolate cravings now, which isn't good. I've been doing really well on watching what I eat, god knows I can't say much about my keeping a date with Burt because I've been so busy, but I am very physically active these days I've been sweating like a mad man at work lifting boxes all day. Well not a date with Burt, but you know what I mean aka my sessions with him. I honestly want to work out with him more but whenever I reschedule with him, my mind goes blank or something happens that steals my focus. I wouldn't blame him if he loses his patience with me, by this point so am I but he's actually been very understanding (which just makes me feel worse) I must make a note in my phone reminding me to text him as soon as I leave Bill's side to rebook him one last time. Actually I think I will make an extended appointment with him to make up for lost time. God knows I've really started to love his company; no one can make me laugh like Burt.

Now I've saved it in my phone I feel more orderly and as though I'm slowly taking control of my life, and I like it. Putting all thoughts of the gym, Burt and chocolate out of my mind now, I need to take things one at a time. Thankfully my hunger for Galaxy has gone and the box of dark Italy's finest isn't of any appeal to me at all. Bill enjoys them on a night with a black coffee; he just raves and raves about them. Unfortunately to me they will always be a mystery as to whether that are that good or not, Bill has never, not once offered me one. So I guess I'll never know.

———⁂———

Heading into reception I forgot that they might enquire if I have an appointment or not. I hope they see sense and know who I am, I'm the soon to be wife of one of their most successful lawyers. I presume Bill has one of the biggest offices in the building after all its only right, he lives for his work so it's no more than he deserves.

Damn security is extremely tight round here, too tight. The amount of sass I'm getting off people on the front desk and the security man takes it upon himself to get involved.

"I'm sorry miss but if you don't have an appointment I'm afraid I'm gonna have to ask you to leave." This man ain't playing games. I'm mortified, I can't have a scene in here. I wanted to get in with little or no fuss (preferably the latter) after all this is meant to be a happy surprise. My cheeks are starting to glow with embarrassment. I have explained multiple times that I am Mr. Swanson's fiancé but to no avail.

Well then if that doesn't impress him then I guess I can always play the dad card. Everyone in corporate law knows who my father is, this should definitely work.

"I'm terribly sorry sir, I forgot to mention I'm Mr. Harold Green's daughter and I was hoping to see Mr. Swanson. I won't take up too much of his time; I'm his fiancé Jill Green." I can't believe that didn't work! He looks completely unimpressed by my statement, and when I mentioned my father's name there was zero recognition on his face. Actually come to think about it he's just a security guard. He won't know the first thing about big names in the world of law. All his job consists of is escorting people of the premises and keeping everyone in the building safe. So I shouldn't be offended. Just as he puts his hands on my arm, my jaw hits the floor.

Is he serious! He's gonna physically remove me out of the building like a common criminal. This isn't how I should be treated at all, just wait till my father hears about this.

Declaring my outrage and out right telling this buffoon who my father is and that I plan on seeing this idiot fired, a man witnesses my humiliation and comes over, as if he's about to get involved.

"Miss Green, my word how lovely to see you. How's your father these days? I haven't seen him in a few months, all well I hope. Um what seems to be the problem here?"

Thank the god's, I didn't realize who this man was at first but I do now. It's THE Frank McDougal. Only one of the most prestigious men among lawyers. He's basically on par with my father, actually I'd say he's a little higher than him. After all he is the chairman of Richman&co. (which is where Bill works, where I currently am now, this could not have been better timing) told you my dad knows practically everyone in this field, even if your just starting out in this business you will soon learn of him and come to respect his name.

"Mr. McDougal thank god you're here. This rude man won't let me past to see Bill in his office. I can't call Bill on his cell because it's a surprise. I've brought his favourite candy with me; I was planning on staying only for a short while. But this great oaf won't let me in all because I don't have an appointment." Rant over.

Within two shakes of a lamb's tail I'm off the hook. Dear Mr. McDougal told the security guard exactly who I am, and that I should be granted entry at any time; day or night. I do love Frank he's always been one of father's dearest friends, they go back centuries. Sorry, old man joke. But they have known each other a very long time. What luck he should have been passing in my time of need, maybe luck is on my side today.

"So sorry about that Miss Green, it won't happen again I can assure you that. Drop by my office later if you have the time and I'll see what I can do for you in terms of an 'access all areas' pass, but in the meantime here take my spare one then you'll never need worry." Love this man. How helpful. I've always been proper and respectful toward Frank when I've seen him at some of daddy's dinner parties. Father warned me on our first meeting that he also is a very important man with an incredible list of clientele. He reeled off a few names and they were all celebrities, which left me as a little girl, reeling. After all I was only eleven years old at the time, but forever after that I would speak to Frank like he himself was and is a celebrity (which my father loved)

Good old Frankie boy, I must remember to send him a thank you note and some flowers as any decent person would.

Access granted

Reputation heightened

VIP treatment

And surprise still in tack

It doesn't take me long to find Bill's office, thankfully all major offices have the person's name plaque on the door. And just as I suspected, Bill's is one of the largest on the floor. That's my man for ya, I'm so proud.

As I suspected it's locked and guarded by his receptionist, whom I have only ever heard about and I am so relieved to find out she's in her sixties and if she's younger than that it doesn't show. She looks up and just as she's about to shoo me away I flash her, my 'VIP access all areas card', feeling like the IT girl.

My god this card is soo cool. One small thrust of it in her direction and her mouth instantly closes. She just nods and looks back down at her typing. Man, I think I will drop into Frank's office afterward; I gotta get me one of these.

When it says access all areas it means it. I assumed the grumpy old woman would have passed me a silver key for the door, but there's a swiper thingamajig on the door and as if by magic I've gained entry. I'm literally in love with my new toy.

Classy is the word that comes to mind, while taking in Bill's office. It's huge and roomy with a killer view. There's his name plate on his desk and the desk it's self is beautiful; a red chest nut color, it looks shiny and expensive. For the amount of hours of his life he gives to this place it's only right his surroundings be comfortable and spacious.

It's not quite as big as my father's office though, I bet Frank's is. I feel so powerful with the magic card key around my neck I know I could have a full tour of this place, and no one would stop me. Telling myself I'm not going to abuse this power I push all thoughts of it out of my head.

I really feel like a naughty child being in here without him knowing. In a way I'm relieved he isn't already here because now I have the opportunity to really give him the shock of his life when he opens that door. I think I want to actually scare him a little (not so much he has a heart attack) just enough so that I can see him jump.

It's not enough for me to just be sat at the right side of the desk; I want to jump out from somewhere. I start giggling to myself at the idea of this and I know I need to find a great hiding spot.

For God's sake there is nowhere to hide, this place is as clean as a whistle with no nooks and cranny's to squeeze yourself into. The only place possible is under the desk. I can easily sit under it; it's just means that I may actually make his heart stop. Could you imagine, he comes in, sits down, starts drinking his coffee, typing up emails and going through mounds of paper work. He's just going about his business quietly until ...BOO!

A pair of hands grab him by his ankles.

I'm literally choking on a laugh and my eyes are watering from this mental image. Suppressing the world's hardest belly laugh I shimmy under the desk with his candy in hand. I don't want to leave it out on the desk. That would give the whole game away.

I don't know what's gotten into me right now; I've never been playful with Bill before. Actually before I met the girls and Burt I don't think I've ever really laughed much before. I'm enjoying this new side of me; I feel more care free and less uptight.

I can't wait for him to come in, I'm gonna hold my breath when he does. I want this room so silent you can hear a pin drop.

I arrived in his office at 12.15, hoping to catch him on his lunch break. When I saw he wasn't here I turned into a big kid and planned on surprising him. The time now is 3.45pm, my back is killing me. I've never sat on the floor for this long before, let alone a hard wood floor. Moving my legs slowly as I've developed raging pins and needles, I try to get into a kneeling position so I can then get up.

What could be taking him so long? So business lunch's last this long? Well from what I've seen of daddy and his clients the answer is yes. They cover all topics and even lead into things unrelated to work like golfing, and fishing and holidays, what's happened in the news... the list goes on and on. When you are just a spectator to these lunch's it can get real old, real quick but I was and still am a daddy's girl, so I handled it well and never let my boredom show. Same as when Bill does finally manage to get away and come back to the office, I won't whinge or complain over how long I've been waiting for him. I mean he didn't even know I was coming.

Regaining feeling in my numb ass and legs, I set about to stand but the distant faint echo of mumbling comes from the corridor. The voices are getting louder with every step closer to the office, and one voice for sure is Bill's. Seeing as I'm already down here it would be stupid to get up now after all this time. I plant my ass back on the now warm spot I have been habiting for several hours and prepare for the moment I have to hold my breath. At the beginning of this I was excited, now I'm just impatient. Thankfully texting Anne and Sally provided me with entertainment while I've been hiding under the desk all this time. They wanted me to text them afterward and tell them how Bill jumped out of his skin when I scared the hell out of him' needless to say they are still waiting for the results.

Finally the door opens and I jump a little, even though I knew it was coming. I hear more than one person enter from the footsteps and I have no wish to make a fool out of myself to a complete stranger, so I'm going to have to wait till they're gone.

"Thanks for a wonderful lunch Billy, the food there never lets us down does it." Come's a familiar female voice. And who the hell calls Bill, Billy? Even I don't call him that, who is this woman?!

A flaw to this desk that I have just discovered is that the wood goes all the way around, shielding me from their view but that's also stopping me from getting a good look at this woman. There's only a small gap between the wood and the floor of which I'm putting my face to the ground in order to get a glimpse of her footwear, not that, that help's much but it's something. All I can see are some fake ass Manolo Blahniks. I see Bill's feet start walking closer to the desk and my heart is pounding so loudly, I'm amazed I haven't yet been discovered. But there is still time.

I feel a shudder around me from a drawer being pulled open and he removes something but I'm not sure what. Could this woman be a client? Does he work with or her or for her? Either way I don't think I'm happy about it.

"It was a wonderful lunch, as always. Then again everything is wonderful with you." The girlish woman giggles and I feel a rock developing in my stomach.

"Well I really need to go Billy; I'm surprised Mr. Hornski hasn't noticed I'm gone yet. I don't want to get fired but how about dinner this Saturday night? If you can get away?" Help! What? Mr. Hornski? Bill flirting? He's been with her this whole time, not at a business lunch. I swallow the bile that's working its way up my throat and I honestly want to dry heave.

"Felicity, Don't go yet. I brought you back here because I forgot to bring it to lunch. Here, I bought you a little gift." I hear her squeal in delight.

"Billy! Oh my god. Billy! These are gorgeous!"

"Real diamond tiffany studs for my superstar." Why isn't the floor swallowing me up. How can this be happening – and right under my nose. Diamonds ... pet names, Billy and superstar? How come he never had a pet name for me? And how long have they been seeing each other? No wonder he hasn't been coming home often lately. It's been getting later and later every day, and I always assumed it was work related.

The delicate pitter patter of her cheap imitation wannabe designer shoes dance over to Bill and I can literally hear the smacking of their lips. EW, holy shit ... Bill's cheating on me with this... this... Fuck no! NO! JESUS CHRIST IT IS. Water has sprung to my eyes and still I'm not making a sound. In less than ten minutes flat, my whole world has turned to shit.

It's Farilyn.

I can't believe it. Bill is literally sleeping with the enemy. It's definitely, absolutely, positively her. I thought I recognized her voice, now I know why. The cheap shoes and working for

Mr. Hornski. This is the worst day of my life. Someone hit the escape button I need to get out of here.

"Billy baby, I can't thank you enough. I love them so much! I need to go now, or I never will."

"One more kiss and then I'll walk you down." They make out one more time and then they hit the road. Closing the door softly behind them, I'm finally able to take the longest deepest breath imaginable.

I need to get my bearings and run. Out of town preferably.

If I thought my legs were numb before, there's no comparison now. My body is defying my wishes and I seem to have turned into a statue. Paralyzed by utter disbelief, and yet I believe it.

How on earth did they meet though?

Something my father said floats back to me. Something about Bill talking to my dad about me finally understanding and agreeing to the prenup, and dad told him I went to Hornski. Father told me Bill and Hornski were acquaintances and that Bill wanted to thank him for helping me get to grips with the document. I bet that's when Bill bumped into Farilyn, when he went to thank Mr. Hornski. That's when Farilyn, sorry Felicity (the evil life ruining whore) will have sewn her web and dragged him in. Sadly for me he fell for it, hook line and sinker.

Speaking of being drawn into someone's web, it's me that fell for it. I fell for the idea that we would be together forever and I would be his queen.

Wanting to run away from what I had just been a witness to, I run out of the office, down the stairs (because I know they will have taken the elevator) I see them French kissing on the front steps outside the building and it confirms everything I already knew. It is her. I wait impatiently for him to come back in so I can make my quick exit. He takes the elevator and as he goes up, I go down.

That couldn't be more to the point of how I feel right now: as he goes up, I go down.

All that's going through my head right now is; what will my mother think. The thought of her sarcastic remarks with no thought as to my mental wellbeing is shocking. I'm going to keep this from her for as long as possible, she's the last problem I need right now.

I can't believe I was going to take my vows to that man. I think to myself as I wander around aimlessly through the streets of New York.

Till death do us part, hell we are parting before we get married, because there is no wedding. Maybe there never was. It's not like any real plans have been made. I know I had several in my head but I could never put them into practice because I was so absorbed in the task of becoming the perfect woman, the perfect wife so that he would hopefully never divorce me. Well fat chance of that, I don't know why I bothered.

Ours clearly wasn't a love meant to last. Surely if it was, the physical and emotional toll of parting should hurt.

Whether you've loved and lost him to another woman, or loved and lost him from this world. Both situations should leave you feeling bereft, agony, mourning and regret. Bitter over the fact that he was stolen from you, you're personal piece of happiness.

But no. Whilst he is in heaven in another woman's arms, I am not in hell. I feel down and hurt and shocked and disgusted but I am not wracked in sobs clutching my broken heart.

As a little girl, I used to watch old black and white movies (you know the ones with real love and romance in? not like nowadays. They're right when they say chivalry is dead, and if it's not then it's hiding from me!) I'd watch these classic beauties scream their hearts out when their lovers died or ended the relationship in any final way. They would cry, scream, curse at the wind and be overcome with grief holding onto a memento or souvenir that their beloved had given them. (You know like a telegram or a hand written love letter. I've always wanted a love letter of my own, but never got one. Like I said chivalry really is dead.)

But I don't feel that way, and I know their acting but their acting from real life, real feelings and real situations. That's what makes them great actresses: their realism.

Anyway I feel hollow, just empty. Don't get me wrong there are tears in my eyes but they haven't fallen over the surface yet. I know I'm a tough woman and you may think of me as a stone cold bitch, but I'm not.

Even the tears that refuse to fall; I instinctively know are not for Bill. They're for me. Selfish I know but I thought I was getting somewhere in life. I wanted the wedding, the dress, the envious stares, and people to whisper " oooh I wonder how much all of this cost, that Jillian Green's a lucky girl" I wanted to be the talk of the town. Now look at me, cheated on with nothing to look forward too.

Oh my god!

There, I knew it! I just said it! I don't love him; I was in love with the lifestyle. The idea of a fairy tale wedding with all the trimmings. It was never once about the groom or my feelings towards him. It was never about LOVE, Ever. How have I only just realized this? Now I really am in mourning. I'm mourning that little girl that believed in love, and the woman I've turned into that believes in money. Nice going Jill.

Chapter Twenty

Seeking Sally And Secrets

As I was running away from Wall Street, I hailed a taxi, jumped in and called Sally and Anne to find out if they were both in the same place. Only Sally answers and Anne's goes to voicemail, which is just like her if she's vacuuming she can't hear a thing.

"Hey honey. So how did the surprise go? I bet he nearly died finding you under the desk!" The line goes quiet and there are no words. Where to begin? I still haven't digested the whole thing myself. Besides becoming hysterical over my cheating fiancé (I mean ex fiancé) in the back of this man's taxi would be even more embarrassing. So I settle on a small cryptic message.

"I'll tell you everything when I see you. I just wanted to know that you're home." I say slowly in an undertone so the driver doesn't over hear.

"My, my, my. This does sound juicy. Righto I'll put the machine on. See you soon." Her and that bloody espresso machine, it's worth its weight in gold to Sally now, we all live off the stuff when we're at work. I suppose in the end it became an ideal purchase (can't say the same for the rest)

Work. Just thinking about it gets me mad. As if I took a day off for this! I really wish I hadn't, but then again: is ignorance bliss? Or is it your version of reality that someone hands you, because they think that you are incapable of handling the truth? Either way he's a liar and I hate liars.

Hurriedly paying and tipping the driver, I make the now overly familiar trip up to Sally's apartment and even I've had the displeasure of bumping into old man Albert more than once. He's such a nosey busy body and I can tell from his peering into the corridor behind me, he is curious as to why I'm practically sprinting up the stairs taking them two at a time.

I have no time for pleasantries, so I pretend not to have seen him and to keep pushing on full steam ahead. Sally must have heard my banging around as she's already at the door greeting me with a smile on her face. Although after looking at my expression she loses the smile, sensing correctly that this isn't the time, the place or even the right day to be happy.

Making my way into her now almost comfortable apartment I take to the couch and gratefully accept the still hot espresso.

"Well, are we going to talk about it?" Sally starts, obviously unsure how to remain quiet for more than two minutes.

One of the blessings of working full time is that you hardly find the time to smoke, but the minute you stop you try and make up for all the smoking time wasted. After today's horror I've already had three cigarettes back to back since walking out of Richman&co.

Chugging back as much espresso as possible and taking a deep breath to help me begin, I start.

"You know Farilyn" it's more like a statement than a question, but with the confused look upon Sally's face I realize my mistake. No one ever called her that, just me in my head. Looks like I'm going to have to start from the beginning for her to understand.

"Her real name is Felicity; she's the receptionist at Mr. Hornski's office. Remember that place where we all met?" still looking blank I go further into detail in an attempt to jog Sally's shit memory.

"Remember the blonde woman who told Anne off for cleaning that chair in the waiting area?" recognition spreads across her face, followed by a big smile.

"Yes! I do remember. Awgh that's where we first met." Sally looks off into the distance; reminiscing full of nostalgia, completely forgetting what is was we were talking about.

"Sally!" I shout to bring her back into the room.

"Yes sorry I'm listening – carry on" honestly I'd say she has the attention span of a goldfish, but comparing her more to Dory out of 'Finding Nemo', would be more appropriate.

"So anyway, that awful blonde tart's name is Felicity. Are you following me?" this is gonna take a while.

"Yes I'm following, what about this Felicity woman? Did she ruin your surprise?"

Precisely an hour later and I've filled Sally in on absolutely every detail of my humiliation. I've covered everything from my previous hatred toward Farilyn or Felicity or whatever you wanna call her, I think I'll just stick to: BITCH.

I've told her all about my being under the desk with a numb ass for hours on end only to discover their love affair. I even told her about the tiffany's diamonds, the wet sloppy sound effects from their heavy make out session and my scurrying out of the building without him ever knowing I was there.

"Holy shit!" I knew Sally's reaction wouldn't let me down.

"Jill no! I can't believe that scum bag did this to you!" Sal's outraged and rightly so, I'm still gob smacked and at my wits end. Where do I go now, what can I do?

"What an asshole, oh that Bill, I ought to go round there and kick his ass! I wanna give him a piece of my mind. And with that cheap slut of all people! Jilly I can't believe this has happened to you, come here give me a hug. This is just the worst thing that could have happened. EVER!" Jeez Sally's turning violent and it's cheering me up to no end. I've never heard her so angry before but knowing she feels so passionate about this on my behalf makes me feel loved at least by someone.

I go in for an enormous hug and when this overly affectionate display starts getting to me and I can feel the tears start creeping into my eyes I try and pull away, before I succumb to crying openly in front of her. Unluckily for me the minute I try to retrieve from Sally's loving embrace, she just pulls me in tighter refusing to let me go. Unsure of whether I am silently loving or hating this, I allow her loving squeezes to continue until she has had her fill and several tears have fallen.

She notices a few small tracks of water coming out from under my lashes and hands me a Kleenex. I'm not choking on my tears or hysterically crying, my sadness is coming purely from my stupidity and naivety. I feel sorry for myself and that's all and actually I'm pleasantly surprised by how little I care that she's looking at me at my most vulnerable state. I don't want to run or hide, being with a friend is exactly what I need right now. It's a shame Anne's not here too; I know she'd be as upset by this shocking news as Sally is. As though reading my mind, Sally says "I'm gonna call Anne and tell her to get round here right now. We all need to be together at this awful time." A sad half smile comes to my lips at how motherly she's become in such a short time. I'm afraid the tables have turned today. I'm the upset child needing her parents to pick her up when I'm down. Sally and Anne, my two mothers. Who could ask for more?

Wanting to call my father and tell him all, purely out of frustration and also I'd like to see if my dad could have a negative influence on the rest of Bill's career. I know it's such a childish way to think, but right now I'm hurt and I don't see why he should get away with this unscathed. Knowing this isn't the right time to do such a thing, I put it off until later when I've had a chance to talk it through at length with my girlfriends first.

"That's funny, she's not answering. She must be cleaning again. God knows that woman can't hear a thing when she's vacuuming." Sally comes to the same conclusion I did. Shame though, I would have liked her to be here, just when I needed her most.

"I'll try again later. What's that you've brought?" Sally asks, pointing to her coffee table where I see Bill's box of chocolates I brought to the office as a mid-day treat for him. I can't believe I've had hold of them all this time.

"They're Bill's favourite Italian dark chocolates. Very expensive, he eats them sparingly, normally saves them for a special occasion or when he intends to really relax. He usually would suck on one for about ten minutes laid in bed next to me, reading the latest Dan Brown novel." I say mournfully. Already I'm talking about him in a past context.

"I'm not a big fan of dark chocolate" declares Sal, breaking into my sorrowful mood.

"Give me a big bar of Galaxy any day." that small smile comes back to my face. My thoughts exactly, we totally have the same taste in candy.

"Well crack them open Jill; he won't be getting them now. He doesn't deserve them. Let's eat his precious candy and laugh at him, that should make us feel better." I don't know how her mind works, but she does make me laugh.

"Are you kidding?! We can't eat his chocolates, he would kill me. These are like his delicacy. Never, ever did he once give me one." her mouth flops open as she gasps.

"How selfish is he. All this time with him and he never shared his candy with you, Jill that's disgusting. And what do you mean he would kill you? He won't ever know will he and even if he does, you're hardly going to feel bad after what he's done to you."

She's right, what am I talking about. He can go to hell for all I care; I hope I never see him again.

"Go on. Let's try one. See if they are all what he's made them out to be."

Needing no encouragement, I tear the box open and take a good look inside. The small dark squares are almost blending into the black tissue paper background. They certainly do look posh but already I can smell just how much cocoa has gone into these things. We peer in for a closer look, both of us pulling a face as we each take one. Clinking our coal colored pieces of chocolate as if this is a champagne toast, we take a bite of the bitter block and simultaneously spit it back out again.

"Ew, how can anyone like this stuff?" squeals Sally.

"I'm glad he never offered me one now, they are horrible."

We are both in complete agreement that they may be one of the worst things we have ever put in our mouths.

Sally storms out of the room and quickly returns with our favourite, a sharers block of Galaxy.

"Here get some of this; we need it to take that vile taste out of our mouths." As if to heal all wounds she sits by my side, snaps the block in half and feeds me the silky creamy chocolate as she strokes my hair. (Sigh)

Who needs a man or a mother when you have Sally.

Really now thinking about it I should have known we were never right for each other, just from our opposite tastes in chocolate. Galaxy's slogan comes to mind and I've decided to apply it to all things in life.

Why have cotton, when you can have silk?

I'm so glad we decided to take the day off today. I know Jill plans on paying Bill a visit at the office, and I think Sally plans to just chill out, but I've decided to come home and catch up on some housework. Poor Richard has had to make do with a less than immaculate apartment. It's actually not as filthy as I expected, he must have done some cleaning himself when I've been out. Richard has always been very good like that, he's just like me: he loves a tidy home.

He hasn't once complained though, at my working so late. In fact he completely encourages it, he said it will fill my days and bring a bit of extra money in which could never hurt, and I feel the same way. I'm really glad he sees it that way because I know a lot of men find it threatening when a woman gets a job, they take it almost like a physical blow to their manly pride. So I'm relieved he's so supportive about it. I'm really enjoying working with the girls though, I feel useful at last.

I enjoy coming home on the night and know that we have both had a busy day, it's no longer a case of me soothing him after a hard day's work, we are a team of equals nowadays. I guess deep down I knew I had more to offer then just being a housewife, but I never would have realized it if it weren't for the girls and this new project. Before my new working lifestyle I would make a delicious meal for two. Admittedly my cooking skills as you know are not at an expert level, but I've always got by on the bits I can do. Pot roast being one of them, its Richard's favourite dish and I used to cook it regularly until recently. I plan on making it tonight though as a nice surprise when he comes in. He doesn't know I've got the day off today so I think I'll catch up on some of this neglected house work and cook us a lovely homemade meal.

Lately our life has consisted of Chinese takeout. He's so thoughtful as to not bother me at work and demand I come home to make his dinner. Usually I come home after he does and the moment I walk through the door the aroma of duck with sweet and sour sauce hits my nostrils and I'm filled with pleasure. Partly in knowing my hunger is going to be satisfied but also because I know I don't have the extra chore of cooking ahead of me after a long day: pure bliss.

Of course it's not healthy to eat Chinese everyday so I am looking forward to this meal tonight. I've already prepared it and I've put it in the slow cooker it'll take hours that way but when it's done it will be succulent.

I try to fill my time with odd jobs, a spot of dusting, a boat load of laundry and ironing, when a fleeting idea comes to my head. I've just remembered, I have all that kinky junk I bought stashed in a draw somewhere. Knowing I'm alone with a bit of time on my hands I have the urge to find them once again just to remind myself of what I bought.

Rummaging through endless draw after endless draw I finally find all the overpriced pieces I was told so certainly would keep Richard interested in me. As it happened he absolutely didn't want to touch me in them, which I'll admit at the time felt depressing to be sooo rejected by your partner, but I was revoltingly drunk and I must have looked a mess. Right now I'm no longer drunk, I'm as sober as a judge and for the life of me I can't remember what I looked like in them. Did I look sexy? It would be nice to know if any of them are suitable, I mean when we get married I would like to take some of this stuff on honeymoon with us if it looks good on me. After all he did spend a small fortune on it; I'd die of embarrassment going back to 'Kinky Couture' in order to get a refund on all this stuff. Plus I have technically worn them so I'm sure they wouldn't do a refund anyway.

Being naughty and daring I swallow my fear and put on each outfit in turn. What I see in the reflection doesn't scare me as much as I thought it would. What with my long legs, slim figure and my red bob cut I do look a little kinky. I'm so into this look, I'm not the type of woman who has a huge ego or well any ego at all, but even I have to admit I look sexy as hell. Swept up in the thrill of turning into a new woman before my eyes I try on my sexy lingerie, after frilly knickers after sexy thong after wig, and at the end I'm stumped for words. Drunk or not, Richard should have wanted me. Guilt runs through me for thinking this way, he's a gorgeous gentleman and the last thing he wanted was for his fiancé to turn into a slut. I'm not a slut though quite the opposite, I'm a virgin so surely if I become sexual with him it can't be frowned upon. I really hope he doesn't think any less of me for attempting to seduce him that night, I meant well but I will never pull that one again until we are married that's for sure.

I'm sexy, confident and relieved to know that those pieces weren't a total waste of money; I'm definitely using them on our honeymoon. I found them tossed haphazardly into the draw, which isn't my style so this must be Richard's handy work.

Taking pride in them now and finally giving them the treatment they deserve, I empty the draw to fill it neatly just the way I like it. After everything is neatly folded I start placing them in the draw carefully. This draw needed a good clear out anyway it's filled with old socks – one with a hole in so they'll both have to go in the trash. There's a box of matches – in case there is a power cut, but they are in the wrong place they should be with the candles. And there's even a magazine called 'OUT'. I've never seen this magazine before, ever in my life. In fact I've never even heard of it. I thought I knew everything about Richard but clearly not if I don't even know what his favourite mag to read is.

Flicking through the pages to see what 'OUT' is all about, I start to feel quite sick. It's for gay men! A dizzy spell takes over me and I sit on the bed to take a breath. Too distracted to think, I give my brain a shake to get my head round this. This must be old; I bet he never even knew it was here, I bet he's never seen this before just like I haven't. Besides Richard isn't much of a reader anyway so this can't be his. Talking out loud I can hear my own insanity, being the only one listening in to my one way conversation, only I can hear my bullshit. I sound like a warped woman willing to believe in anything but the truth, because reality is often too hard to swallow. Refusing to be that woman I become desperate for answers and begin to ransack the place, and I know just where I'm heading to: his desk that has a key hole on each drawer. He's always told me I can clean anywhere I like except his desk; only he is allowed to go in there. Out of respect I did what he asked but now I can't stand it, I want answers. Jiggling and pulling on each draw, none of them give way. I guessed as much, it turns out all draws are locked as I expected. All of a sudden the desk in which I never spent a moment wondering about has become the centre of my world. The huge vastness of the object practically gloating at me for we both now know it is holding a deep dark secret in its chest. Using everything I can get my hands on, hair grips, knifes, and even an ice pick to break open my torturer but nothing works. Shuffling around on his desk for a paper clip or anything that might help, I land upon the answer to all of my prayers.

The key.

What luck, I can't believe he's left a key out, I know it wasn't intentional as it was buried among folders and stacks of papers and envelopes but the fact is I have it. Now I know I can get the truth, but I'm suddenly afraid of what I will find. Taking my time to unlock the first draw, I breathe out all my anxieties because there is nothing inside but a fountain pen. One down two to go. Unlocking the second one I begin to feel foolish upon finding nothing more than a stapler and a box of paperclips. Last one, please don't fail me now. Slowly turning the key I have a dreaded feeling that this is the one, the draw that will change my destiny if I am to marry Richard or not. "Please let it be empty." I whisper to myself on repeat. "Let it be empty."

It's not empty. There it is, my worst nightmare: a packet of opened condoms buried deep within his draw. Picking up the packet I peer into the contents. My heart falls through my stomach. The condom packet tells me that it held six condoms, looking inside the box I only find two. How much more evidence do I need?!

Under the condom packet I find the rest of his stash of magazines for gay men, such as 'The official New York City pride guide' and 'The Advocate' and 'PASSPORT' I know that one sounds safe but you're wrong. It too is a gay men mag! Taking each mag to hand I skim through quickly before the pictures burn my eyes. They don't just contain gay porn it's everything about the LGBT community: fashion, stories, style, culture, life, pride events etc. All of a sudden everything makes sense. I never saw this coming but now I think of it, it's all suddenly so clear why he's so neat, clean, smells good, helps round the house, does everything his mother commands and is always far to understanding about the lack of sex in our relationship. He is more than willing to just let me sleep, he's even talked me out of it the one time I tried to be sexual 'Taking it slow' he said! 'Don't want to rush you' he said! 'No sex before marriage would be so romantic' he said!"

Everything from the dramatic wedding, the explosion of glam and glitter, and how it excites him more than me, suddenly makes sense (too much sense) all this time he's been nothing more than a gay best friend to me and I believed he loved me, but clearly he's been making love to someone and a man of all people. It's the ultimate blow. The biggest deal breaker, no matter how much it hurts. Shoving all the evidence into my bag, I know I can't be here when he gets home, this is too much for me to deal with alone. The urgency is in me to run for the hills and by hills I mean to Sally and Jill. I need them for they are my friends, my family, and right now they will have to be my therapist's too.

Chapter Twenty One

Life Is A Cabaret

The buzzer rings so loudly causing Sally and myself to jump with a start.

"I wonder who that could be. Anne said she was making a lovely home cooked meal for herself and Richard. It can't be Anne it sounds too urgent." the buzzer rings in a constant panic, being pressed over seven times before Sal makes it to the intercom.

"Hello? Who is this?" Sally's unsteady but curious voice floats out onto the dimming street.

"Sally, it's Anne. Please let me in right away" without hesitating Sally buzzes Anne into the building, whilst turning to me with a look of worry on her face.

"She sounds really distressed Jill. Something must have happened." Both of us are riddled with concern and I'm almost relieved to have something fresh to think about to momentarily distract me from my own problems. Even I could hear the emotion in Anne's voice and I'm almost certain she is or has been crying; I keep these thoughts to myself as to not further alarm Sally.

Bursting in past us come's a weeping Anne. I've never seen

Anne cry before and I must admit the sight has me unnerved. What could have happened? The suspense is killing me.

"Anne, honey what's wrong?" the mother in Sally emerges again. "What's made you so upset?" Sal's voice has drastically changed from high pitched and slightly ditzy to low and comforting. Almost to a whisper. Almost like a child's lullaby.

"I don't know, I don't get it. How could this have happened? We were so happy. How could he do this to me?! What did I do to deserve this? This can't be happening." Anne has turned into my worst nightmare; an out of control, over emotional woman that looks crazy, irrational and overdramatic. I guarantee whatever has happened between her and Richard it will in no way hold any comparison over what my day has been like.

"Sshh, hush now everything going to be ok. Just relax, tell us everything and start from the beginning." Anne is hyperventilating and it's hard to hear a single clear word. Trying to decode Anne's problem becomes too much. Glances are going back and forth from me to Sally, but neither of us have any clue. Anne finally gives up, becoming exasperated by our dumb looks; at last she thrusts forward everything she was trying to tell us.

"Magazines! GAY Magazines!" chanting this over and over while she rocks her body in distress, wrapping her arms around herself as if to shield her from the pain she is currently enduring. I become firstly amazed then bewildered, then baffled and then intrigued. Not one of us has any idea what to say. Perusing through each gay glossy mag, comes a new level of shock.

Ok maybe her day is on par with mine after all. I didn't believe I could ever feel sorry for anyone today, not today, the day when my life turned to shit. And yet I stand corrected; it's true what they say: no matter how badly you think you have it, someone out there always has it worse. Fact.

Unable to comprehend what Anne must be feeling all we can do is cuddle up to her and follow her lead as we take a seat on the floor. All three of us in motion, rocking slowly back and forth holding tightly on to one another; reminiscent of the aftermath of an earthquake. Only this time there are no survivors.

From the dimming of the day we carry on talking well into the darkness as night falls. Hours upon hours have passed and both Anne and I have had a missed call from our (former) partners. I allowed mine to go to voicemail and the sound of Bill's lying cheating voice immediately puts my back up and my skin on edge. The message was merely informing me that he has to work late again tonight and for me not to; as he puts it "wait up". This has become a very regular saying, recited by Bill almost daily, now I know why. Anne refused to answer hers as well. It's so typical that now they should want to reach out and get in touch, they don't usually make the effort; the universe has a sick sense of humor. Richard on the other hand didn't leave Anne a voicemail, he just dropped her a quick text. A short to the point message asking where she is, when she will be home and that he's had to take the pot roast out of the slow cooker because it smelt like it was burning.

Needless to say these grueling hours that have sped by, have consisted of Anne spilling her guts about everything. The gay magazines, the open hidden packet of condoms, his excitement over a glam wedding, the way he does his hair and the way he never touches her.

Sally and I took that to mean that their sex life isn't up to scratch which I can relate with, but in fact we couldn't have been further from the truth. Anne revealed her deepest secret of all; she's a virgin! Honestly the minute she said it I instantly believed her. The way she would never comment on her sex life, the way she blushed and cowered while we were shopping in 'Kinky couture'. I mean it makes all the sense and I can't believe I never figured it out for myself. Complete horror was written all over our faces when she told us this, and then she led on to tell us about her one and only time she tried to seduce him. That night we were drunk after sex shopping. All this time I believed I was the only one that had a shit time that night, but now I have been fully informed by both of them that no one got laid that night and we all wound up alone and miserable in our beds.

Absorbing Anne's information Sally and I took turns to inform Anne of my personal hell today. Telling her that I'm being cheated on by Bill with a cheap blonde tart, and the creature's name is Felicity. I reminded her all about the receptionist at Mr. Hornski's office that tried to make a fool out of her, and Anne knew exactly who I was referring to.

Whining, complaining and often crying yet I'm the only one slightly keeping it together compared to these two. Trying to show support to Anne I offer her my place, if she'd like to stay with me for a while until we can all figure this stuff out and plan our next move. My rational brain has already kicked in and my mind is working overtime on sussing out where to go from here. The only place I know I will never go back to live again is Bill's. I'm away from there now for good and I intend on keeping it that way. Just like my daddy always says "Nothings final until you have the ring on." and once again he's been proven right. Now I'm so grateful to have my small apartment on the Upper East Side, admittedly it's no haven on Lexington Avenue, but it is going to be my place of sanctuary. I feel it only right to offer help to a friend in need especially when that friend has nowhere to go and is already having a hell of a time.

"Yes please, jeez I never even thought about that. Where

am I going to live? What am I going to do? Everything has to be cancelled; all the arrangements for the wedding have to be undone. I'll have to call my family let them know, and the worst part will be confronting Richard that I know everything. Then I'll need to find my own apartment but I don't have the money to pay for it. Oh god my life is over!" freaking out and her mind spinning out of control we both advise her to cool down and not everything can be put into place over night.

"We will try and wrap all our heads round this tomorrow but in the meantime let's just go back to my place and try and unwind." I say thinking rationally.

When life gives you lemons you make lemonade. When your husband's-to-be are cheating on you, you need Vodka. We need Vodka.

You probably think I'm a raging alcoholic but it's absolutely not true. Since working on Sally's place none of us have gotten drunk the night before for work reasons; we want to keep sharp. And from all the hard work we have done and then the added baggage of our futures being shattered; I'd say we are entitled to a night of binging.

Sally begs me to let her sleep over at my place too, she appears to be in just as much pain as us and her soothing words have been comforting us both, so naturally I want her there. Once outside we hail a cab from Sal's building, we file in and give the cabby my address then speed off into the night.

We stay up all night talking, getting the Ben and Jerry's out, binge eating junk food (temporarily falling off my diet for one night only) we start mellowing out. I've started to keep this place fully stocked with over indulgent supplies because this always seems to be the place we fall upon during hard times. A few sniffles come from each of us at different times, but the vodka is a temporary cure for pain. As it happens I believe all doctors should recommend Vodka occasionally as a strong sedative for when the world gets too much. Or have I just developed the mentality of an alcoholic?

Any way the initial shock of everything seems to have subsided much to our relief and the night seems to have taken on a funny turn. Sally makes joke after joke at how lucky we are to have escaped them. That they probably have little dicks and don't even know how to use them, and that every time I did it with Bill I faked it. She's kind of right for the most part, it was never mind blowing. Sally tells Anne that she was lucky not to have given her virginity to a man that clearly doesn't deserve her and that this is a blessing in disguise. I also agree with this, could you imagine having waited for thirty-seven years of her life just too accidently give it to a gay guy?! It's awful but she must be inwardly thankful that this happened while she is still pure. In all seriousness I'm far more blown away from the fact that Anne hasn't had sex not once in her life more than I'm shocked that Richard is secretly gay.

The drinks keep flowing and the mood has been lightened by everything Sally says and does to cheer us up, mixed with the sensation of no longer caring what the Vodka shots seem to have done to us. In my drunken haze I take stock at what I've got. Life isn't so bad really is it? I have my own apartment and I have two great friends, I have a father you adores me and I adore him and on top of that I have a sense of worth from the job we've been doing. And even somewhere in all of that, lies Burt. He really has become a confidant of sorts and I do consider him more a friend than a trainer. I'd like the girls to meet him properly; I think they would also really like him too.

Looking to Anne and then to Sally it strikes me again just how much these two have come to mean to me and how much they have changed my life. If it weren't for them I'd be licking my wounds alone without any comfort from a friend. Life has drastically changed in the short time I have known them, and yet it feels like forever. They are more like sisters to me than friends (which secretly I've always wanted a sibling, as an only child it was often very lonely when my father wasn't around; playing with an au pair had its advantages but nothing could compare with having your own sister of a similar age. Now I feel life has delivered them to me at last. Better late than never) after tears, emotional spills and dreams of our fantasy weddings now crushed, Sally (with too many Vodka's in her system) wanders around my apartment, swaying slightly left to right until she stumbles upon an old acoustic guitar in my bedroom. It was bought on a whim when I had romantic ideas of being able to play just like Dolly Parton. In truth I have never took the time to learn; now it has become a lovely ornament coated in a thick layer of dust. Sally emerges into the lounge looking triumphant. She improvises on the spot and writes a silly song to keep the laughter going. Learning to laugh about how bad things are really is the best medicine of all, and the perfect remedy to quick healing. Of course all things take time and our problems won't disappear overnight. But learning to laugh at one's own misery is a strong personality trait, so Sally helps lighten the mood even more with a drunken song, about being in denial about your boyfriend being gay.

"Here Anne I'll write you a funny song to cheer you up, it goes like this. I hope you like it. P.s I'm not a professional guitar player." Sally slurs, with a shot in one hand and dusty guitar in the other.

"You are really into your own reflection
But that's because you are perfection

And we both love one direction
And we both know you get an erection
When you see ha...aa...rrryyy
I know he makes you soo ha..aa..ppyy!"

After a verse Anne and I scream at Sally to stop while we hold our stomachs laughing.

"What? I was hoping you'd see the funny side to it. Come on Anne; there must have been a few times you wondered about his sexuality!"

"I suppose it's a fair question Anne. I know it doesn't fix anything, but wasn't there a part of you that knew? I mean just the fact he was willing to wait till marriage proves he's not a normal heterosexual red blooded man." Sally sniggers openly at her own comment.

"That's not true. There are a few romantic, virgin men out there in the world that want to find the right woman, before giving themselves physically. Such as Christians; don't they wait till marriage? And wear purity rings until their wedding night?" says Anne "I just thought he was a romantic."

"Well you were wrong." Sally states aggressively.

"Sally your being really hard on Anne right now, what's gotten into you?" I ask, appalled for Anne's sake.

"I'm sorry; I just think it's funny that you couldn't tell. All men LOVE SEX! And I feel if there's a serious lack of sex in your relationship then he's either cheating on you, gay, or impotent and that's my black and white, but very realistic take on the world. I just wish you had said something in the beginning. I would have sussed it out for you and saved you the trouble. I'm also being kinda heartless because I'm angry at him and at Bill ... even Allan." Sally puts her head down in stress.

For god's sake don't tell me we have a full house of losers

right now. Please don't tell me Allan's turned bisexual. (I'm just picturing the worst case scenario) He's cheating on Sally with a man and a woman while he's on the road. Things round here just couldn't get any worse!

"Shit Sal-" Anne says "not you two!" I panic.

I hold my breath in wait for the response...

Sally distracts us to get us off the topic, she plays her whole song that she started and names it 'Rose tinted glasses'. And it works. We quickly realize she isn't in the mood to discuss what's going on with her and Allan, but in time I know she will. In part I'm thankful she chose not to drop another problem onto our heads on this night. I think one more negative thing, even in the smallest degree may have catapulted us over the edge. I have been left curious though; maybe she's just missing him, like always.

Chapter Twenty Two

Rose Tinted Glasses

Here's a tasty little jam I have titled 'Rose tinted glasses'
"You're always so good to me
And at night we both just sit and read.
You're always so understanding about my migraines and such
Because we both know you're not into sex much
But that doesn't bother me
Because I refuse to see clearly

Thank god for my
Rose tinted glasses
My rose tinted glasses

You are really into your own reflection
But that's because you are perfection
And we both love one direction
And we both know you get an erection
When you see ha..aa...rrryyy
I know he makes you soo ha..aa..ppyy

That's why I need my
Rose tinted glasses
My rose tinted glasses

I love the way you fix my hair
I know you only do it because you care
But haters say
It's because you're Gay
But they don't know you like I do
Because you love me, and I love you
All I need is you and my...

Rose tinted glasses
My rose tinted glasses

　　"Jill you really should be harmonising with me on the chorus part!" Sally demands.

"You're my best friend until the end of time
All the girls stare because your mine
And everyone knows that I'm a 2 and you're a 9
But why should I care, that's fine...
Because life is good all the time, with my

(Time for the chorus!)
Rose tinted glasses
My rose tinted glasses

I love the way you look in my eyes
And I love the way we wear the same size
How many women can say he wears her clothes?
In fact he picked her whole wardrobe
You even gave me my first pair of

(EVERYBODY!)
Rose tinted glasses
My rose tinted glasses

I know the rumours
I've heard them all
But I don't care we have a ball
The best moment of my life was our wedding day
And even then I heard them say
"How come she doesn't care that her husband's gay
How badly did they get it wrong?
Even though you chose to dance with your best man to our
     wedding song
I know I'm being daft, I'm being silly
But come to think of it
I've never seen your Willy ...

But that's ok, I'll get by
How could I not, when I've got MY!
Rose tinted glasssssssessssss
My rose tinted glaaaa.aaaa...ssseess.

You love Beyoncé, Britney and Christina
And you have quite a bitchy demeanour
For some reason we are always talking about cocks
And you'd rather take me shopping than play with my box
But I don't care I think that rocks...
I promise I will never take off
My rose tinted glasses
My rose tinted glasses

The day I caught you in bed with a man
You said it was ok; it was all part of the plan
That Mike was helping you look for fleas
But Mike just happened to be on his knees
I think he meant lice
Well isn't that nice
But why was Mike dressed like Fanny Brice?

(Now the strumming slows down to a sad rhythm)
I don't think about it for too long
I just wipe away the tears and carry on
Deep down I knew something was wrong
I think that's why I wrote this song
About my
Rose tinted glasses
My rose tinted glasses.

Chapter Twenty Three

The Cinderella Complex

'm reading 'The Cinderella complex' in my oversized, plush dark purple, velvet chair. This piece of furniture is so old and doesn't go with the rest of my simple décor at all. It tends to stand out in every way for me. It's shabby looking and well worn, it smells a little musty probably from a build-up of dust over the years and my neglect of hardly ever coming back here to check on my apartment; but I still love it. The velvet chair is so big it's more like a third of a couch, it's the one thing I've kept as a souvenir from my childhood and the funniest thing is it was never where I sat as a child. This chair was where my father would sit every morning and every evening. I'd watch him with fascination as he thumbed the day's newspaper. The look of concentration on his face always amused me; he'd wrinkle his brow, not blinking for what felt like an hour. At his side would be (what I thought at the time to be) the world's biggest coffee mug. Fresh hot and steaming, I'd see the steam rise above the mug and strong mocha aromas would come floating by my small nose. Sometimes dad would catch my eye when I was staring at him in wonder, he would drag me on to his knee, kiss me on the back of the head and allow me the last quarter mug full of his favourite drink. Just remembering the last time I felt that content brings tears to my eyes; because in truth it hasn't happened since.

The book was suggested to me by Google. I typed in 'Feminist books' and it was the first one to come up. With 'Cinderella' in the title it was enough to sell me on the idea; little did I know it would change how I think about everything forever. It's funny, honest, brilliant, and to the point. This Colette Dowling is some woman to have written this, but also it's exactly everything I feared. I believe every word that's written, I constantly feel myself unconsciously nodding against my will; Colette couldn't have hit the nail on the head more if she tried. Women really are afraid of becoming completely independent. Even the independent women out there in the world would always prefer a man to fall back on should life become a challenge. Not only was Bill the man I had set my sights on and was only too happy to live in his successful shadow, but the book has also taught me about how dependency grows in little girls from a very early age. A lot of it is due to how the girl perceives her parents and also how they treat and molly coddle her; this starts her dependency issues off in the first place. As women, we are doomed at the start and once all this becomes clear all in one go it's completely mind boggling. 'The Cinderella complex' has pointed out very vividly that my father is something of a crutch for me. Even to this day I do what he likes, what he thinks is right for me, and I do it all to please him. I've never truly sat down in a quiet room and asked myself "so Jill what is it you want? Do you want to marry? Or do you want to see the world? Would you like a career and make money to do the things you want? And if so, how are you going to go about it?" Thinking in-depth about my life choices, about my lack of a mother and how my father has come to mean everything to me (almost too much) I'm starting to see a pattern emerge. In my head I'm a self-assured, reliable, and capable of hard work woman with a huge personality. But in real life I tend to act accordingly to please which ever man is around me.

Take my father for example, the minute he tells me something or suggests something, I act as if it's the law and act on it straight away; no questions asked. Same with Bill, with Bill I think there is (or rather was) a certain element of fear there. I could tell when he didn't want to talk, which was always. If he needed something doing he would bark orders and I'd act like a puppet being controlled by my strings. It's only been since reading this fantastic book that I've suddenly realized that I had strings to be controlled by. In part it's obvious to me now that the reason I become so placid with the man in my life at the time, is because that's how I act towards my father. I've always seen it as an act of respect and that it's just how you're meant to behave around men that are important in your life. They say jump and I say how high. I love my dad so much and that won't ever change, but the fact is I know I have changed. I've been feeling it for a while now and I know that I need to be free to be me. Now that I've got the message loud and clear, I guess it's time for me to face it and start fresh. With what's left of the work, we are still occupied in a small way these days even though it's almost over. It's still reassuring to know that we all do have skills and I can make a career for myself. I just need to face the fire and be my own keeper. Thanks to Colette Dowling I know that now, and I think deep inside me I knew it all along.

Anne is crying into her pillow day and night. I still can't create an emotional gut wrenching spill on a level that Anne is on. My slight depression is rapidly turning into self-confidence and forcefulness. If anything I feel angry at myself for playing the dummy for so long. I've offered Anne the book when I'm done reading it but her vision is completely impaired from the constant tears. Anne is definitely in a worse condition than me, that's why I've given her my bed. I'm using my velvet chair to sleep in. It's not overly comfortable as I am a tall woman but at the moment it's the only place I find peace. For the majority of the day I let Anne sleep in between her sobs. Sally and I take it in shifts to talk to her and pull her out of her funk but we have both since agreed she just needs time. After all she has had an incredible blow to deal with. Richard has been blowing up her phone day and night and you can tell he's really concerned (as well he should be!) he is clueless as to the damage he has done to Anne and for that we can never forgive him.

Anne's been on the phone to her parents, Sally and I over-heard her hyperventilating on the phone part shrieking, part fighting for breath. She's informed everyone that the wedding is off but she won't tell them the reason why. She's still ada-mant about facing him on this. Confronting him in person as to why he lied, why the pretense, and why keep her in the dark for so long. The few times Anne has been coherent all of her statements are baffling questions. The only way she'll ever find peace in her mind again is if she gets full closure.

Sally and I often talk late at night about Richard and why he would want to hurt Anne by keeping himself locked in the closet. If he can't face his sexuality surely that's his problem, as awful as it sounds it's the truth. Anne is the one who has been hurt by all of this and for that he should be ashamed. I think what the most painful part of it all for Anne is she really loves him. That's where she and I differ. Through endless analyzing my own thoughts for once I finally had the courage to admit to myself that there was a never true feeling between Bill and I. The romantic illusion that I had created in my head was that I would be someone's wife. A big someone's wife at that. Plenty of money, great apartment with a small amount of power. And the killer was my father's approval. That's what sealed the deal for me, since the first time I met Bill it was through my father. It was almost like my dad had dropped off a boyfriend for me. Signed, sealed, delivered. I never questioned my feelings or emotions towards Bill not once because my father's word is the law. If he is deemed worthy by my father than naturally I assumed this must be the perfect guy for me. It just goes to show that no matter how good anyone's intentions are; sometimes you just have to think for yourself.

Anne on the other hand never felt obliged to be with Richard, he was of her own choosing and I guess that's what makes it all the worse. As I said whenever he does call, Anne can't bring herself to answer but she wants him not to worry. She's asked me and Sally to take turns answering his calls to throw him off the scent. Each time I did it I had to grit my teeth to prevent me from tearing his head off down the phone. I hold back for Anne's sake and tell him she's working late tonight so don't wait up. Yeah that's right Bill's line that he uses on me all the time. It finally became in handy for something.

Bill still sends me that text each day just after lunch time and I'm almost convinced he has it saved as a template so he doesn't need to write it daily. What can I say he's a business man that knows all about the importance of time management. He has no idea I was there under his desk that day and all I can think is that his receptionist didn't care to be the bearer of bad news and kept her mouth shut, which I appreciate. I still haven't figured out how to tell him what I saw, how I feel or that we're over. I'm sure I will find a way to let him know soon, but for now I'm in no rush. All that matters at the moment is self-healing, getting cozy reading books, taking a few days off work so we can just chill out and be there for each other.

I've since confided part of my troubles to Burt through texts. He messaged me one day out of the blue and asked when I was planning to come in next as its been several weeks. My text to him was short and vague, and from that he could sense there was something wrong. It took me several texts to explain as much as I could but as always his kindness and concern gets to me. I started by being cautious over how much information I was going to give him. I texted him some flakey bull shit like "can't come in at the moment, had a lot on recently but will hopefully see you soon". Several messages later and I must have been coming across as mysterious and strange. Normally these days our texts are quite funny and personal, just chit chatting about life. We have actually become really good friends and that's why I decided to open up to him in the end, even though it was embarrassing to talk about it to a man. Burt was like a dog with a bone and once he felt like I was dragging my heels and not really getting to the point, he called me. Reluctantly I answered not sure where to start.

"Sounds like you need to talk about it, so I thought I'd call. You mentioned something about you being single again? Is that right? So do I finally have a shot now?" he adds with only the slightest bit of sarcasm and both of us give a little chuckle at his direct words.

"Burt don't make me laugh right now, it's not the time." My half-hearted giggle subsides when I hear Anne crying in the background, it immediately sobers me up. Even Burt can hear it.

"Who's crying? Is everything alright? No. clearly it isn't, I'm sorry that was a dumb question. Are you able to go for a coffee? I get off in an hour, then we can talk properly" knowing instinctively that this isn't a date, that he's just being a nice man and a good friend, I accept. We agree to meet at one of his favourite coffee shops which so happens to be called 'Coffee cake' which is the same place where Anne and I met Allan for the first time.

I tell the girls that I'm heading out for a walk to clear my head and Sally edges to come along to.

"Well don't you think one of us needs to be here for Anne? I mean, what if the phone rings, you'll have to answer it." I can tell I've struck a chord with her and she nods in agreement.

"I'll pick up some doughnuts while I'm out ok. I won't be long." I say it as soothingly as possible, I hate to leave Sally in the lurch right now, and after all it has been both of us as a united front to take turns checking up on Anne. Trying to get her to eat, trying to get her to talk and trying to make her laugh. Ok so that was mainly Sally's department but I do attempt it myself sometimes. Her crying has lessened but she's definitely still hiding from him and the world right now. She's doing a lot of sleeping but Sally and I agreed that she needs her rest. Thankfully her appetite has improved dramatically in the last few days and now she eats what is being handed to her. Once Sally bought her a novel to read and without even looking at what was being given to her she put it straight into her mouth. She is in a complete daze most of the time, but we are seeing slight changes in her behavior. It's so mad that the first night we were here we were all laughing and drinking Vodka and at the time we felt almost carefree, even Anne was enjoying herself. But since that fateful night her attitude has spiraled downhill, I guess the Vodka wore off and her reaction to everything that's happened has finally sunk in.

Anne is still hell bent on confronting Richard face to face, she says the reason she is sleeping so much is just to get her strength up to go and see him. To me, that takes a strong woman to do something like that. I have no intention of ever seeing Bill again if I can help it. I went to sneak into his apartment the other day to get my things, and before I went I did a mental check list of the things I knew I needed from there. After racking my brain for an hour I realized there really isn't anything to take. A few pieces of jewelry that he bought me which he can keep (or better yet give to Felicity) and a few sexy pieces I bought just to please him, not that he ever really cared about the amount of time and attention to detail I made for him. Then again men never really notice the things you do for them; it tends to go right over their heads.

Arriving at 'Coffee cake' fifteen minutes early I take it upon myself to buy doughnuts in bulk for me and the girls before Burt gets here. The only reason I didn't want Sally to come with me is because I knew for sure she would embarrass me and call this a date. She still probably would have tagged along to be our third wheel and more than likely put me and Burt on the spot. I didn't want to admit where I was going because she would have tried to see the worst in what we are doing and we are only going for coffee as friends, nothing more.

Burt arrives and joins me for coffee; he pays, even though I offer to cover the bill for both of us. It's strange even something as mundane and normal to me as that has changed. Ordinarily I wouldn't even have thought to ask to pay my own way much less his; but due to the book my mentality has completely transformed. Even Burt seemed astonished that I had asked to pick up the tab, I guess my usual image has been one of a high maintenance, self-loving bitch. Well that woman is dead and gone, thank god.

Time flies so fast when I'm with Burt, we've already been here for a couple of hours and I have covered more than the basics. I told him the whole thing; surprising Bill at work and hiding under his desk just to find him dallying with his mistress. Whom incidentally turned out to be my arch enemy. The animated faces I pull and the drama I put into the story captivates Burt's attention. I see his eyes get big when I drop a twist in the story; even I've come to slightly enjoy telling the story because that's exactly what it feels like now. As though it didn't happen to me, I'm just gossiping about some poor bitch that has the world's worst luck.

When all is said and done Burt looks utterly amazed.

"Wow you've really been put through the mill haven't you? What shit luck to find out that way though. I mean you went to surprise him and then witnessed all that, that must have been awful. I don't know about this Bill guy but if you ask me he sounds like a damn fool to have let you go. Clearly he doesn't know what a catch he's got, and I bet this new woman of his isn't half as gorgeous as you are. Jill I don't know what to say, you weren't kidding when you said you've had a lot on. I'd say I'm sorry for your sake but to be honest I think it's for the best that you've found out what kind of man he is before you married him. This way you've actually seen it for yourself instead of taking someone else's word for it. This way there is no way he can deny it." Burt talks sense.

"Yeah you're right, I think I'm finally starting to see it that way. I don't want you to feel sorry for me; I don't feel sorry for myself anymore which is good. Also I think seeing what Anne has gone through recently has kind of put me in check, she's having a far tougher time of it than I am."

Peculiarly I don't even have to remind him who Anne is. He refers to her as "the red head you were with the first time we met" he's got a great memory. He becomes curious as to Anne's situation and I tell him all. I don't feel I am betraying Anne by divulging her secrets to him, after all he doesn't really know her and he definitely won't go around telling everyone of Anne's humiliation. Putting my now excellent story telling spin on it, once again I've made it sound like a juicy novel rather than a real woman's broken heart. I end the story by telling him she's bracing herself to sit down with him and talk it through, she intends to call him out on it and Burt's jaw drops several inches. He is literally gob smacked; he did not see that coming.

"That's insane, my god what the hell! How did he manage to hide that from her? This Anne sounds like a very strong woman to be able to do that. And she's right to want to understand better, he owes her an explanation." Seeing how appalled Burt is for my friends makes me soften even more towards him.

He's a lovely man with a great sense of humor and he knows just what to say to make me laugh, but I also like this. Being able to talk like adults and confide in each other is what everyone needs.

We talk until they begin to close for the day, every topic has been covered from his work to mine to cheating partners, to friends, to him hoping to leave his job soon, to me wanting to officially end it with Bill. For me it's already over but he still has no idea, which gives you a clue as to how often he comes home, because he still hasn't noticed that I'm no longer there. Burt has made a few occasional flirtatious comments that have given my ego the pat it needed, I know he isn't pressurizing me for anything he's just given me compliments and making me feel better about myself. Deep down Burt is a gentleman, he can see that I need space romantically but I do want and need friends, the more the merrier and Burt is included in that.

Now being so close and so comfortable with each other we actually kiss on the cheek on parting. It took me by surprise but I didn't dislike it, actually it was quite nice. He offers to pay for my cab and I violently refuse, man I really have changed. It's enough he bought the six fancy coffees we've just consumed but I'm finally breaking free from being dependent on men starting now, and even something this small counts. He walks back to his place; he said he only lives a few blocks away and I wave at him from my cab window. I told him he's welcome to visit me at my place if he dare risk it with three women that are slightly less than happy right now. He took my address and said he'd drop by soon, maybe tomorrow after work and that he'd bring doughnuts.

You know your life is bad when your personal trainer is encouraging you to comfort eat. Awgh to hell with it, who cares if I gain a tiny bit of weight? What with no wedding to plan and no man to make love to why do I give a damn? The answer is I don't!

———⁓ᴡᴏᴏᴄᴠᴏᴏⱦᴏᴏᴏⱳ———

I'm back at my apartment, I thought I'd stay here the night. In truth it's because I miss my bed. Curling up next to Anne has been necessary for both of us but now she's all better I feel she needs her space. It feels like it's been too long since I've been back here by myself, whenever I'm here it's to work with the girls and now it's all over. We've sold the very last box of unopened goods just this morning and we've already sent it off. This place has never looked cleaner, fresher, or bigger in size and has never seemed less like home to me, in fact it never was home. I feel as alone as I would be if I were single, and I know getting married won't change that. How my life is now, is how my life will be even with another ring on my finger. Sometimes I often think that's all I'll get out of this marriage; a piece of jewelry. Shouldn't there be more than that?

I told Jill that I was planning on staying at my place but that I'll be back tomorrow, first thing. With an empty tomb of an apartment I suddenly get goosebumps all over my skin and feel the prickling of my hairs begin to rise. Regretting my decision to be home alone I hesitate to go back to Jill's apartment, at least there's back ground noise, people to talk to, a cozy couch and company there. But I decide to stick it out and put the T.V on; there must be something good to watch at this hour it's only early on in the night. I flick through each channel until I find an old looking movie called 'Gone with the wind'. I've heard of it before but have never seen it and the info button tells me it only started five minutes ago and it lasts for another three hours and forty-three minutes. My word! This is literally the longest movie I've ever heard of, but it should entertain me for the rest of the night.

Wrapping myself in my old raggedy sheets and blanket on my bed, I settle into my body mold the mattress is indented with from my previous life of teleshopping. Nearly four hours later and I'm crying my heart out, the end of the movie was so heart breaking. I hate to give you a spoiler alert in case you haven't watched it but the little girl dies! I'm overcome with emotion and I'm shocked at how much I enjoyed it. I've never really been one for old movies, I prefer colorful Disney Pixar characters with happy endings but I guess that's the child in me talking. But this movie! This has definitely appealed to the woman in me. Scarlett is my new idol, relating to her pain I think we have the same sadness in common. The men that we love aren't with us. At times like this I would love nothing more than to just cuddle up to Allan, but as always he's nowhere to be seen. A text just isn't the same as having someone to hold you tightly. Moments such as this are something that Jill and Anne just aren't good for, you can't replace all types of physical affection with friends. Not just sex, but you need a lover in your life for the cuddles, for the tickling and touching, for the kisses on the end of your button nose, for the spooning late into the night. Actually I did accidently do that with Jill several times when she stayed with me; actually I did it regularly to Anne recently too. She never pushed me off or told me to stop once; with the shit she's been going through I assumed that all soothing forms of contact were welcome.

Anne's more or less fixed now, in the sense that she's not crying anymore. She's up and about, cooking and cleaning, being as proactive as possible. From all the time she has spent in the only bed in the apartment it seems to have given her a kick up the ass. She's been buzzing round Jill's apartment like a busy bee; she was actually the one that forced us all to get back to work at my apartment, which we were only too happy to do. Anne even offered to make a simple dinner for all of us, Burt included. Jill has been seeing a lot of Burt recently he comes round after work just to drop off coffee and doughnuts quite randomly. Me being me I ushered him in and we got to talking. Anne and I both love him we think he is fantastic but then again I knew Jill should have given him a chance when I first saw him. Of course then she was with Bill, but now that that's over I hope she makes time for Burt. Jill assures me she just wants to be friends with him at the moment and I agree. I think we all need to clear our heads and concentrate on ourselves for a while. But we do love Burt; he's become great company for all of us, we have become a fantastic friendly foursome.

Turning off the T.V to avoid temptation to slip into my old ways (I promised Jill I wouldn't buy a single thing, it was actually the condition she made me agree to, otherwise I don't think she would have let me out of her apartment) thinking back on my shopping habit I always knew it was something that distracted my mind. It preoccupied my brain, by doing something. Being hypnotized with shiny new products that I had no need for was just my way of dealing with my loneliness, as sad as that sounds. I always knew that was why but couldn't admit it, even to myself. Lying in the dark, feeling separate from the whole world and now with no nocturnal distractions, all I have to keep me company are my thoughts. Thoughts that won't let me sleep, thoughts that force me to face reality. I'm lonely.

I focus on the positives of life. I've found a sense of worth and I know what line of work I want to get into. Simon at the call centre has filled me in on what to expect in a call centre (at Jill's suggestion, only this time it was just for a chat, no purchases I promise) and I feel confident that I am capable of working as a telesales advisor. He agreed; after all this time of getting to know me, he believes I'm exactly what any call centre is looking for. A fresh, chatty, vibrant person with real people skills, apparently he thinks I have the full package. I'm excited about the future, for the first time I know I can do something, and I love having something to look forward to. The only thing I'm not enjoying right now are my conflicting emotions towards what's to become of mine and Allan's relationship.

Once upon a time I could (just barely) handle it, the loneliness, and I believed it was my lot in life to feel this way. So in love, and yet so alone. Purely from the companionship I've shared with Anne and Jill, I've seen what my life could be like. Why do I always have to be alone when I have someone I love in my life? Maybe I would have more fun and maybe even more company if I were available, and not committed to another. Being faithful has never been a problem for me and I believe it's the same for Allan. He loves me too much and also there is no way he would ever find the time to cheat on me. I know in my heart that he will be faithful to the end. But that's just it; maybe the relationship needs to end.

I hate to see it end but I know the relationship we have, is not enough for me. Surely it's not enough for him either. They say the hardest thing is to let go of a loved one, and just the thought of it is breaking my heart. I need to aspire to bigger and better things and have a full life, whether I'm alone or not, I want to be more independent and have an actual life. The decision to break my own heart has been in the works for months, I just never could face it. It's been in the back of my mind for some time now, possibly even before I last saw him. Seeing him again brings the pain back tenfold. Once I really believed that distance makes the heart grow stronger and the statement still stays true to this day, but with an enormous love for someone so out of reach; comes terrible heartache. It's as though in the end it will be easier to just let go. I don't long or care for the single life, I've always enjoyed the company, love and affection from others; sadly Allan will never be able to work from home, or be a nine to five guy, which is unfortunate because it would be the ideal life for me. My dream of him being at home just as much as at work is just that: a dream.

Wishing for something that will never come true just fills me with dread, upset and disappointment; and no one wants that. In the midnight hours as I lay here, wide awake, I shed several silent tears, for I know what I have to do. I can't wait until the next time I see him, by then I will have lost my nerve and all my love for him will overflow. It will become physically impossible to break our engagement, his heart and my own. Acting out of impulse I grab my phone to get the message to him the best way I know how to get in touch with him: via text. Admittedly it's not the nicest way to break up with anyone, let alone the love of your life. Nevertheless it's the only way. Face to face would kill me on the inside and a handwritten letter wouldn't be appropriate; he never stays in the same place for too long, moving from hotel to hotel for months on end. The letter could wind up in anyone's hands. No the decision has been made. A long winded, emotional, honest text explaining what I feel, what I want and what has to be done has to be typed up now or never, for I know I'll never sleep until it's done. I love him but I can't live like this anymore, it's killing me.

Chapter Twenty Four

The Broken Love Letters

To: Allan

Darling

I love you more than what is possible. I firstly want you to know that. I've never loved a man as much as I love you. When you're due to come home I can barely sleep the night before, I'm too excited! But when you let me down or become too busy, the pain is too much. You'd think I'd be used to this by now, but I'm really not. This isn't your fault I want you to know that. I want you with me all the time, forever and always. There's a selfish part of me that wishes you didn't work. I know that sounds so ridiculous, everyone needs to work, even me. I'm beginning to see that now. I know that you love what you do but I'm afraid our part time relationship no longer works for me. Before I used to put up with it because I loved you so much, I still do but there are more sad moments in this for me than happy ones. I think the most I have seen of you in one year was 6 times! To you that probably seems like a lot. To me though, I've since realized that, that's not nearly enough. I want

242

and need more in life. I'm breaking my own heart by doing this, which makes it all the worse, but we need to break up. We're not getting married.

I'm so sorry baby; please don't think you've done anything bad to me because you haven't. I hate to do this over text but I don't know when we will see each other again and I didn't feel like this could wait. Also the thought of calling you to talk about this would have made me cry hysterically to hear your voice; this really is the hardest decision I've ever had to make. I don't know what I'm looking for in life but I know what I don't want my life to be like, and that is the reality that I'm living right now.

I hope you understand and don't hate me for wanting more. I'm not asking you to choose between me and your work; I'm asking you to let me go so I can have a life of my own.

I'll love you forever

Please forgive me xxxxxxxxxxxx

After much delay I finally hit 'send' with a heavy heart. Hitting send brings a lump of emotion to my throat, but also relief. In a small devastating way I know I've done the right thing. No matter how awful it was to take the plunge. The message is delivered in five texts. Done. I've ended my dead end relationship in a few texts; this definitely isn't my proudest moment. Dread fills me and my tears blinded me as I wrote the whole thing, they overflowed and many hit the screen of my cell. I had to wipe it clean several times in order to get the job done. But now it's done. I'm so emotionally drained I will sleep like the dead now, silently, deeply and with no disturbances.

It was kind of weird that Sally chose to be alone, and go back to her apartment last night. I didn't stop her; I reckoned she wanted to see what the place feels like now that all the boxes have gone. It was really a miraculous moment to see how much we had achieved in such little time. Filled with pride, when the last box was collected by its new owner we came back to my place for several glasses of pink champagne. It was actually the first big purchase any of us had made with our earnings, it was pretty expensive stuff but we split it three ways so it wasn't so bad. The cool refreshing taste of accomplishment went down well and all our spirits were uplifted. Looking around her practically empty apartment made me emotional; it was a moment of realizing it was over. I don't know what exactly was over, but there was definitely a sense in all of us that something was done. Mixed between happy delight in finishing the job and empty hollowness and not truly understanding where it was coming from. In mine and Anne's case I think it was a symbol of us closing the chapter where our relationships were. Even Sally seemed cool and distant, and still seemed that way when she told me she wanted to sleep at her place on her own. She probably enjoyed her new clean surroundings and slept better than she ever has done before.

With there being no work to be done, I become restless and my hands become irritable as though they should be doing something. Unfortunately I've finished the wonderful book I was reading and with Anne back on her 'A' game my place has also never been cleaner. There is nothing for me to do and it's really getting to me. Searching and searching in my mind for any little thing that needs seeing to it dawns on me the inevitable that I've been putting off; until now. Telling Bill that I know he's cheating on me, that I've moved out and that we are SO over.

He doesn't deserve a thoughtful face to face conversation, quite frankly if I ever see him again it will be too soon. I'm not calling him and listening to the creep's ridiculous attempts of lying or trying to deny it. I just need a way to have said it and eventually he will know it but it doesn't demand an immediate response; or any response really, I'd much prefer if he didn't.

A letter; a letter is the solution I'm looking for. I can write it and drop it off at his apartment. Well that's settled and it gives me something to do for now. Grabbing a notepad and a pen I sit down in my now favourite spot and conduct the beginning of the letter in my head before putting pen to paper.

Dear lying, cheating scumbag.

It's your ex fiancé Jill, I'm writing this letter to you to tell you we are over. For good. I went to surprise you in your office sometime last week and was hiding under your desk, only to find you making out with a fake blonde by the name of Felicity. Don't try and deny it I heard everything; I also know you call her your 'superstar'. Why did you never have a pet name for me? Was I not good enough? At my disbelief that you would do this to me, I had no other way of handling this other than to tell my father. To say the least he's absolutely shocked and furious. I'm not implying he'll threaten you or anything but let's just say you're a moron to have made enemies with my father. And obviously the wedding is off! I wish you and that cheap tart well, in fact I believe you two deserve each other; just like flies round shit you two go hand in hand.

Besides from my blatant shock and disappointment I felt that day I want to thank you. I've been living in a dream, protected by highly powerful men with real money and because of that I've become spoilt, high maintenance and completely dependent on you. But that time is over now. I want to thank you for popping my disillusional bubble and for forcing me to face reality. The reality being that we never loved each other, we were comfortable by association.

Now I'm done with the bubble, and I'm done with you.

I'm on to my next chapter and I'm aiming for bigger and better things and hopefully one day I too will be someone's superstar, but for now I'm fine.

Unkind regards

Sincerely not yours

Jill Green

p.s don't wait up!

With a smirk on me lips I lick the envelope shut and address it on the front 'To Billy' hopefully he might think it's from his lady fair.

Making one final trip to the place of doom I cautiously slither into his penthouse and hold my breath on the off chance I've caught them at it in bed; I pray they don't hear me. A few footsteps into the place and I realize even 'Billy' wouldn't be that stupid to bring her back here where he believes I'm still at home waiting for him. In his mind nothing has changed and I'm still in the dark about what's going on. Little does he know I have been enlightened and know everything.

Placing my honest/sarcastic letter onto the satin sheets of the place where we once used to make love I waste no time in getting the hell out of here. Every piece of the place feels tainted and weird, like I never belonged in the first place. It just goes to show once again how little I cared for him because again, I'm not crying, I don't feel like I'm losing my home and I don't miss him at all. Leaving everything I owned there because it would be like taking memories of him with me, and I want a clean slate a fresh start with fresh memories. I scuttle out to the hallway with speed and lock the door behind me.

Shoving my copy of his key under the door I breathe a sigh of relief. I feel a weight come off my shoulders and I can finally exhale. Suddenly the urge to skip down the stairs instead of taking the elevator has come upon me, and I just go with it.

Skipping merrily all the way down the stairs I become out of breath and slightly dizzy from this rush of exhilaration, when I find myself out in the New York air I suddenly notice it's a gorgeous day outside. How come I didn't register how beautiful the colours of fall were on my way here?

For once I was blind, but now I see.

———~~∞∽⌒∽◯≺∞⌒◯~~———

Ok no more avoiding this, it's been long enough. I'm thinking with clarity, maybe it's because I have the place to myself. Sally apparently slept at her own place last night and Jill has just gone out too, she said she's just posting a letter. I've wanted to confront Richard face to face over this since the first day I raided his desk. Hoping to find peace and acceptance in what he has to say, I'm eager to see him now. I've just text him telling him I'm coming home and he sounded happy to hear from me; well that's the impression I got from his text. Shaking with nerves and anxiety I bundle up in one of Jill's winter coats for the air outside is icy fresh considering it's only fall.

Outside of our once happy home, I inhale so deeply I feel as though I could combust. Psyching myself up to face what lies ahead, and that's exactly what I pray for; no more lies ahead. It's gonna be hard to believe anything he tells me at this point, but I pray that my naivety has been broken enough for me to detect between the truth and falsehoods.

Walking in cautiously it takes me some time before I can give him eye contact; it's so hard when someone is being so sickly sweet. I can't stand it.

Richard sees me standing hesitantly in the doorway, not daring to fully become submerged with the room. Wanting to run screaming from this awful scene that will inevitably commence, but I stand my ground even when he comes over to kiss me on the head (as always) once upon a time I considered it sweet even, now I see through to what it has always meant: I don't want to kiss you on the lips.

"Hello darling, man where have you been hiding!" he beams at me sounding all chipper. "Work has been keeping you so busy; I feel I haven't seen you in ages. How are the girls? Tell you what, you can tell me everything over lunch. I was gonna fix myself a chicken salad, do you want some?" he's so clueless to how I feel right now. Food is the last thing on my mind, I just want answers and I want them now.

"No." I say rather sheepishly. He turns to me looking baffled.

"Really? You've always loved my chicken salads." Richard says looking perplexed. That wasn't the only thing I loved that I won't be having anymore.

"Richard we need to talk. Can we sit down please, this isn't easy for me." only now have I dared look up into his eyes to show him that somewhere deep inside of me something has surely died.

"Okay" he gives me a dry laugh and swallows hard; I can tell he's already nervous. There must have been a part of him always terrified that one day I would realize that our relationship is built on lies.

"This sounds serious, is this about the wedding." He looks at me hopeful, whilst he sits on the couch with crossed legs sipping a white wine. This is how we used to spend every Saturday, emotions start creeping in and the pathetic part of me which obviously for now still exists says: I'm gonna miss him. Richard was more than my romantic interest, he was my best friend.

"This isn't about the wedding. In fact there isn't going to be a wedding." I let this simple shocking statement sit with him for a few seconds before I give him the full details as to why.

"What! What do you mean there is no wedding?! What's happened?" He looks genuinely upset and crazed by this which makes this even harder for me. I think in the past few days I started to hate Richard and even built up anger towards him. For some unknown reason all my hatred and fierce feelings have been drained from me, maybe it was all that crying that has done it but I no longer want to scream at him. I just feel sad and hollow in the pit of my stomach.

Without saying another word I empty the contents of my handbag, which carries all the evidence of his sexuality which he was no doubt missing since I've been gone.

Locked in a deadly silence I hear him swallow and his cheeks redden with humiliation. Averting my eyes at all costs I hover above him, stood up erect and him still sitting on the edge of the couch with eyes to the ground.

I refuse to break the silence first it's him that needs to start some serious talking. The longer the silence the more I know his brain is ticking over, probably trying to come up with a reasonable lie that he will try and feed me. But I'm done with all the bullshit; I've had enough of the pretense. At this point I'm no longer searching for the truth because its etched all over his miserable face.

After precisely seven of the most awkward intense minutes known to man, Richard finally makes his opening statement.

"Where did you get them?" really? Are we really doing this? He and I both know the answer to his ridiculous question. It's such a weak question I'm not even going to bother answering it. One glance at my face and he sees a slight shake of my head, which tells him not to bother making nonsensical small talk, I'm really not in the mood.

"Anne I ... I ...I'm sorry. I don't know what else to say." A single tear leaves it's shiny mark on Richard's handsome face.

"Have you told everyone yet? Am I already a laughing stock to your parents?" what an odd train of thought to have. Instead of giving me answers as to why he's with me, if he's gay and why he's lied for so long the first thing that comes to his head is, is he the talk of the town. Besides even if I had told my parents I think the furthest thing they'd find about the situation is that it's funny.

"I haven't told my parents anything yet, only my friends know, that's where I've been. And this is the reason I haven't been back home." His head flops directly into his open hands as he starts to sob hysterically. I'm in pain watching him; I've never seen him this way. So raw and emotional it pulls on my heartstrings for him which isn't what I wanted to feel, it's me who is the victim in all of this and I need to make him aware of that before he makes this all about him.

"Stop crying please. Richard look at me right now! You lied to me! YOU'RE GAY for Christ sake! Is that all you can think about? Yourself! How about how I feel, does that even bother you?" my calm façade has slipped, I couldn't hold back any longer. It's taking me too long to get answers; he needs to make me understand before I lose my mind.

"I'M SORRY! I'm so so so sorry Annie. I hate myself for what I've done." I can just about make out what he's saying. He's crying so hard with both hands burying his face. He faces me for a brief moment and I see tear stains and red circles have already formed under his eyes from crying so much. The piece of me that loves him wants to take him in close and kiss each tear away, but now there is another piece of me; and this piece wants to be held and kissed by the man that loves me.

I slump on the opposite end of the couch so we are not that close that we are touching, but suddenly all my strength has dissipated.

"How long have you known?" I ask not knowing what else to say.

"Forever." he wipes his running nose with his sleeve and finally faces in my direction and stays there. "I've never, not been gay Anne. I hate that you've been caught up in all of this but I had no other choice." His words puzzle me, sensing my confusion he continues.

"You've met my mother; she's a real religious woman. A catholic, like you. I came out to both my mother and father when I was fifteen years old, my mother said I was never to mention such things and that I must have the devil in me to think that way. I left it for another year or so until I found a boy that I really liked, at the time I thought it was love and I just wanted my parents to accept me. I tried once more to tell just my mother this time that I meant it when I said I was gay. I told her I was sorry but it was something I had no control over and I begged her to love me regardless of my faults. Anyway it back fired, she told me if I didn't force myself to change she would cut all ties with me and refuse to acknowledge me as her son. That terrified me so much I didn't know what to do, but I knew she meant it, she meant it with every fiber of her being. After that she made me read from the Bible for four hours every day before bed, she said god works in mysterious ways and with help from the bible maybe he will hear my mother's prayers. From that moment on I loathed myself, I always was made to feel that my attraction to men wasn't normal and I was in some way dirty. My mother made me promise her that one day I would provide her with grandchildren. She said I am her only child and it's my responsibility to give her a grandson or granddaughter and a daughter in law, she said she wanted me to make a family for myself like any good catholic man should. I mean I love kids so the thought of it didn't repulse me, I'd love to have a family just not in the traditional sense of the word." At last he's opening up to me and the picture is becoming clearer.

"Growing up I had several girlfriends, good clean respectable girls, big church goers. These were the types of girls my mother approved of. Sex was naturally never an option as the majority of them where waiting for marriage so I never had a problem trying to get out of being intimate with a girl, which made things easier for me." he gives me a dry laugh and we are both emotional wrecks by this point. Richard trying to find the funny side in all this just adds to our hurt.

"That is before I had to deal with my little drunk Annie that night, you nearly gave me a heart attack. Coming at a gay man like that, I was so shocked it was so unlike you to do something like that." He laughs heartily through his tears, a real belly laugh remembering the image of me, drunk and horny sky diving on him. The memory makes me chuckle reluctantly.

He looks at me full of love and nostalgia. Reaching over slowly to take my hand into his, I cringe. Every moment of this has hurt my heart.

"I wanted you as my wife Anne because you're the sweetest, kindest and gentlest person I've ever met. And I hate myself for hurting you, you're my best friend and I can't tell you how long I've wanted to tell you the truth but I knew you couldn't understand. I hate that you know now because that means I've lost you. But I'm almost relieved this has happened; now I can sleep at night knowing that I'm not going to be the one that takes your virginity. You're so special Anne, you deserve the guy of your dreams a real stud. Not a faker like me, I was selfish to have kept you for so long and for hiding the real me from you. I hope one day you can forgive me." he wraps up his speech looking defeated and drained.

"Why did you let me believe we were forever?" I ask softly almost a whisper; my voice has become hoarse from grief. "Why did you keep me for so long?"

"Because I love you. I love you more than I intended to. When we first met I knew you were the kind of girl my mother would approve of but I didn't really take into account that I would become emotionally attached to you the way I have. That's the thing about love; it comes in all different varieties. I did love you, I do love you Anne. Unfortunately just not the way a husband should love his wife and for that I'm sorry."

I cry for him, for the boy that was never allowed to be himself, I'm crying for dreams now lost and the marriage that we'll never share. And lastly I cry for myself for loving the wrong man. Maybe I've been too naïve and too innocent for my own good. If life is a lesson, then I'm surely learning.

Chapter Twenty Five

Fresh Starts

I t didn't take Allan too long to receive my texts. What added to my pain was that he didn't really fight for our love, he kind of agreed to our splitting up almost immediately. He told me repeatedly that he loves me and can't believe we've lost a good thing but at the end of the day even he had to admit that managing a long distance relationship is tough, too tough and in most cases down right impossible. He said he hates what's happened between us but understands why I'm unhappy. He told me that I can keep the apartment forever if I want; he said he'll keep paying the rent for me which was sweet.

See what I mean; Allan is a sweetheart that has done nothing wrong. He's just too busy to be with anyone right now; that's his only crime. The reality of the situation was that there was never any point him having a home at all, considering he lives like a gypsy with no permanent address. The only reason he made the occasion trip back to New York was purely and only to see me; the one he left behind. In hindsight, no matter how much he loved me or I loved him, our priorities couldn't have been more different. His main concern was work, that's his passion and what he lives for. The thing that keeps him going day in and day out, I was almost his afterthought.

Of course he loves me I'm not denying that, but realistically I was last thing on his list. For me it was completely the opposite, Allan was the first, middle and last on my list of priorities, the only thought that constantly consumed my mind. Maybe it was from a lack of anything else going on in my life, but even when I was at work my mind would regularly wander back to him. Wondering how he was, how his day was going and if I'd hear from him that day. I mean it's no way to live to be obsessed with anyone but Allan's mind never wandered much to me, he was too focused on the thing he loves to do in life: work. I've decided now that it's time I do the same.

Finding a job is already on my new list of priorities; Jill's helping me in my job search so we both have something to occupy us at the moment. After an in depth talk with Jill she's agreed to let me live with her and Anne until we all figure out our next move in life. It was a shame I had to decline Allan's very generous offer of letting me keep the apartment but as I told Jill it only holds sad memories for me now. It's so strange how life has worked out, if we hadn't sold every box I would have had a real chore on my hands by this point and would have had to move everything into Jill's tiny apartment that can barely fit the three of us, let alone anything else. She agrees that the three of us living together, even though it's cramped, is what we all need right now; love, trust and companionship.

And yes it is official, Anne has moved out and Jill has taken her in too (which is nice), and Anne told me everything that had happened when she went to finally inform Richard of her findings. Apparently it was a really awful emotion moment between them, and she said he didn't even try to deny it, which is something I suppose. The only thing that I felt relieved about is he supposedly said sorry, like fifty times and was crying hard, as he should have been. If he had handled it any other way he would have had me to deal with. I still hate him for what he's done to her (even though I still haven't met him) but she hasn't started crying again (thank god) but she's definitely become with-drawn from real life. It's terrible because she had made such great progress recently; she was lively and talkative and just seemed very upbeat and content. That's the thing with putting on a brave face; if you get real good at it you can even fool yourself. We aren't forcing her to open up; we are all just being really understanding of each other and attempting to stay positive. Jill is the main source of strength that Anne and I are trying to absorb.

Every time a text comes through we all hurry to check our phones to make sure it isn't us. Each time it's Richard, she tells us that he's just constantly begging for her forgiveness which is sweet but it's also annoying as hell. She's only just found out and now her life has completely changed, in my opinion he is asking for way too much understanding far too quickly if you ask me. Anne herself said she can't respond to anything at the moment, she just wants to find herself and deal with her feelings before she forgives him. He shouldn't get off that easy anyway, just so he can clear his conscious. Richard offered to move out and stay with a friend for a few weeks if she wanted to stay at his apartment without him there, he was willing to do that for her. She refused his offer and knew she'd rather stay here with us. She said she just knew there was nothing left for her there anymore. It's his place and it fills her with dread now, it's no longer home.

―――✦―――

I've kept at my online business with eBay. Business isn't

booming because I've got hardly anything to sell. My apartment was pretty minimal to begin with, so my selling isn't to the level it was when we cleaned out Sal's place. I want to buy things old and new then sell them on for a profit. With the work we did for Sally it was far easier than what I'm doing now. With Sally, all her packages were already there, bought and paid for with someone else's cash but I'm not so lucky. I want to blow all my earnings on getting in great stock that I know will sell well, but there's something stirring in me that's telling me I'll need this money for a rainy day. Almost sensing that something big is gonna happen; what exactly I'm not sure. With my new independent attitude I've already promised myself I'll no longer accept handouts from my father, it's time I learned to rely only on myself. A passage I read from Collette's 'The Cinderella Complex' has stuck with me.

'Men are stretchers. They may generate their own brand of anxiety by skating out on the thin ice beyond their god given capabilities, but at least they get to the middle of the pond. Women are shrinkers. They pull back from their possibilities, aiming well below their natural level of accomplishment.'

That's been my entire life in a nut shell, and I'm sure many women have said the same. I'm now going to aim for my natural level of accomplishment and even higher if I can reach it.

I've been waiting for an angry text or phone call, but in the days after I went to Bill's apartment to drop it off, the only text I keep receiving is the now-famous template text I have come to despise. What an idiot. He has been officially dumped and I moved out weeks ago, and he still has no idea that I've gone. Just goes to show how much time he used to spend with me, it's ludicrous the amount of time he used to stay away from home. I've since wondered if Farilyn was his first affair, but I have a feeling that is a stupid question. He spends most of his time at 'work' but really he could have been using that excuse every time he had a new mistress, I'm such a loser not to have seen it coming. I have since told my dad everything and he went ballistic! He actually suggested having a word with Frank the chairman about working on a way to get him fired, without Bill being able to call it 'unfair dismissal'. As my father turns into a cunning man creating a plot, or situation to drop Bill into, I stopped him before he went any further.

"No dad, I don't want you to do any of that. He's not worth it. I'm down about it but I'm not broken hearted and to be honest I'd prefer for him to be fearful for the rest of his days about bumping into you or your friends. He knows he's made an enemy out of you; I included it all in a letter; which he hasn't yet read. What a jerk, even now he's probably fooling around with her on his desk and believes I'm at home pacing by the door waiting for him to come home. What an idiot I've been pap. I'm angrier at my own stupidity than what he's done to me. So promise me you won't waste your energy on him, I know I won't"

My father goes on to tell me how grown up I sound and his voice became emotional and he said he's so proud to have raised such a strong woman, which made me feel like a little girl again getting praise off my father. But that's just it, he never did raise a strong woman, he brought me up to be a daddy's girls, high maintenance, spoilt, lazy and now I think I can probably admit all together not really a nice person. Life has turned me into a strong woman, the book and my new friends have all guided me to see the light and make a change. At some point I guess we all need to realize this, as women deep down we all expect to be saved by a gorgeous man that will look after us till our dying day. As women we believe it is our right to do nothing, marry a rich guy who worships us for reasons unknown to anyone. 'Let him do all the hard work' we think. He's the man, he's meant to be the provider and I'm just the dainty pretty little thing that plays house and shops with his credit card.

How far we have fallen from the days of the suffragettes, burning our bras and making statements, causing trouble and demanding to be heard. Us women can be very complex creatures, most of the time we declare to be independent doing it all for ourselves. We declare it proudly and watch our friends and family forn all over us, telling us how strong and capable we are. Clearly so clever and made of strong stuff and we just bask in the glow of it all, like I did with my father. The minute he praised me I enjoyed the attention, I loved the stroke to my ego but why do women expect it? Men go along in life doing practically everything by themselves, especially if they are not married. Why is it they don't expect or even crave attention or a giant fan fair in their honor when they pay their bills? When they put in overtime at work? When they pick up the dry cleaning, get to work early, sleep alone, buy their own apartment and live by their own rules? A boy never came into the world knowing or wanting to be relied upon. He never knew that one day he would be obliged to take care of his wife. And a girl never came into this world expecting to be any different from the boy, it's called childlike innocence. It's only from our surroundings and the way children are treated that lead to this kind of mess. If you treat your children the same no doubt the outcome will be different, but as far as little girls go I think it would be beneficial if we changed the way we protect them, making them believe they really are as fragile as china and the only way to feel safe is in a man's arms. This I don't think should be allowed anymore. The amount of single New York women there are just goes to show that marriage isn't a certainty, it was never guaranteed but parents never tell us that.

When I was a girl both my parents at separate times would say things along the lines of 'you're gorgeous Jill your gonna have men lining up for you' or 'the man you marry will be a very lucky man' and even 'Jill is gonna be a heartbreaker when she's older, it's gonna be hard for her to pick just the one husband'.

It was engraved in my brain from the start that, that was the way life should be, we are never told different and most definitely never the harsh reality of 'well honey only when two people love each other do they decide to get married, it isn't for everyone you know. Some people go through life and never find the right person for them. It's all just a game of chance meetings.' Heaven forbid a six year old girl should hear that for the first time, it would burst her make believe bubble forever.

But now however I feel it may just be a case of being cruel to be kind.

Feminism is all about equality of the sexes and yet no matter how hard we try it will always be woven into the fiber of our beings that women need a provider, and men are that provider. They are expected to be strong and earn enough to keep the woman in a life style that she has become accustom to, probably due to her dad, who in turn treat her like a princess and gave her everything in life she wanted. No wonder women like me find it hard to start again and become independent when they've had a dad like mine. But I'm doing it regardless, I need to start again.

I'm enjoying my new found freedom; I often pick up groceries for me and the girls. Anne is still very much the cook in residence but we all pitch in with a little task she thinks we will manage. I know I sound like a fruit loop but I take pleasure in shopping for groceries, there's something about being in control of what I choose and the paying for it at the till part leaves me with a fuzzy glow about me. I often look around and at the line of people behind me, just so they can take a good old look at the sassy head strong woman who has come out alone to pick up some groceries and is paying for it with her own cash.

One day I return home to find Burt on my couch, sat between the girls and there all laughing animatedly at a joke I've missed. The thing with Burt is that I completely trust him around them. He is a friend to us all, and truly has become a part of the furniture round here. They rave on about him all the time, but I know he just wants to be a friend to them and he still feels rotten over what Anne has been through, he often brings us all flowers which is really sweet. I think he's the only man any of us want to be around at the moment.

It's become tradition that all of us have dinner together; this is actually turning into a daily occurrence which we all enjoy. Burt's routine now is to finish work and then head on over, usually picking up several bottles of wine on the way. Last time I worked out with him was about a month ago, he's never pressured me to go back but I think it's because we see plenty of each other now anyway. What with me hoarding every penny I've made I'm trying to live on a budget for that 'save it for a rainy day feeling' is still with me and I can't shift it. Through my budget cut I've since realized paying for exercise is ridiculous and an added expense I could really do without, no matter how much I want to help save Burt's job. I'm surprised to find him here before me, normally the food has been cooked by the time Burt shows up and he helps to dish it out (not wanting to feel like he's taking advantage of us) but he's here already. Over an hour early.

"Hey stranger how come you're here so early?" I ask pleasantly surprised.

Burt looks up from his three way discussion and runs over to help me with the bags with a huge smile on his lips.

"I quit!" he hauls all the groceries into my small kitchen still grinning as if he'd won a ton of money.

"What! You quit? What happened?" shocked he would leave his job so soon, I thought he was gonna leave when he found a new job. "Wait does this mean you've found somewhere else?" I start smiling for him thinking hopefully we have something to celebrate tonight.

"Well kinda. The start date isn't official yet but I've been talking to an old friend of mine back in London and we've been discussing going into partnership together for years. Anyway he's been approved for a loan to start up his own gym and he asked me if I would want to help him run the place. Can you believe it, just when I needed something new this happens." He looks excited and breathless and I'm so happy for him.

"Wait does this mean you're moving back to London?" he puts his back to me to unload the shopping and deliberately hesitates answering my question for as long as possible. "Yeah." comes the smallest voice in the world.

"When?" I ask ever so slightly devastated. Besides Anne and Sally, Burt is my only other friend. I can't believe he's going.

"Like I said we haven't set the date, he has to get ready and open up the place first. There are loads of things to sort out, buying all the equipment, signing all the paper work, advertising, all that kind of stuff. But in the meantime he needs me there to help out. I'm leaving for London next week." He finally turns to me to look me in the eyes and I try to hide the fact that I'm miserable.

"Wow, that's brilliant, I'm so happy for you. Have you told them?" I ask, referring to the girls talking quietly in the next room.

"No I wanted to wait till I saw you, thought you'd be happy to know I won't be around to annoy you anymore." he gives a small laugh only I don't join in. I really don't want to put him off the idea but I'm really sad to see him go, and clearly it is written on my face.

"Hey, come on now. It's not like you to get upset." Everyone has always believed that of me. "I'll send you postcards and hopefully when I'm settled down there you and the girls could pay me a visit. I'll show you round London, we'll make a fun weekend of it." At this I smile, already picturing it. It would be fun. I've never been to London in my life.

"We will definitely have to do that, my Dowager accent will blend in there won't it." He gives a sudden burst of laughter and immediately adopts his butler accent trying to add levity to this upsetting news.

At dinner Burt announces the news to the girls, they both have the same attitude toward it as me. Happy for him, Sad for us. We all congratulate him and tell him how much he'll be missed. At this he starts squirming in his seat from all of this attention, and tells us how much we have come to mean to him and that he will miss us too. He said he intends to call whenever he can and he tells the others of our plans to go see him once he has everything straightened out in London.

"Yes, yes. Oh man we have to do that I've always wanted to see the London eye." Sally says too excitedly nearly spilling her wine all over the place.

"Yes and Big Ben, Jill haven't you always wanted to see Big Ben?" I nod emphatically, I know I'm going to sound ignorant here but I have no idea who Big Ben is.

"I bet there's loads of sightseeing to be done in London." Sally looks at Burt and he fills us in on the delights that London has to offer.

"It has the same stuff New York has; only people say New York is far more fashionable and modern than London, which I suppose is true. They both have theatres and designer shops-" my ears perk up at the mention of designer shops "They both have busy streets and lots to see and do, only London has Buckingham palace, Trafalgar square, The Royal Albert Hall and Westminster Abbey."

"That's right, you have a royal family! Girls we have to go, I wanna go so bad. Jill can we?" why Sally is asking me I'll never know. I'm not her mother, when is she going to realize that?

"You guys should just move to London with me, it would make things easier for all of us. I think you could all do with a break from 'The Big Apple', there's really nothing tying you here anymore." Burt says between shoveling in another fork full of Anne's amazing pasta dish that we are all addicted to. "Beside how will I live without Anne's incredible pasta dishes, I may die!" Anne loves the compliment and we all enjoy the joke, only one of us doesn't know it is a joke.

"That's a great idea! Why don't we?" Sally stares each one of us in the eye with the question. "Why don't we move to London, Burt's right what the hell are we staying here for?"

"I was only joking Sal, you three are New Yorkers by heart." Burt wolfs down the rest of the pasta on his plate and happily accepts a second helping when Anne offers to fill up his plate.

"Sal we can't just head to London on a whim, what would we do there?" Anne asks as she fills up Burt's plate with what I like to call the world's biggest spoon.

"Well my work is online so I can take it anywhere, you can look for cleaning jobs over there and Sally can start applying to call centres in London, Sally's right why shouldn't we move?" everyone around the table stares at me like I'm growing another head. "What? I think Sally is right. Burt, please don't think we are stalking you to your new job it's just that... I don't know something about this feels right." the girls look on at me in wonder.

Even I can't believe my own ears, I'm not an overly spontaneous person and when Sally just mentioned it I thought it was funny. But on second thought why not?! We all need a clean slate; we all need to begin again. A new place, a new life, a new me.

What was once an offhand remark from Burt, has now completely dominated the entire night's conversation. Even Burt is looking at us with hope in his eyes, praying that we mean it and not just full of silly fantasies. He tells me of all the charity shops and auctions that I could visit to get stock for my online shop and I'm in love with the idea. We are all exhilarated and terrified at the prospect but just as work once did for us; it's a project for us to stick our teeth into and something new to focus one. And god knows we all need that. Making plans and arrangements of how we could possibly pull this off, it looks as though this could definitely be happening.

As I look around the room I see a spark in all of our eyes that I've never seen before. We are all alive and animated with conversation, filled with excited and for the first time in what feels like forever; looking forward to the future.

—⁓⁓⁓⁓⁓—

Burt calls me the following afternoon and asks me to take a long walk in central park with him. It's the perfect luxury for him with him not having to work at the moment, that he now has the opportunity to bask in a glorious day walking through the stunning grounds of central park in the fall when all the leaves have turned golden brown.

Meeting him at the park we give each other a small kiss on the cheek, this has become a regular thing now and I've always secretly enjoyed it and look forward to even that smallest bit of affection. As predicted the conversation jumps straight to talk of moving to London. I don't mind though, the girls had me up all night discussing details on how and where we should live. We even went to the extremes of looking online for a potential place to live in London that are in good neighborhoods but are also reasonable in price. We already agreed that we will all continue to live together, not just to make things financially easier but also because I don't think any of us would care to be without one another.

"Are you being serious about coming to London? I know you and the girls could do with a fresh start but are you certain this is what you want, and what they want?" Burt is such a sensitive thoughtful man now that I know him better.

"Yes I'm being serious. Me and the girls have talked about it none stop since you left, and the more we think about it the more it feels right." I tell him, to assure him that this is really happening.

"Well as long as you're sure then maybe we should start looking for flats near to each other. You know just in case you three need me for anything. It will make things easier to have me close at hand." His uncertainty in his voice makes him sound vulnerable and timid. We both know he's testing the waters to see if we will stay in touch once we've made the move. Instead of just agreeing with him, I want him to know that he is not needed but that he is wanted.

"Yeah that would be ideal, plus it will make it easier for you to travel to our place for our dysfunctional family meals." I say only half joking. Ours really is a family of sorts, an adoptive family that I have picked up on the way through life. And Burt is a part of that family now, no matter how cheesy it sounds.

We both chuckle at my joke but when he looks to the ground in an effort to avert my eyes, I know he's not taking in the beautiful colours of autumn. He's subtly avoiding my gaze because I can tell that it hit a cord within him knowing we want him in our lives. I want him in my life.

The air is crisp and the wind becomes stronger, I love the feeling of wind in my hair like this. The feeling of cobwebs literally being blown away, being scattered throughout the park like the fallen leaves on the ground, only not as pretty. It's strange that the death of a leaf in pretty, that the colours are so attractive. Death is not forever with nature though, next year in summer the trees will be in full bloom with the brightest green leaves you've ever seen. But that is just like life really, now that I think about it you have to cut off the dead ends in life in order to make way for the new. Such as getting your split ends cut off, the reason for this is to refresh your hair and give room for new growth. Soon your hair becomes young and fresh looking and more vibrant than it's been in months. Same as the fallen leaves, they've had their time, now it's time for a fresh start. Just coming to this conclusion as we meander through the park on this colorful, chilly day, I find it hopeful to know that fresh starts are wonderful. I pray that mine will be the same.

———∿∽⊙⋇⊙⋇⊙∽∿———

This is crazy; I can't believe it's really happening everything is underway. The girls and I have decided to throw in all our earnings from the work we did and it's enough to buy our plane tickets and pay for a luxury hotel for a few nights but we are struggling for cash for somewhere to live, so I've decided to raise extra funds by selling all my furniture and stuff that's in the apartment such as the bed, couch, and even the Dolly Parton guitar just for some much needed cash. Along with it went my canary diamond to the nearest porn shop. They robbed me blind on the price, I still got several thousand for it but I know they grabbed themselves a deal. They must have seen me coming, or have known my desperation for cash because no matter how I tried to haggle they barely moved from the figure they first offered me. Still I'm going to treat this as my 'stock' money. It'll help towards getting my business off the ground when I get to London.

I've called my father and told him I want to sell the apartment and move to London. Dad freaked out over the idea of his one and only daughter moving to another country but he believes I'm a strong woman now and is reassured to know I will be living with friends. He also goes on business trips to London from time to time and we can always call. He said if I need him he is only a flight away and I know he'll take it for me; to him I will always be his little girl. As his final gift he tells me to sell the apartment to the highest bidder and keep the money to go towards my new life. My new Feminist ways start to protest to my father's generosity, but in the end I give in. I know I need every last penny I can get my hands on. Also it occurs to me that by not marrying Bill I have saved my dad a fortune, because the wedding I was going to plan would have cost somewhere around three million dollars. I don't bother getting in touch with my mom, she'll find out soon enough if she makes contact with father. Now with a bit of financial security I've become really excited for the move, we all are its starting to feel real.

Putting the apartment up for sale, I got a buyer within two days, that's New York for ya! I got around $700,000 for the apartment and I had already sold every single thing in the place, there were a few nights of sleeping on the floor but we were all far too hyped up to care. With the money I made I had enough to buy a small three bedroom terrace house on Charminster road in London, Anne and Sally helped pick it out. They put what little they could toward the place which wasn't a lot but I allowed it so they didn't feel as though they were living off me. It's crazy, the price for our new house was almost exactly half the amount for my apartment in New York, so far so good and we got it at a steal! A house too for god's sake! We even have a teeny tiny garden which Anne is already mentally planning what flowers she intends she plant there. Burt's plan is to live with his friend in his spare room at his apartment (sorry I mean flat as Londoners call it) until he finds the perfect place for him, plus its saving him money.

My old place is now completely empty and Anne being Anne has cleaned the place from top to bottom and it looks great. Looking around at the bare rooms I feel sentimental over losing this place. This place in the short time of using it has had more memories in it than Bills place ever had for me. I've lived with friends here; we've had small intimate dinner parties here. We've had laughter and we've had tears, we've been drunk and we've been desperate (sigh) the story these walls could tell. Also I find it hilarious that Bill never responded to my letter, I know he still hasn't read it because I got a copy of the template text just last night. I'm so done with seeing that same message that just this morning I decided to change my number. I desperately needed a new number and now I'll never know what his response was, and quite frankly I couldn't give a rat's ass.

In the weeks leading up to the big move we switched where we did a job search for Anne and Sally, from New York to London and already Sally has two interviews in call centres lined up and it actually stated 'no experience needed, as full training will be given' how lucky is that. And a woman with blatantly a great amount of wealth is looking to hire a neat and tidy house maid to clean her seventeen bedroom manor home on a regular basis. Anne said the wealthy woman's name is Beatrix and they've had several phone conversations, it's looking promising and they have arranged to meet the day after we arrive. Everything's tied itself up so neatly; this really couldn't have gone better if we tried.

All of us are traveling straight to London with nothing more than a suitcase or two each, (talk about being light travelers) Burt promised to meet us at the airport as he had to go over early to help his friend set up shop, but he plans to be our tour guide and he even offered to help us unpack (not that there is really anything to unpack) the only piece of the past I've brought along for the ride is my tatty old purple velvet chair. You didn't think I'd sell that did you! I'm not that heartless. It's been shipped over and will get there before us, Burt has the keys to our house and he's waiting for my chair to be delivered. It still feels so weird to say we have a house. It's so weird that we were born and raised here in New York, all of us, but have absolutely nothing to show for it other than some clothes, jewelry and make up. That's all we've brought, it's easier this way. None of us have anything holding us here, no sentimental attachments to anything or anyone (except father but I know him, he won't stay away too long he'll visit every chance he gets) as for me I have no wish to ever return back here, even for a day. Sure the park is gorgeous, the shops are fabulous and the food is amazing but I'm done with New York.

I can't wait to start fresh and in London of all places, hey if it's good enough for a queen then it's good enough for me. At last I feel as though I'm finally becoming the girl I used to be. The one that believed in big adventures and real love, who knows I may still get my happily ever after but in the mean time I intend to enjoy my newly found independence, as I'm sure we all will. Hopefully moving away and starting a new life in London will be the best thing for us.

I've got what I came here for. I've found real love in these two amazing women. I've learnt money is not the most important thing in the world and it should never replace real love in a marriage. I feel as though I've grown and I'm ready to move onward and upward: this isn't the end, this is just the beginning.

We're moving to London BITCHESS!!

Epilogue

'The woman who believes in herself does not have to fool herself with empty dreams of things that are beyond her capabilities. At the same time, she does not waver in the face of those tasks for which she's competent, and prepared. She is realistic, well grounded, and self-loving. She is free at last to love others – because she loves herself. All of these things, and no less, belong to the woman who has sprung free.'

- The Cinderella Complex